Praise for *Bingo Barge Murder*

"Chandler launches her first Shay O'Hanlon caper with panache. Coffee, romance, murder, and dog all make for Minnesota nice-nice."
—*Lavender Magazine*

"*Bingo Barge Murder* is a solid first entry in the Shay O'Hanlon mystery series. Chandler writes with a wonderful sense of place, plenty of humor, and a crisp pace. The best part for me were the characters, which were so richly drawn that they felt like instant friends. This is a great read from the very first page!" —Ellen Hart, author of the
Jane Lawless series

"Chandler's debut is fast and funny … crammed with memorably quirky Minnesota characters." —Brian Freeman,
bestselling author of *Immoral*

"Jessie Chandler delivers a fresh murder motive in this engaging debut mystery." —Julie Kramer, author of *Stalking Susan*

"What do you get if you if you line up Shay O'Hanlon, owner of a café called the Rabbit Hole, a scrumptious police detective named JT Bordeaux, a computer genius drama queen, and a murder at the Pig's Eye Bingo Barge? If you said a rollicking, fast-paced black-out game of mystery and suspense, I'd have to yell—BINGO!"
—Mary Logue, author of *Frozen Stiff*

"If anything happens to me, I want Shay O'Hanlon on my side! *Bingo Barge Murder* is a fun read with an emotional depth that sneaks up on you. The characters are interesting and quirky and the location is unique and well-developed. I hope this is just the first of many adventures for this 'Tenacious Protector' and her pals."
—Neil Plakcy, author of the Mahu series of mysteries

Praise for *Hide and Snake Murder*

"Chandler follows up *Bingo Barge Murder* with another tricky plot fully worthy of your suspension of disbelief." —*Lavender Magazine*

"Fast paced and witty. It is peopled with wonderfully colorful characters, making it a strong second novel in the Shay O'Hanlon Caper series." —*Lambda Literary*

"After reading her novels, I have come to believe Jessie Chandler is the illegitimate child of Raymond Chandler and Dorothy L. Sayers. She's funny—and she's good!" —Lori L. Lake, author of the Gun series and the Public Eye series

"Wild and wacky *Hide and Snake Murder* will keep readers guessing all the way to a slam bang finale."—Carolyn Hart, *New York Times* bestselling author

"*Hide and Snake Murder* takes us to the beginning and end of the Mississippi, New Orleans and Minneapolis, capturing the quirky charm of both cities. It's a rollicking read with an entertaining cast of funny and fascinating characters. You won't be able to turn the pages fast enough." —J.M. Redmann, author of the Goldie award-winning novel *Water Mark: A Micky Knight Mystery*

"Jessie Chandler makes me laugh. A talented storyteller with a deft hand at pacing, she writes rollicking, raucous adventures that are sure to entertain." —Julie Hyzy, bestselling author of the Manor House mysteries and White House Chef mystery series

"Shay O'Hanlon can't say no to a friend in trouble—even a pain-in-the-ass one like her old buddy Baz. One miserable night, he comes to her with a story of mayhem, murder, and a purloined toy snake. Bad guys want the snake, and Shay realizes that the mysterious toy holds the key to some serious malfeasance. When more of her friends become endangered, Shay has no choice but to find the snake before the criminals sink their fangs into everybody she knows. The trail slithers down to New Orleans, where the street performers know more than everybody else, but where success only leads to deeper mystery—and more danger. Back in Minneapolis, new helpers enter the picture, but are they true, or do they speak with forked tongues? Jessie Chandler doesn't just write twists in this novel, she writes twists within twists. Scaly thugs, venomous crime bosses, and the mingled scents of jasmine and gunsmoke constrict tighter and tighter around tenacious Shay as she follows the mystery to its surprising conclusion. *Hide and Snake Murder* is a unique story of zany friendship, tentative romance, and the deadly face of today's underworld."—Elizabeth Sims, author of the Rita Farmer mysteries and the Lillian Byrd crime series

Praise for *Pickle in the Middle Murder*

"*Pickle in the Middle Murder* has all the beloved characters from the first two capers: sweet Coop, tough old broad Eddy, adorable Rocky and, best of all, this time we find out what's behind JT's air of enigma. There is some dark stuff here as well as the jokes, chases, and knock-about, but that only makes us root even more for these wonderful characters. If you only read one Twin Cities pickle-based murder mystery this year, make it Jessie Chandler's. Oh, and the dogs—Dawg and Bogey—only just manage not to steal the whole show. Great fun with a big heart: I loved it."
—Catriona McPherson, award-winning author of the Dandy Gilver Mystery Series

THE SHAY O'HANLON SERIES

Bingo Barge Murder (2011)
Hide and Snake Murder (2012)
Pickle in the Middle Murder (2013)

JESSIE CHANDLER

A Shay O'Hanlon Caper

Chip Off the Ice Block Murder

MIDNIGHT INK
WOODBURY, MINNESOTA

FIRST EDITION
First Printing, 2014

Book format by Bob Gaul
Cover design by Lisa Novak
Cover illustration © Gary Hanna
Editing by Nicole Nugent

Midnight Ink, an imprint of Llewellyn Worldwide Ltd.

This is a work of fiction. Names, characters, places, and incidents are either the product of the author's imagination or are used fictitiously, and any resemblance to actual persons, living or dead, business establishments, events, or locales is entirely coincidental.

Library of Congress Cataloging-in-Publication Data
Chandler, Jessie.
  Chip off the ice block murder: a Shay O'Hanlon caper/by Jessie Chandler.—First Edition.
    pages; cm.—(The Shay O'Hanlon series; #4)
  ISBN 978-0-7387-3939-7
  1. Murder—Investigation—Fiction. 2. Minneapolis (Minn—Fiction). I. Title.
  PS3603.H3568C45 2014
  813'.6—dc23
                    2013046326

Midnight Ink
Llewellyn Worldwide Ltd.
2143 Wooddale Drive
Woodbury, MN 55125-2989
www.midnightinkbooks.com

Printed in the United States of America

ACKNOWLEDGMENTS

There are so many people who lend a hand in the creation of a book. All the usual suspects have returned, and from the bottom of my heart, they have my undying thanks.

Lori L. Lake, Patty Schramm, MB Panichi, April, DJ, Pat, Angel, Mary, and whoever I'm forgetting... I'm forever grateful for your assistance, and in such a short timeframe. I couldn't do it without you all.

Lastly, I write caper stories and occasionally take the liberty to alter reality. The St. Paul PD and the St. Paul Winter Carnival are two of my latest victims. No offense or disrespect intended.

The events of this book take place at the beginning of 2012, a few months after *Pickle in the Middle Murder*.

ONE

"SHAY! HEY, YO—PHONE!"

"Hang on a sec," I hollered and cringed as the reverb hurt my ears.

My upper body was crammed inside a two-tier glass display case, where I was wiping up pastry crumbs left from a busy New Year's Eve afternoon. If I wasn't careful, this simple project was going to leave me hearing impaired.

More garbled yelling spurred me to rapidly finish up, but I misjudged my withdrawal and cracked my skull sharply against the top edge of the display.

"Ow!" I yelped and tossed the damp rag into a sink along the back wall of the café with a little more force than necessary.

"SHAY! TELEPHONE!"

"Coming!" I yelled, and stomped into the kitchen/storage room of the Rabbit Hole, the Uptown Minneapolis coffee shop I co-owned with Kate McKenzie. The woman herself was currently leaning against a wire rack of supplies impatiently tapping the phone receiver against her leg. Her attention was on the screen of a fifteen-inch TV we'd recently mounted above the sink counter. It was tuned to a channel with coverage leading up to tomorrow's Rose Bowl.

Kate was a whirling dervish I loved like a sister. Tonight she was itching to blow out of the café and get on with the business of celebrating New Year's Eve with her squeeze of the week. Her short hair was currently electric pink, and her cheeks were almost the same color, probably from frustration that I hadn't heard her.

I grabbed the phone she thrust at me. "This is Shay."

A gruff voice cut through background noise that sounded like lots of people in a tight space. "It's Whale. Your dad left your number for emergencies, and I've got a fucking emergency. He was supposed to be here to open at eleven. Still hasn't shown his face. It's busier than shit. To top it off, the fucking Summit Brewing delivery guy needs payment before he can unload. We're almost out, and if we don't get this shipment, there's gonna be a lot of pissed partiers."

Whale? What kind of name was that? And where did my father find these people? My apparently absent parent ran the Leprechaun, a blue-collar neighborhood bar in Northeast Minneapolis. He loved to consume what he sold and periodically hopped off the responsibility merry-go-round, riding a multiday bender instead. To my knowledge he hadn't performed one of these stunts anytime recently, so getting this call was last thing I expected, especially with the potential profit from a Saturday night New Year's Eve on the line. The problem was, each time I thought I had my old man figured out, I learned how very wrong I was. He had some serious balls to fall apart on the busiest drinking day of the year.

While I hadn't picked up an abnormal affection for firewater from my father, I had inherited a healthy temper with a fast-burning fuse. My rope was exceptionally short when it came to dealing

2

with his excessive alcohol consumption, and now I bounced hard at the end of it.

"Hang on," I told Whale more sharply than I intended, and muttered, "I'm going to kill him." I checked my watch. 3:27 p.m. Kate and I had closed early in honor of the holiday, and we were almost done cleaning up.

Kate had managed to tear herself from the TV to focus on my conversation. I covered the mouthpiece and said to her, "My father picked today to no-show. I need to head to the Lep. You okay to finish up? Front's done except for the mopping."

"Oh, shit, Shay, I'm sorry. It's fine. Get outta here." Kate was well acquainted with my father's alcohol-induced shenanigans. It wasn't the first time she'd pick up my slack because of it, and it probably wouldn't be the last.

Into the phone I growled, "I'm on my way. Do not let that delivery guy leave."

Whale raised his voice against the muted roar of the crowd. "I'll do what I can."

There was a click and dead silence on the other end as I opened my mouth to respond. I pulled the handset from my ear and stared at it in disbelief. "That jerk hung up on me. Whale. Jesus." I slammed the receiver into the cradle. "Of all the days for my father to crash the gravy train."

Kate straightened up. "Get going, I've got this. And good luck."

At that moment, Bogey, my bloodhound and flunky ex-police dog, ambled into the kitchen. His nose was twitching and a string of drool trailed to the floor from the corner of his mouth. He plopped himself on his haunches and whined a yawn, his droopy brown eyes flicking from me to Kate and back again in hopes that something edible might come his way. I'd forgotten about him and Dawg, who was probably still in the same position—upside-down and sound asleep in front of the fire—as he'd been a half hour ago.

"Oh crap. Kate, can you—"

"Yeah." She cut me off with a wave. "I got 'em. Scoot."

"Thanks. I'll swing by and pick them up later." I gave Bogey a pat and grabbed my jacket from the hook behind the kitchen door.

Behind me, Kate muttered, "Holy crap."

Her tone stopped me cold. "What?"

"Check it out."

I turned around and followed her gaze to the television. A breaking news banner filled the bottom of the screen and a talking head took up the rest. Kate upped the volume.

"—in an large chunk of ice." The picture cut to a stock image of massive blocks of ice awaiting carvers from some previous Winter Carnival. "Our sources tell us the body is that of a man, but we haven't received official confirmation."

The news anchor reappeared. "Once again, if you're now tuning in, a body has been found encased in a rectangular block of ice in St. Paul's Rice Park near the area where workers have been feverishly preparing for the 2012 St. Paul Winter Carnival's ice carving contest."

The anchor looked up from his notes, his expression both incredulous and stern. "We have a crew headed to the scene, and we'll keep you updated as we learn more." With a grim smile, he signed off and football coverage resumed.

"Damn," I swore softly.

"That's horrible."

"No kidding. Nasty way to go." I shuddered. "I'm out of here. Thanks again."

After another quick scratch to the top of Bogey's bony head and a few treats from my pocket, I made tracks out the front door, exchanging warm, coffee-and-spice-tinged aromas for an Arctic blast that slithered down the back of my neck.

My feet squeaked, irritating and loud, on the snow-covered sidewalk. I gingerly did the Minnesota shuffle—the peculiar waddle Midwesterners adopt to keep upright on ice and snow. I hustled as fast as I dared toward my new-for-me-but-previously-owned 2005 Ford Escape. The vehicle was a replacement for the pickup I'd totaled after smashing into a clothing donation bin last fall.

A slow-burning rage bubbled up to simmer right below my rib cage. I cranked the engine and thoroughly cussed out my liquor-loving father. My partner, JT, and I had miraculously managed to finagle six consecutive days off in a row, and we were booked into a bed-and-breakfast up in Duluth starting tomorrow. It'd been a little over a year since I'd started seeing JT Bordeaux, a detective with the Minneapolis Police Department, and we were planning an anniversary of sorts. If I had to delay my mini-vacation, my father was going to be in some even deeper shit.

The ride between the Hole and the Leprechaun didn't take long. Street parking was at a premium, and the lot next to the Lep was full. Whale was right; the bar was busier than a tow lot after a snow emergency.

The Summit beer truck was still backed up to the rear entrance. I let out a mental breath I hadn't realized I was holding. My dad lived on the razor's edge of being unable to pay the next month's bills when they were due. To lose out on beer sales on New Year's Eve would put a serious dent in his prospects.

I trolled the neighborhood streets and eventually found an open spot a block and a half away. After locking the SUV, I trudged to the bar. We still had a long way to go before this unusually cold and snowy winter released its grip. The dwindling rays of sun did little more than blind people as it reflected off the white stuff.

We'd suffered through a couple of recent snowstorms where a combination of freezing rain and slush with rapidly plummeting temps had resulted in unevenly icy roads, sidewalks, and parking lots. You could get bucked right onto your ass if you weren't careful, and sometimes even when you were. We'd probably be dealing with dangerously bumpy ice-coated surfaces for the rest of the snow season. Happy frickin' New Year.

I pulled open the Lep's heavy wooden front door and stepped into my past. The familiar scent of booze and a lesser odor of ancient cigarette smoke engulfed me. No matter how long smoking had been banned in bars in Minnesota, the acrid smell would not go away. It seemed to have seeped into the very core of the old building. It didn't help that half the time my father didn't enforce the legislation.

I squinted as my eyes adjusted to the dim lighting. The din of drunken revelers was at an all-time high. Within a few steps, my ears hurt.

Dark paneled walls were lined with memorabilia from my father's barge rat days on the Mississippi. A highly polished, antique oak bar ran down one wall of the space, and tables and booths were scattered on the other side. There was room for a twelve-by-twelve dance floor if patrons cooperated in rearranging the furniture, but not much dancing usually happened here. Just a lot of heavy drinking.

The place was well and truly packed. Faces I'd never seen before were four deep at the bar, and every table was occupied. Most of the regulars knew better than to come to the Lep on the last day of the year.

Led Zeppelin's "Dazed and Confused" blared from the same beat-up jukebox that I grew up with. That it still functioned was a minor miracle. I scanned the room and glimpsed a head of short, spiky hair bobbing through the crowd. Jill Zats, a longtime part-time server, worked her way through the throng toward the bar. She expertly balanced a round tray of glasses and empty bottles above her head. Her skill at fending off wandering hands and groping advances while keeping a friendly smile plastered across her face was legendary. If it were me, I'd be doing a whole lot more slapping and much less serving. Good thing I was into coffee and not booze. At the café I only had to deal with someone who was tripping on a caffeine buzz instead of inebriated, pawing patrons.

Jill, wearing an uncharacteristic frown, threw a quick wave my way before she was snagged by a customer. I pushed through the crush and managed to work my way behind the bar.

Whale—whose name actually fit him well, since he was huge in all ways—was frantically taking orders, mixing drinks, and making change. Sweat poured from his shiny bald head. The white bar rag slung over his shoulder and the navy T-shirt beneath were both stained dark.

He acknowledged me with a curt nod and finished the drink he was working on. Liquid sloshed onto the bar top as he slammed it down and snatched the bills out of the waiting customer's hand.

Whale lumbered toward me, his bushy eyebrows nearly colliding above the bridge of his nose. His eyes were squinty, his mouth pinched. "You Shay?"

"Yeah," I shouted.

He flung the rag from his shoulder to mine, the end grazing my cheek before it splatted wetly against my jacket. Fumbling behind his back, he pulled the apron off and tossed it at my face. "I quit," he shouted. "This is ridiculous. Tell your old man I'll be in next week for my check."

I swatted at the apron as he fired a ring of keys at me. They smacked me in the chest and fell to the floor.

"Wait a minute—"

"I'm done." With that, Whale shoved past me and pushed people out of his way like a human snowplow, headed directly for the front door.

I managed to extricate myself from the apron and stood staring, open-mouthed, at his retreating back. "But you can't…" I held out a hand, then dropped it.

A voice and a poke in the arm yanked me out of my shocked stupor. "Lady, looks like you're in a mess, but I need payment before I can unload that beer in back." The speaker was a burly man with a buzz cut, wearing an insulated flannel jacket on his back and compassion on his face. He shrugged. "Sorry."

"Okay, hang on." My brain was two steps behind. "Goddamn it," I muttered and bent to scoop up Whale's keys and slide them into my pocket.

"Hey hotness!" a guy shouted from halfway down the bar. He had a silver New Year's Eve party hat sitting cockeyed on his head. "Where's me drinkie? Are you a Leprechaun?" He dissolved in laughter that would make a donkey proud.

"Shay!" Jill hollered over Mr. Happy's braying.

My head snapped from the man to Jill, and in that moment I took in the full impact of Whale's departure. I was stranded with a shitload of drunk or on-their-way-to-being-drunk partygoers who wanted more booze—right now—and a delivery guy who needed god only knew how much money. Patrons up and down the bar were staring at me, holding up glasses and money and waiting for service.

My first inclination was to tell them all to go to hell. Thankfully, before I did something really stupid, autopilot kicked in. I pulled off my jacket, stowed it under the counter, and hustled down to Jill. She looked at me with wide eyes and a tired "here we go again" grin.

"Long time no see," I yelled in her ear. "You have any idea how my dad pays the delivery guy?"

"I think usually by check. Not sure. I'm only around on days like this, when all hell is breaking loose."

"Don't suppose you know where he keeps his checkbook?" Why would she? It was a long shot, but it couldn't hurt to ask.

Jill was about to answer when someone grabbed the shoulder of the green Henley I wore and yanked so hard that my ribs slammed into the edge of the bar top. I grunted in pain.

It was Mr. Happy, and he wasn't smiling anymore. "I wan' a beer and I wan' it now!"

Laying hands on me was a very bad idea. I'd been doing everything I could to keep my anger in check, and now Mr. Happy was about to meet Shay on a rampage. Fury pounded a heavy beat through my veins. I grabbed the collar of his sweatshirt with both hands and yanked him half over the bar. "Touch me again and this will be your last new year."

He grabbed my wrists in alarm, unable to prevent me from shaking him like Dawg doing a death rattle on one of his stuffed toys.

"You." Shake. "Got." Shake. "That?" Shake.

"'Kay. 'Kay. Sorry. Leggo." He tugged against my grip. "'Kay, I said!" His eyes rolled back in his head. If he puked on me, I was definitely going to rip his drunken ass apart.

My gaze flicked to the linebacker-sized kid standing next to Mr. Happy. He looked like he was on the wrong side of twenty-one, and that dinged my caution bell. I pinned him in place with narrowed eyes. "You with him?"

The kid had the courtesy to look sheepish and simply nodded.

"Get him the hell out of here. I don't want to see him again to-night." I straight-armed Mr. Happy and shoved him away from the bar.

His buddy caught him before he hit the floor.

The crowd had surged away from the trouble. As Mr. Happy staggered toward the front door, they flooded back, refilling the open space.

I'd reached my limit. "LISTEN UP!" I shouted at the top of my lungs. The noise decreased by a couple decibels. I hopped up on top of the bar and repeated my command. When I thought most people were following directions, I bellowed, "PLAY NICE OR GET OUT. I PROMISE TO DO MY BEST TO GET YOUR ORDER. PLEASE BE PATIENT!" The more I shouted, the more the bar quieted, and there were some rumbles of acquiescence. In a lower register I rumbled, "THANK YOU!"

I hadn't even jumped down from the bar top before the cacophony ramped up again.

Jill yelled, "Damn, Little O, you haven't lost your touch. And no, I have no idea where your dad keeps his financial stuff."

"I'm outta practice, but it comes back fast. What do you need?"

She rattled off a list. Fortunately bottled beer rounded out the bulk of it. I hustled to the cooler under the bar, scored the requested bottles, popped them, and set them on the waiting tray. Then I slapped three well drinks together and sloshed them onto the tray. I was rusty, but my skills were on the way back.

"Thanks," Jill shouted over her shoulder. She hefted the tray and was immediately swallowed up by the throng. The crowd surged against the bar, looking thirstier by the second. I took a deep breath and caught sight of the Summit delivery guy still waiting for payment.

Shit.

My head felt like it was about to explode. I worked the rabble as fast as I could down the length of the bar toward the delivery man, feeling like a broken typewriter. I wasn't sure of my father's current prices, so I made them up as I went and eyeballed the liquor I splashed into glasses.

Before I reached the end of the bar, a tall woman with long, straight, honey-blond hair, wearing a black leather motorcycle jacket pushed up to the counter and flashed a bill. I stopped in front of her and tilted my head, waiting for her order.

"Whiskey, neat. Top shelf, if you have it." Her voice was resonant, her demeanor friendly.

"Sure." I grabbed a bottle of Knappogue Castle and a glass and poured.

"Looks like you've got your hands full."

"You can say that again." I pushed the drink toward her.

She held a twenty in hand, back far enough that I'd have to make an uncomfortable reach for it. That pissed me off. She said, "Is Pete O'Hanlon around?"

I let a fraction of my irritation color my tone. "No, he's not. It'll be fourteen bucks."

Still she held onto the bill and leaned in close. "When will he be in?"

Who did this chick think she was? "Look, I have no goddamn idea. Please give me your money so I can get your change and move on. If you haven't noticed, I've got a few people waiting here."

Both her eyebrows rocketed skyward. She handed me the twenty and held both hands up, palms out. "Hey, take it easy. I didn't mean anything." She shot a quick glance down the length of the counter and back. "You the only one on?"

Would this lady leave already? "Yep." I slapped her change in her hand.

She dropped the six bucks in front of me. "It's New Year's Eve. You're never going to make it at this rate."

"Tell me something I don't know." I turned away before I gave in to my desire to punch her and moved on to the poor delivery man, who by now had been waiting forever. I said to him, "I'm so sorry. How much do you need?"

He told me and settled on his stool, apparently content to nurse a half-full mug of beer. I quickly drew another and slid it down the bar toward him. He grabbed the handle and nodded his thanks.

I yelled, "I'll see if we have enough in the till to cover it."

My heart sank when I popped the drawer beneath the bar and made a quick cash calculation. The total didn't even come close.

I stuffed the money back in the till and stood, ignoring the couple of college-age guys a few feet away who were howling for their drinks. My left eye started to twitch, and I pushed my fingers against my eyebrow.

"Hey!" a voice hollered. I wasn't surprised to see the biker-jacketed woman who'd so handily summed up the totality of my life moments ago trying to get my attention. She no doubt wished to ensure that my knowledge of the shittiness of my current lot was complete.

"What?" I bellowed and shot her a drop-dead glare.

She bit her bottom lip. "I know how to pour. Been slinging liquor for years. I can help you out if…" She trailed off with a raised eyebrow and a shrug. She looked far too young to have been "slinging liquor for years."

Did I want to keep trying to hold the masses at bay, knowing it was only going to get busier as the night went on? And I had to find some way to pay the Summit dude. Desperation clawed at my core. It was time to wave the white flag. "Okay, yeah." I met her compassion-filled eyes and felt like a jerk. "I could use a hand or three. Look, I—I'm really sorry."

With a shake of her head she stopped my bumbling apology and made her way around the bar.

Things were happening too fast for me to track. I felt like hell for being an ass. For the life of me I couldn't figure out why this woman would want to dive into my nightmare. However, I wasn't about to argue.

I jerked a thumb under the counter. "Apron's down there if you want one. Mixers in the cooler." I pointed at the squat silver refrigerator tucked under the bar. "Garnishes on both ends and the middle of the bar. Wait staff down on the far right. Right now I'm free pouring. If you can find the jiggers, go for it." I quickly ran down the prices I'd been charging. "And hey, name's Shay. Thank you."

She stuck her hand out, and I shook it. Her grip was firm and sure. "Lisa. Lisa Vecoli. Glad to help."

I wasn't in any position to question why she didn't have anything better to do on New Year's Eve. I clapped her on the shoulder, helped a couple more people, and watched Lisa do her thing. After she poured her first drink, I could see she was confident and capable. I hoped she was as proficient with money as she was with booze.

"Lisa," I called as I handed an honest-to-god Shirley Temple to a short, round lady with curly dishwater-blond hair. "Can you hold the natives at bay while I go find a way to pay that delivery dude at the end of the bar?" I wasn't sure if I could trust this chick or not, but right now my options were pared down to one.

Without missing a beat, she said, "Sure. I'm good." She flipped the bottle she'd been holding high over her head, caught it, and proceeded to add it to the drink she was making.

Show-off.

Whatever the case, I was grateful. As long as she didn't rob me blind.

I hustled through a swinging door into the kitchen. A ghastly stench assailed my nose and I pulled up short. I took a second, deeper sniff, but the odor had wafted away. It was probably an olfactory hallucination. I was feeling quite like I'd lost most of my senses anyway.

Two more steps and I was out the back door. The cold hit me like a slap in the face and sucked the breath from my lungs. I ignored it and charged around the corner of the building. My footsteps echoed against the wall as I pounded up a set of exterior stairs that led to my father's second-floor apartment.

At the top, I stopped short. Maybe my dad was inside but something had happened to him. Maybe he'd finally had that stroke I'd been worrying about for years. I reached a tentative hand to the doorknob, expecting to find it locked. I jerked my hand off the metal as it twisted in my palm, then turned the knob again and swung the door open.

My heart leapt from my chest and landed securely in my throat. I pushed the door wider and peered into the dim apartment. The front door opened directly into the living room, with an open kitchen situated in the back. To the left a hall led to two bedrooms and a tiny bathroom. The light above the stove was on, and that was the only illumination in the place, save the glow of various electronics. Every time I came here, I was thrust back to my childhood, and the ghosts of the past roared into my head. It was so hard to believe Mom, Dad, and I had once lived in this cramped place.

The faint tang of burnt toast lingered in the air. I flipped on the light switch next to the door, and a few of the ghosts disappeared.

"Dad?" I called out. My heart triple-timed. I did not want to walk down that hall and find my father. But my feet had a mind of their own. I slowly stepped farther inside. "Dad?" I called again, louder.

I took a calming breath and moved across the floor and turned on the hall light. *Just do it, O'Hanlon. Go to your parents' room and look inside.* My late mother had been gone for the better part of my life, and I still couldn't think of that room as my dad's alone.

My dry throat clicked as I swallowed hard. Before I could talk myself out of it, I marched to the first door, reached in, and hit the light. "Dad?"

I stuck my head around the doorjamb. For a minute I thought I was going to hyperventilate. I concentrated on even breaths as I scanned the room. The bed was made—my father was a tidy drunk—and the rest of the room looked organized and neat like it usually did, minus any bodies.

Emboldened, I moved on to the room that had been my own. I didn't need light to see that it was void of my father. The bedroom was largely unchanged from when I'd moved out. Same twin mattress topped by the same old patchwork quilt. The same desk that had seen me suffer trigonometry and term papers sat in the same corner.

Nowadays, my old room was an emergency crash pad for the pals my dad played poker with—on the rare occasion they actually admitted they were too drunk to drive home.

The bathroom was the last place I checked. I flipped the light on and did a quick once-over. No one home there either.

I steamed back out to the living room, breathing easier and a little miffed at myself for getting carried away. However, nothing about this night was anywhere near normal.

Back to the task at hand. I needed to find the checkbook, post-haste.

The metal TV tray next to my dad's recliner seemed a good place to start. After shuffling magazines and almost spilling a half-full glass of some questionable liquid, I gave that up.

Next I headed for the desk by the front door. It was a beautiful piece of furniture, hand-carved and inlaid by my grandfather. Bills and unfolded statements were strewn across the top. I sifted through the mess, noting that the dates on a number of the bills were past due. I tried to remember if my father had complained recently about his cash flow.

At the bottom of the stack of crap was a typewritten sheet that looked like it had been balled up and flattened out again, maybe more than once. A business card was stapled to the corner. I was about to pass it by when I caught the words *Intent to Purchase* at the top of the paper. I pulled the piece of stationery from the pile and scanned the first few lines.

> *Dear Peter O'Hanlon,*
>
> *This letter expresses the mutual interest in a transaction currently in negotiations between the following parties:*
>
> *Buyer: Subsidy Renovations Inc.*
> *Seller: Peter James O'Hanlon*
>
> *This document outlines the potential terms of the sale of the property known as the Leprechaun Bar and its respective holdings to be negotiated and finalized at a later date.*

I sank into the chair and stared at the letter in disbelief. No way would Dad ever sell the Lep. He loved his bar, and I didn't think it was just because he was a drunk. Although that did help. But seriously. He wouldn't consider it without talking to me beforehand.

Would he?

And what was Subsidy Renovations? As I perched on the hard wooden seat, I recalled my father mentioning some time ago that he'd been approached by someone who was interested in the property the bar was built on. I remembered he said he laughed in the guy's face and told him that it would be over his dead body that he'd let them tear the place down and build a parking ramp or some other unnecessary "un"-improvement. Then he said he'd kicked the man out of the bar.

Maybe he'd reconsidered. I knew his funds were tight. Were his finances that bad? My father and I were going to have to have a heart-to-heart whenever he decided to show his face again. After I killed him, that is. I folded the letter and pocketed it, fully intending to confront my dad with it when I saw him.

I hit the drawer on the right side of the desk and rifled through it, finding nothing but writing utensils and three tins of peppermint Altoids. I shuddered to look at them, their smell reminding me of all the years my father sucked on the potent little white disks in an attempt to hide the odor of alcohol on his breath.

Next drawer down I hit the jackpot. I snatched out a blue vinyl-covered checkbook and flipped to the register. There was barely enough in the account to cover the cost of the beer downstairs. Right now, it didn't matter. I scribbled out the check. With a lift of my shoulder, I scrawled my father's name and entered the numbers into the register. It would have to do.

I locked the door and hustled down to the truck where the delivery man was now waiting, his hands stuffed in his armpits. I thrust the check at him, and he pocketed it with a grunt of thanks, white vapor billowing from his mouth.

"You know where to put the product?" I asked.

"Sure do," he rumbled. "Been delivering here the last year or so. I'll leave some in the cooler and bring the rest down to that aromatic cellar. You wanna do a count?"

"Nope. Do your thing. Oh—if you don't mind, stick the invoice on top of the microwave."

"Can do."

"Thanks so much for your patience." I started for the back entrance, but I realized I should probably update JT on the current state of affairs—and the probable state of our vacation if my father didn't pull his head from between his butt cheeks and materialize.

The humid air of the kitchen blasted me as I stepped across the threshold and blocked the screen door open. A fresh wave of impotent fury fogged my brain. I tried to breathe through the haze while I speed dialed JT. The display on my cell read 5:15 p.m. There was still time to salvage this night.

Cold tendrils of air wafted in from the open back door, swirling around as the delivery guy hand-trucked in his first load. A shiver worked its way up my spine.

I leaned against the stainless-steel counter waiting for JT to either pick up or for voicemail to kick in. The phone rang, and something other than cold air hit my nose. There was that smell again—like a sour, backed-up drain. I took another sniff, scanning the floor for the location of the suspect drain. A bucket of water dumped down the pipe should fix that little problem.

The sound of my girlfriend's voice jolted me back to awareness. "Babe, hey, I've been meaning to call." JT sounded exasperated and slightly out of breath, and I forgot all about stinky drainpipes.

"Sorry if I caught you at a bad time."

"No. I'm sorry. Trying to tie everything up so we can head out tomorrow, and things aren't playing out as easily as they should."

Here we go. Time to add a healthy portion of guilt to my slow boil. I was truly going to murder my father when he showed up. "Yeah. About that."

There was a pause on the line. "Uh-oh. What."

I gave her my thirty-five-cent version of the latest events.

"Shit."

"You said it."

"Want me to head to the Lep if I ever get done? At least we won't have to spend the dawn of the New Year apart."

"Sure. Thanks. I'll call you if anything changes."

JT rang off, and I headed back into battle.

———

The hands on an old Lucky Strike neon clock above the bar read twenty-five after nine. Still no Pete. He was almost certainly holed up in some dingy tavern, shooting Jack or Jim.

One good thing I hadn't realized was that my father had actually thought through at least some of the logistics of staffing the Lep for this big-ass holiday. In addition to Jill, he'd scheduled two additional servers to come on at seven. That considerably lightened the work in front of the bar, and Lisa and I had fallen into a comfortable rhythm as we poured beer, popped tops, mixed drinks, and made change.

The reveler's mass mood was rowdy but congenial, and that made me breathe a whole lot easier, although I still felt edgy that a bouncer wasn't working the front door. I wondered if that had slipped my dad's mind or if he'd been planning on handling that aspect of things himself. By unspoken agreement, both Lisa and I were careful to card anyone who looked remotely on the down side of twenty-one. She was an ass saver.

I was in the middle of making a screwdriver when someone thwapped me on the shoulder. I nearly pulled a repeat of the Mr. Happy performance on the thwapper before I recognized the shaggy hair and grinning face of my best friend, Nick Cooper, better known to the masses as Coop.

"Hey!" I leaned forward and stifled a shout of glee. "Thought you were partying with the Beans." The Green Beans for Peace and Preservation was an environmental organization dedicated to the green cause. Well-intentioned, often jailed.

He hollered, "Heard you were in a spot. Figured there was no better way to ring in the New Year than to hang out at the Lep." He looked around. "Pete hasn't shown up yet?"

I shook my head.

"What can I do?"

Music to my ears. "You wanna card the little girls and boys and bounce whoever needs bouncing? First dibs on the hot chicks."

Coop's grin grew. In the last year or so, my meek friend had turned from a somewhat wussy pacifist into a pacifist who wasn't afraid to confront trouble with an appropriate level of ferocity. Since he'd recently split ways—on friendly terms—with his enigmatic ex-cartel-running girlfriend, he was more than happy to cavort with potential playmates.

Into Coop's ear I said in a somewhat lower register, "Who told you what was going on? Kate?"

"No. JT called and said you might need a hand."

Oh, but I loved that woman.

"In fact," Coop said, "here she is." He stepped sideways and, holy crap on a cracker, there was my girl in the flesh. A purple scarf wound around her neck and was tucked into the front of her navy blue pea coat. Her cheeks were red from the cold.

I couldn't help but grin like an infatuated teenager. "Hey!"

Coop waved a hand and threaded his way to the front door.

JT wedged herself up to the bar. Wisps of chestnut hair had escaped her once-neat ponytail and floated around her cheeks. "What's a girl gotta do for some attention around here?"

Unmindful of the audience, I cupped her face and gave her a brief moment of some very appreciative attention. Apparently the crowd was too schnockered to care, because there was absolutely no reaction.

She leaned back with a smile. "Coop heeded my cry for help. I tried to rope Kate and her gal toy in, but they had a better offer."

I laughed. "Figures."

A tall, alcohol-deprived carouser sitting next to JT started getting feisty. The woman had on a cone-shaped New Year's hat and periodically blew a kazoo at me. Prior to JT's arrival, I might have ripped that kazoo out of her mouth and tried to shove it down her throat. Now instead bringing a potential lawsuit on my father, I finished making her drink, grabbed the kazoo from between her lips, and dumped it in her martini. I handed it over with a satisfied smirk.

She slapped a bill on the bar and, with her kazoo-laden drink in hand, backed cautiously away from the insane bartender.

I returned my attention to JT, who was watching me with an amused grin. "What can I do?"

"Make the rounds? Pick up empties, wipe tables?"

"No problem." JT pushed back from the bar as she unwound her scarf and shrugged out of her jacket.

I exchanged her winter wear for a bar rag and tossed it to her. She snagged it out of the air and disappeared into the throng.

I was elbowed back to reality by a well-placed shot from Lisa. She yelled, "Who was that?"

21

"Girlfriend," I hollered.

"Not bad." She grinned and moved on to another customer.

For the better part of the next two and a half hours, Lisa and I worked nonstop. As the countdown neared, I tried to keep an eye on the time so we could turn up the volume on the two TVs that were mounted above the bar. We were ten minutes from the New Year, and I finally felt like we might make it to the end of the night.

I handed off the last of the latest round of drink orders to one of the servers whose name had flown in one ear and straight out the other. She was a fresh-faced, college-aged kid with a strawberry-blond French braid who seemed reasonably capable. She shouldered the loaded tray with practiced grace. I wondered what she wanted to be when she grew up.

"Hey!" A hoarse voice shook me out of my very momentary reverie.

I turned toward a balding, narrow-faced man with a bulbous red nose who was crammed like a sardine against the bar. From the look of him, he appreciated his alcohol.

"What can I—" The rest of my query died in my throat when I caught sight of the wallet he was holding out. Instead of showing me his driver's license, the wallet contained a police shield. In the blink of an eye, multiple thoughts raced through my head, a dead father leading the chase. My jaw snapped shut.

He squinted at me, looking remarkably like Popeye the Sailor Man.

I waited, inanely wondering if he was going to speak out of the side of his mouth and ask me for some spinach. When the words came, they weren't about spinach. "Peter O'Hanlon here?"

Okay. If my father was dead, would they be asking for him? I had no idea. I quickly scanned the crowd for JT, without success. I said, "No, he's not."

Popeye shifted his eyes from one end of the bar to the other as if he thought I might be hiding my dad in plain sight. His gaze pinned me again. "Know where I can find him?"

I leaned close. "If I could find him right now, I'd probably kill him. What's going on?"

His breath was hot on my cheek and smelled like a combination of cigarettes and wintergreen. I wondered if he used mints like my dad did to hide the evidence of his lapses.

"I need to talk to him."

"Don't know what to tell you. I haven't seen my father today."

"Your father?"

"Yeah, Pete O'Hanlon's my dad. Did you pick him up again?"

Popeye gave me a sharp look. "No. Should we?"

Well, hell. I was too busy to play twenty questions with the law. The clock on the wall read 11:56. If he wasn't here to break the news to me that I had a dead daddy, I didn't have time to deal with him. "Look," I said, "I don't know where he is. If you find him, please tell him to get his ass back here." I was about to move on when the man stopped me with a hand on my wrist.

Irritated, I swung back to face him. "What?"

Popeye pulled me toward him and again put his lips next to my cheek. "Your father own a gun?"

A gun? What kind of question was that? My dad used to keep an old revolver under the bar for emergencies, but as far as I knew, he'd never pulled it out. Whether it was still there I had no idea. "He used to," I answered warily. "Why?"

Popeye flipped his business card at me, like a surly TV detective. "You call me if he comes back, okay?"

I picked up the card. Emblazoned across the top was SGT. ROBERT DESILVERO followed on the next line by SAINT PAUL POLICE DEPARTMENT, with HOMICIDE DIVISION printed below that.

Holy cow. Homicide Division? My head snapped up to meet Sergeant DeSilvero's eyes.

"Call me." He backed up and faded into the masses.

Any further thought I had on what transpired were lost when the floor literally started vibrating from the stomping of feet and thunder of voices shouting down the seconds to the new year.

It didn't look like 2012 was going to be getting off to a very good start.

———

It was past three in the morning when JT and I hit the sack. Exhaustion made my body feel heavy and lethargic. JT clicked off the bedside lamp, and the mattress sank down as she crawled in and rolled to face me. She propped herself on her elbow, silhouetted against the window behind her.

"Okay. You've been weird all night. What's going on?"

My emotions were a jumble. Throughout the last twelve hours, too many thoughts and feelings I couldn't deal with had been whirling through my brain. At some point I'd shunted my misgivings deep into my mental dungeon, a place that was reserved for stowing away the crap I didn't want to deal with. I had long ago honed the ability to block out everything but the most immediate issues and deal with whatever situation was most dire, but a part of me knew I couldn't compartmentalize like that forever.

At the Leprechaun tonight, we'd been so busy that I hadn't had a chance to tell JT about the visit from Sgt. Robert DeSilvero of the SPPD. Or about the letter that was burning a hole in the pocket of my pants. So I cranked up the moat gate and let out some of my confusion and fear. As I talked, JT's hand settled gently on my ribs, warming the skin through my T-shirt. Her touch often kept me grounded, and it did again now as I haltingly explained things.

"So," I said, "I have no idea what the cop wanted aside from the gun thing, which I don't get, and I still have no idea where my god-damn father is." I blew out an irritated breath, concentrated on JT's thumb as it traced abstract patterns on my side. "Oh, yeah, and there's the little matter of a letter I found on Dad's desk. A note of intent regarding the sale of the Leprechaun."

JT's hand stilled its calming movements. "Sale of the bar?"

"Yeah. I had no clue. He never mentioned that he was thinking about selling. I think that'd be something he'd tell me." I dropped my voice a few octaves, mimicking my dad. "*Oh, by the way, Shay, I'm selling the bar and moving to the Keys where I can live in the mangroves and fish to my heart's content.*" JT gave a small chuckle.

I pushed my head into the pillow. "You know, earlier this fall, or maybe it was sometime in the summer, I remember Dad mentioning that someone had stopped by—a developer of some kind, I think—and asked if he ever thought about getting out of the business. Dad told the guy to take a hike. Although I suppose he probably used a bit more colorful language that that." I allowed a small smile. "I know he loves the place. I can't see him selling out to anyone."

For a couple of moments we were both quiet. With a yawn, I added, "I wonder if he's been having money trouble. There were a few past-due bills on his desk."

It was too dark to make out JT's features, but I could feel her eyes on me. I reached over and slid my hand lightly across her cheek and tangled my fingers in her hair. She was the rock in my oftentimes one-step-away-from-crazy life.

She leaned into my touch, turned her head, and kissed my palm. "I don't know what to say about this sale thing, but I can do a little poking and see if I can find out what St. Paul is sniffing around for."

I yawned again, my eyes watering as I started to unwind enough to feel sleepy. "I'd appreciate it."

There were still so many unanswered questions. Why was Lisa Vecoli looking for my father, for one? Where on earth was he, anyway? Another thought slithered into my consciousness and I stiffened. "Oh, crap."

JT's hand tightened. "What?"

"The B&B we had for tomorrow in Duluth. I'm so sorry. I don't think I can go right now."

"Don't worry about that. I'll call in the morning. Who knows, maybe your dad is back home sleeping off one hell of a New Year's Eve."

"We can hope."

JT settled onto her side close to me, her arm resting across my abdomen. "Shut the mind down and sleep, babe."

I obediently closed my eyes. My last coherent thought was how lucky I was to have found the kind of love JT offered. It was a once in a lifetime thing, and I knew it.

TWO

SUNDAY MORNING ARRIVED BRIGHT and early. After a fast breakfast with JT, I called Kate to tell her I'd be on the way to recover the canines. She answered after four rings, mumbled, "'Kay," into the phone, and hung up on me. She must have had a doozy of a night.

JT took off for the station at half past nine, intending to see if she could find out why St. Paul PD was nosing around Minneapolis territory. I added a mental note to check around when I got to the bar and see if I could find the gun Sergeant DeSilvero was so hot for.

Initially, I'd briefly thought about closing the Lep for the day if my father hadn't miraculously reappeared to open up himself. However, the sad state of my dad's financial affairs, guilt at the thought of abandoning him in his time of need, and worry that something really bad might have happened dictated that I be a good daughter and bring home his bacon.

It took Kate three minutes of my pounding on her door and barking dogs to get her ass out of bed and let me in. She muttered something incoherent, made a U-turn, beelined down the hall into her bathroom, and slammed the door. In the brief glimpse I'd had, the poor thing looked like she woken on the bottom side of hell—one of her eyebrows had looked singed—and her face was whiter than the dingy snow outside. Whatever party she'd attended must have been a doozy.

From Kate's place the dogs and I headed toward Uptown and Pam's Pawhouse. A longtime Rabbit Hole customer named Pam Pine owned the place, which was a doggy daycare and pet boarding business. With her genuine smile, huggy arms, and bottomless pockets of treats, both the mutts adored Pam. JT and I did too, not only because she'd come to love our pooches almost more than we did, but because she was a flat-out huge-hearted human. She trained Dawg and Bogey on Canine Good Citizenship—an American Kennel Club program—teaching both JT and me the ins and outs right along with the dogs. Her patience was infinite, which was a godsend because none of the four of us were stellar students.

Dawg and Bogey were scheduled for their own special vacation with Pam and her canine-loving staff. This morning, JT and I discussed the situation and decided there was no reason for our mutts not to enjoy their vacation, even if our getaway was in question. As they say, it's a dog's life.

I pulled in and parked in front of the Pawhouse, a squat brick building painted orange and green. Dawg sat up straight and pressed his nose to the passenger window, fogging it with his hot, rather fishy breakfast breath. Bogey lifted his head and woofed once from the back where he'd stretched out, his bulk taking up the entire bench seat. Unless he knew for sure there was something worth getting up for, he wasn't going to bother.

I uttered the magic words. "Hey guys, we're gonna go see Pam! Where's Pam, huh? Where's Pam?"

Bogey huffed and lumbered to his feet. Dawg's butt wiggled so hard I could feel the car shake. I grabbed the bag I'd packed with dog food and a couple of their favorite blankets and followed the mad charge to the front door.

A reception desk sat near the entrance of a large, light-chartreuse-painted room that was bisected by a white plastic picket fence three feet high. Behind the fence seven dogs of varying ages and sizes happily bounced around, chewing on and chasing each other. A collapsible yellow tunnel took up one corner, a wall of crates waited for naptime, and various toys were scattered across the floor. This was one place where the four-legged undisputedly ruled.

A long hall down the back held posh boarding suites, a well-equipped groomer's room, and offices. Out back was a fenced-in yard the size of a basketball court that provided hours of pooch playing pleasure.

As I was dragged through the glass doors, Pam emerged from the back. Her eyes lit up when she saw Bogey and Dawg.

"My boys are here! Happy New Year!" A gigantic, delighted smile spread across her face as she dropped to her knees. I released the leashes and watched the dogs deliriously scramble into her arms, tongues washing her face, slobber flying. The drool didn't faze her in the least, and after some very soggy puppy love, she glanced up. "Good to see you too." Pam's smile faded. "You look wiped. What's wrong?" Each of her arms was full of dog, and she kept her hands on their heads as she straightened and looked warily at me.

"Long story. My dad's at it again."

"Oh, oh. Lay it on me."

I did, and when I finished, she shook her head. "Shay, I'm so sorry."

I gave her a wan smile. "We decided there was no reason to deprive Bogey and Dawg of their fun. Besides, maybe he'll be at the bar with some ridiculous excuse for his absence. We can only hope, right?"

"Absolutely." She looked down at the two sets of adoring eyes glued to her every move. "Let's get these two situated and you go see if you can reclaim your vacation." She held out a hand and I most appreciatively gave her the mutts' bag. She said, "We're good here. Go forth and find your father."

I saluted her and made my exit.

———

Snow flurries periodically spewed from the heavens as I pulled into the Leprechaun parking lot. I exited the Escape, hit lock on the fob, was rewarded with a grating beep, and trudged to the rear entrance of the bar.

At the door I stopped and took a good look at the old building. At one time I'd helped my father paint the structure white with Kelly-green trim. It sure didn't feel like it had been that long ago, but the condition of the peeling paint told the real story. Had it been five, maybe ten years ago? Time went by so fast, and it only accelerated the older I got.

Was Dad actually considering selling out? Was he somewhere out there, dead from hypothermia and an overload of hooch?

Maybe he was home. I liked that idea a whole lot better.

I headed up the stairs and rapped my knuckles on the door. Waited a few seconds and knocked again.

No answer, but I'd expected that. I let myself in and did a fast scope of the apartment, which was as devoid of life as it had been the night before.

I pulled the front door shut and locked it. Cold air stung my cheeks and the covered stairway shuddered under my weight as I descended two at a time. I needed to focus on one problem at a time or my head was going to explode. *Forward, Shay, don't look back.* The first order of business was to get the bar up and running by noon.

I keyed the lock, and the kitchen door skittered open with a reluctant squawk. I stepped inside and experimentally swung the door back and forth a few times. It screeched with every movement. Huh. My dad was usually anal about upkeep. Normally he would have attended to such an easily fixable issue—a couple of squirts of WD-40 should take care of it.

I thought about that.

The rundown façade of the bar, the sticking door, and the ungodly stench that assaulted my nasal passages as I stepped inside made no sense. Had I been so caught up in my own life that I'd neglected to see telltale signs my father was slipping? Was I somehow responsible for this because I hadn't been paying attention?

I forced myself to focus on the here and now and forget the rest. First things first: I had to refrain from throwing up all over the tile floor. The malodorous fumes that choked me as soon as I stepped inside had to be coming from the drainpipe under the sink. My eyes watered and I clapped a hand over my nose. I headed into the bar itself, where the smell faded, and wandered around turning on lights, TVs, and ceiling fans. What had the delivery guy said last night? Something about the aromatic cellar. Maybe the source of the problem was coming from there.

I headed back into the kitchen to the basement door. I pulled it open, and nearly gagged again.

The chunky brick wall was rough against my fingertips as I groped for the light switch. With a loud click, a single bulb illuminated a narrow stairway. Cautiously, I made my way down the steep steps with the collar of my sweatshirt pulled over my nose and mouth. Four light fixtures hung from the ceiling and did little to chase shadows from the cobwebby corners of the subterranean space. The cellar was definitely not a favorite hangout. I had always gotten the creeps whenever I descended into the dank dimness, and today was no exception.

My father stored the bulk of the liquor and other odds and ends down here. It was cool in the summer, cold in the winter, and usually smelled of must and liquor. Now those odors were overpowered by sewer stench so strong I nearly retched every time I breathed in.

Cases of booze were stacked on rolling wire shelves that lined the perimeter of the room. Each shelf held a hand-printed card with the type of liquor or beer that was stored there. The Summit driver had stacked a double row of boxes containing the popular ale down the center of the cellar. Otherwise everything else looked in order except for the back right corner of the damp space. The shelving had been rolled away to create an inverted square. An old window fan sat nearby, plugged into an ancient brown extension cord coming from a receptacle embedded in the closest light socket.

I rolled one of the shelves out of the way and took two steps closer. My hand was back over my face, and I sucked the tainted air through my mouth. Black sludge had oozed up from a four-foot crack in the cement floor. The sludge had started to creep across the cement.

My father must have been using the fan to try to disseminate the smell. I didn't hold much hope that it would do much good, but turned it on anyway. We needed the Roto-Rooter man in a very bad way.

THREE

THE MINUTE HAND ON the Lucky Strike clock edged ever closer to the twelve as I hustled to finish prepping the bar. After chopping celery stalks, I topped off the olive and cherry containers in the garnish trays.

I was about to unlock the front door when it dawned on me I'd forgotten to pull the start bank from the floor safe in my father's office. Last night when I put away the New Year's Eve proceeds, it was a huge relief to find he maintained his security interests by never changing combinations or passwords. They were all still they same as they'd always been.

In less than a minute I was back behind the bar, stuffing bills into the till drawer as I tried to remember what else I was forgetting.

Then it dawned on me. The gun. I'd entirely forgotten to look for my dad's revolver. I ducked down and sifted through the detritus under the bar. Where I thought my old man used to stash the weapon now shelved extra glassware and a dishwasher. I systematically searched the rest of the area without success. It must be stashed else-where these days. Whatever.

With a frustrated grunt I straightened.

12:02 p.m. Show time.

The deadbolt on the heavy, windowless front door retracted eas-ily. I gave the door a good shove to make sure it was open.

As it swung outward, I heard a grunt, followed by a thud and a muffled "Oof!"

"What on earth?" I muttered and I warily stuck my head around the door.

The first thing I saw on the ice-covered sidewalk were the soles of a pair of black snow boots. I'd face-planted a probable customer with the door.

"Oh my god. I'm so sorry." My heart hammered hard against my ribs. *Way to go, Shay. You've now given your dad a personal injury lawsuit in addition to the problems he already has.* The per-son was probably going to whip out a mobile phone and dial 1-800-411-PAIN.

"Shay! What are you doing here?" My vic was apparently a woman, and she batted at the fur-lined hood of her poofy black coat to push it away from her face.

"Agnes? That you under all those layers?"

Agnes Zaluski was an old friend with a troublemaking nephew. The previous spring we'd bailed said nephew out of some fishy water, and Agnes had taken a platonic shine to my father. Or, to be more specific, had taken a shine to the card games he conducted in his back room. It didn't hurt that Agnes enjoyed her vodka as much as my father enjoyed his scotch. Two peas in an alcohol-infused pod.

I said, "I'm so sorry. Are you okay?"

"With the exception of my bruised nose, I'm fine. Help this old lady up."

I slid my arms under her armpits and hoisted her to her feet. Despite her years, Agnes still towered well over my own height of five-seven.

She wobbled a little and I hung on as she regained her equilibrium. "Easy."

"I'm okay. Nothing new to this ancient posterior of mine." With a grimace she patted her jacket-covered butt and gave me a shove toward the door.

Once we were safely inside, Agnes hiked herself onto the closest bar stool and shrugged out of her Pillsbury Doughboy replica jacket with a resounding "Uff da." She draped the coat over the adjacent stool and rubbed her hands together. "So where is that scallywag father of yours?"

"Wish I knew. He no-showed last night and still hasn't come up for air."

Agnes squinted, her thin face reminiscent of Professor McGonagall's from the Harry Potter movies. "Really? He was raring to go for New Year's Eve! Night before last he was preoccupied during our game trying to make sure everything was in order." She leveled me a calculating look. "How about a little squirt of the hard stuff since you bowled me head over keister?"

"Sure." I rounded the bar. There wasn't much involved in fixing Agnes her "squirt." I dumped a good amount of vodka straight into a glass and asked, "Did you have a good game?"

"It's poker. You know how poker is. It's always good. Especially here."

I did know. My dad and his weekly games were legendary.

I placed the shot in front of her, and Agnes tossed it back. She didn't flinch as she swallowed.

"Have you been playing often?" I asked, genuinely curious and a little surprised, although I shouldn't have been. The previous spring I'd distracted Agnes from her nephew Baz's shenanigans by stowing her and Eddy Quartermaine—the woman who owned the Victorian that housed the Rabbit Hole, and my pseudo-mom—with my father while Coop, Baz, and I nearly got ourselves executed during a drug cartel shootout.

My dad, in usual form, had organized a back room poker game on the fly, making both Agnes and Eddy very happy. It was no secret Agnes loved poker almost as much as she loved her Stoli, but I hadn't realized she'd become a regular participant in my father's circle.

"Oh yes." Agnes muffled a belch behind her hand. "Every week."

"Did Dad seem okay? Not depressed, or … " I trailed off and shrugged.

"Pete was darn-tootin' good. He won, which added up to a whopping booty of seventy-six bucks. When I left, the bunch of them were talking about Roy's kid's chances running for mayor of Minneapolis."

Roy Larson was one of my father's closest friends. He was a Twin Cities fixture and a real character. He claimed to be a many-times-removed relative of Herbert Sellner, the man who invented the Tilt-A-Whirl. Every August when the State Fair came to St. Paul for twelve days of deep-fried food on a stick, carnival rides, and meltingly hot weather, Roy repeated the tale of Herbie's debut of the venerable Tilt-A-Whirl at the 1927 Great Minnesota Get-Together.

Roy's son Greg, while not quite as quirky as his dad, was still an odd duck. He was a few years older than I was. We'd gone to the same high school, but he had graduated before I landed there. His run for mayor was interesting in light of his father's political and rather unique business history.

Roy Larson had started his business career as the owner of the bar that would eventually become the Leprechaun. My father purchased the joint from him back in the Seventies. Roy sold out to finance a failed bid for the highest office in the state, going up against the very popular Rudy Perpich. He was soundly trounced and quietly retreated back into the business world, eventually managing to build himself something of an empire in the development and production of biodegradable kitty litter. Larson's Super Clump Flush-Away Cat Litter was a regional semi-success, as long as you were careful not to put too much of it down your toilet.

Personally, I wondered if Greg was running for mayor to try to fulfill his dad's lifelong—and lost—dream of holding political office.

I asked, "Who else was playing that night?"

"Let me think." Agnes searched her vodka-soaked brain and ticked names off on the fingers of her right hand. "Me, your dad, a young coot—Brian Eckhart, I think his name was. Roy, the Vulc, and..." Her lips pressed together so hard that the red of her lipstick stood out in stark contrast to the white, bloodless ring of wrinkly skin around her mouth. "Who else?" Agnes frowned and tapped her fingers on the bar top.

Brian Eckhart was an ex-cop who now worked in security. He met my dad a couple years back after responding to an attempted till tap at the Leprechaun. Although he hadn't managed to track down the potential robber, Brian had become a regular after-hours poker participant.

The Vulc, better known as Mick Simon, was a river man who worked with my dad on the Mississippi. He looked like a year-round

Santa Claus. Somewhere in the late '90s or early 2000s, he'd been Vulcanus Rex, the St. Paul Winter Carnival's God of Fire.

"Oh!" Agnes startled me out of my own reverie as she tried to snap arthritic fingers. "Harvey Benjamin and Limpy Dick." She nodded. "That's it."

"Who's Harvey Benjamin?"

"You haven't heard of old Hemorrhoid Harvey?"

"Can't say I have." Nor was I sure I wanted to.

Agnes scrutinized my face. "Don't suppose you would. You're too young. But you just wait." She chortled in a rather terrifying way. "Harvey's the owner of Benjamin's Drugstore in Richfield. Kind of like Merwin Drug in Robbinsdale. Not that Merwin's is there anymore though," she said wistfully. "Oh, Merwin's. They had the best soda fountain in the back. When I was a kid, we'd head there for malteds after some hot and heavy necking at the drive-in. Hoo boy." She shuddered and fanned her face.

Thinking about Agnes making out with someone was as bad as thinking about my parents having sex. Agnes patted my hand. "Benjamin's focuses on the needs of us senior types," she said. "He has some of the best hemorrhoid creams anywhere. That's where he gets his nickname. Now if only Harvey would put a soda fountain in ... "

Agnes droned on, extolling the virtues and pitfalls of ice cream, butt cream, and eventually denture cream. I certainly didn't need to know in such stark detail the bodily malfunctions of the senior set, but out of respect I did try not to make a face.

I nodded and smiled and turned my mind to Limpy Dick instead. His name was actually Richard Zaros, another guy who'd worked with my father back in the day. He was probably one of the most eccentric and definitely the craziest of my dad's friends. Long ago, he'd lost two fingers in a barge accident. Another time his left leg was pinned and crushed between a barge and a pier. It had to be removed below the knee. Now he was one half of South Africa's Blade Runner.

During the time that I'd talked to Agnes, a few additional patrons had drifted in. A number of them were wearing the drooping, squinty-eyed look that indicated a whopper of a New Year's Day hangover.

A college-aged couple sauntered to one of the booths at the back of the bar, and three slack-faced guys parked themselves a few stools apart from each other at the bar. All these customers were a good thing, but they made me feel trapped. What I really wanted to do was look for my dad. I refreshed Agnes's glass with another squirt and wandered off to make my father some money.

———

Things picked up considerably by late afternoon.

Agnes had caught a cab some time ago. It was a good thing, because her complimentary shots were putting a serious dent in the Stoli bottle.

I pulled an on-the-house pitcher for the Shamrock O'Taters— one of the co-rec broomball teams my father sponsored—and weaved through the crowded floor to deliver it amid catcalls and friendly insults. Earlier in afternoon, the Taters won a game against a rival neighborhood tavern, and the crew was in full celebratory mode. For a long time, I'd played broomball with the Taters, until Kate and I sponsored our own team through the Rabbit Hole. Now, when I had an opportunity to hop into a game and work my aggressions out on the ice, I tried to pick games against them. The crew all still liked me, but it didn't take long before a friendly rivalry ensued.

Instead of taking a few minutes to sit and catch up with my ex-teammates, resentment and duty coiled around each other. Duty propelled me to keep working. Of course, rancorous pangs really shredded my gut when I thought about the cozy, unoccupied room at the bed-and-breakfast in Duluth where JT and I were supposed to be getting away from it all.

My father was a selfish bastard, and I was worried sick about him.

Along with the buzz of chattering voices, the heavy beats of "American Woman" thumped in the background for the fourth consecutive time. Whoever was plugging the juke had a serious case of relationship woes.

I snagged empties and pushed chairs in, straightening up as I made my way behind the bar. Beer bottles clanged loudly against each other as I dumped them into the recycling bin. I scanned the customers lined up on bar stools, assessing who needed help, who had reached their limit, and who needed a refresh.

A man animatedly waved a folded bill in front of me, and I pivoted toward him. Before I could move, someone put a hand on my forearm.

I was surprised to see Lisa Vecoli tucked up against the bar.

"Hey," I said and I swung back to face her. "You recover from last night?"

A smile crinkled the corners of her eyes as she surveyed the room. "Oh yeah. It's been awhile since I've had that much fun."

I couldn't tell if she was being serious or sarcastic.

She finished her assessment of the crowd, probably looking for the presumably preoccupied Pete. "I assume if you're running the bar, your father still hasn't turned up?"

"Nope." I gave her an apologetically wry grin, still not understanding why she was so damned determined to talk to my dad. "What is it you need him for?"

An emotion I couldn't identify flickered across Lisa's face, and for a moment I thought she was going to spill it.

"It's . . . well, it's a story."

"Hey, lady!" The guy who'd tried to flag me down was getting antsy. "Can I get some help down here, for chrissake?"

"Hang ON!" I yelled at him and refocused on Lisa. My customer service score was going to be in the toilet.

She said, "Tell you what. Let me give you a hand and later on maybe we can sit down and talk. But," she nodded at Mr. Impatient, "let's get him taken care of before he goes all whoop on your ass."

After Lisa's successful audition last night, I'd be an idiot to turn her down. I was going to have to pay her well for her services.

Forty-five minutes and a number of happier patrons later, we'd conquered the masses and worked ourselves into a sort of equilibrium. I wondered what JT was doing and if Coop was on his feet yet. They might still be wiped from New Year's revelry, but at least they were free while I was stuck here taking care of Daddy's business. When my father showed his face, he was going to get a serious piece of my mind. If I had any mind left.

During a lull in the action, I leaned against the edge of the bar, stuck my lip out, and blew air onto my damp face.

Lisa propped herself next to me. She grabbed onto the edge of the countertop and arched her back with a groan. "I have to admit I'm not used to being on my feet so many hours at a time anymore."

I wondered what she did now, but she'd obviously tended bar sometime in her past. She hadn't lied when she'd said she knew how to pour. I was sure the lull in thirsty customers wouldn't last long enough for a conversation beyond "pass me the Jim Beam," so I simply said, "I hear you." My own body felt as if I'd climbed the rock wall at the gym fifteen times too many. I allowed a half-smile and took a critical look out at the main floor. There were actually a few empty bar stools, and maybe half the tables were occupied. The tide was starting to turn in our favor.

The front door opened. Agnes tottered in with Eddy, Rocky, and Tulip in tow.

Hallelujah! More help had arrived. I'd gotten so busy I hadn't said goodbye to Agnes, and here she was with people who could help me keep things, including my sanity, together.

Rocky, a savant of some kind, lived above the Rabbit Hole in my old one-bedroom apartment with sweet, quiet Tulip, his balloon-animal-creating bride of three months. Rocky and Tulip's whole situation still stunned me nearly speechless every time I thought about it. But as wacky as the two of them were, it was cool to see them happy.

As motherly stand-ins went, Eddy took the prize. She was a second mom to all of us, actually, and I loved her dearly. I couldn't help but admire her eccentricity—like the hot-pink low-rider sneakers she was currently wearing that Coop had given to her for Christmas. She gave me hope that I could be as cool as she was when I became a Woman of a Certain Age and retired. Not that I was guaranteed a retirement at all, considering the way the economy was going.

"Shay O'Hanlon," Rocky said, his green plaid aviator hat pulled low on his head and a delighted smile on his face. "Happy New Year! Did you know that the first recorded celebration of the Eve of the New Year goes back four thousand years? Four thousand years, Shay O'Hanlon! That is a very long time."

Rocky was a round little man somewhere in middle age—maybe forty-five?—with the personality of a sweet teenager. His savantish

43

specialty was facts. He had a photographic memory and knew a bit about almost everything, and that was no exaggeration. If he came across something he wasn't familiar with, he'd dash right to the computer and Google the hell out of whatever it was until he gleaned all there was to glean. Then he enjoyed sharing his newfound knowledge with the rest of us—whether we wanted to know it or not.

I laughed. "No, Rocky, I have to admit I didn't know that."

Tulip was looking cute as could be in a red down jacket with an attached hood and a black-and-pink striped muffler wrapped about fourteen times around her neck. She was actually a little taller than Rocky, a fact he adored about his wife. Tulip was an exotic cross between Queen Latifah and Carol Burnett, with a good dose of Creole thrown in. I think it was the brash red hair, dark skin, and curvy build.

There was certainly no sense of shortcoming between the two of them. They simply delighted in one another. In turn, they were usually a delight to be around, although on occasion the rapid-fire fact sharing sometimes made my head ache.

When Tulip smiled, her entire face lit up, her eyes crinkling with good humor. She said, "To add to Rocky's most entertaining factoids, there are thirty-two thousand two hundred and fifty-six LED lights on the ball that drops in Times Square on New Year's Eve. It weighs a whole bunch. Eleven thousand eight hundred seventy-five pounds, to be exact."

Rocky's head bobbed enthusiastically. "And there are two thousand six hundred and sixty-eight crystal panels—"

"Come along, kids," Eddy said, smoothly interrupting the flow of Rocky's patter. "Let's help Shay out in the kitchen." Eddy hustled Rocky and Tulip into the kitchen.

When Eddy returned, she valiantly squirmed her way aboard the stool next to Agnes. She said, "Set those two on some cleaning in back. Your father does okay, but the joint sure could use some Rocky and Tulip elbow grease. Who ever knew they could have so much fun working together?"

The two could happily spend hours at working on this or that. They did a remarkable job, too.

"See," Agnes said to Eddy. "Told you Shay was here."

Eddy cut dark eyes toward Agnes. "I didn't doubt you, Aggie." Eddy half-turned and scanned the floor. "But you said she was pulling her hair out, and it looks to me like things are under control. You do have an inclination to exaggerate, ya know."

Agnes and Eddy were great friends, but they had a tendency to squabble like a couple of thirteen-year-olds. I could tell they were about to launch into a full-tilt bicker fest. I repressed a grin and got ready for the fireworks. It was humorous to watch, at least when their arguments weren't getting in the way of extricating ourselves from some death-defying situation.

"Pshaw, you old woman," Agnes said. "I only exaggerate when it doesn't matter. You should've seen it in here earlier. Plum crazy, it was." She squinted at my barkeep counterpart. "Who, may I ask, are you?" Subtlety truly wasn't one of Agnes's strengths.

Just like that, the bicker fest was derailed.

"Lisa Vecoli," Lisa answered.

I said, "She's the one who hauled my keister out of purgatory last night, and she came back today for more fun. She's either a serious sucker or a deranged do-gooder."

Lisa gave my hip a friendly nudge. "I'm a sucker for a pretty woman in distress."

I laughed. "I don't know about the pretty part, but I was certainly in a hell of a lot of distress."

Was Lisa flirting with me? She *was* a hot little package. Long hair hung in a braid down her back. A white T-shirt stretched tight across her chest, and worn blue jeans hugged her assets. I might have had a spark of interest if my life and my heart weren't so happily enmeshed with JT's.

Then I recalled why she'd appeared—not as an angel sent from the distillery gods—and thoughts of any potential flirting flew right out the front door. I glanced sideways at Lisa with a curious frown. "Time to fess up. Why are you looking for my dad?"

That was a question I so wanted to hear the answer to. Too many people were asking for my dad, and I was at a loss for a reasonable answer to give any of them. Three pairs of curious eyes locked on Lisa.

She blinked a couple of times. I could almost see the cogs turning in her head. She said, "It's a long story. I'd rather save it for a quieter moment." She indicated the bar with a jerk of her head. "Bad timing." It was the same excuse she used last night, but I had to admit it was valid. We'd almost certainly be interrupted as soon as she got started.

Eddy waved a hand before Lisa had a chance say anything more. "We can listen to her saga once things are squared away here in this old pit. Shay, you need to see if you can rustle up your father. Aggie, you go on in the back and see what those two kids are up to. I'll help Lisa here dole out the booze."

"Eddy," I said with alarm, "you don't know how to tend bar."

"You hush, child. I didn't know how to run a coffee shop either, but I do now."

Good point. She'd gone from drinking Folgers to pulling espresso shots with a finesse that rivaled my own.

I looked at Lisa to see her reaction to Eddy's idea. She shrugged. "I'm okay to stay. Go on and see if you can track your dad down."

With that, I was summarily dismissed. It was almost five o'clock, and I wasn't sure who'd be around to talk to, but I'd give it the old college try.

I searched for my car keys while Lisa gave Eddy a rundown of booze-slinging basics. I don't know why Lisa seemed so trustworthy, but she did. Besides, Eddy was there to cover for me. Nothing bad would happen with her holding court at the Lep.

My mother had picked her friends well before she died, leaving both my dad and me in capable, loving hands. If I couldn't have my mom, Eddy was the next best thing.

———

Before deciding which of my father's favorite hideaways to investigate first, I wanted to make a quick run-through of his apartment and see if I could find that damn gun. Once I knew where it was, I was going to feel a hell of a lot better.

Ten minutes later I came down the steps empty-handed. I'd checked the obvious places and struck out. The search I'd conducted was decidedly haphazard, but before I let myself get too wound up, I figured he could've sold the thing or given it away.

During the failed search, I settled on tackling Rudolph's Bar-B-Que in Uptown first. Rudolph's opened in '75 and was still going whole hog serving comfort food and, of course, barbecue.

The huge, multipeaked, alpinesque restaurant occupied the corner of Lyndale and Franklin. The neon pink, yellow, and purple barbershop-style "Rudolph's" sign was awesome. It reminded me of a figurehead on the bow of a landlocked ship.

One of Rudolph's longtime bartenders was a guy named Beezer. He and my dad went way back, with liquor being the common denominator between them. Beezer had corralled my father more than once during one of Pop's marathon blackout sessions.

A gigantic hulk of a man with a barrel-sized beer belly and the kind of ear that separates the good barmen from the best, Beezer could listen to the current woes of an inebriated patron, pour a drink for another customer, and tend to waitstaff at the same time. He had that special touch that scored him premium tips. Beezer was why Rudolph's was one of the first places my dad headed when the funk hit.

I was happy to see Beezer was indeed behind the bar. He was all smiles as I walked up, but his grin faded when I asked if he'd seen my dad. He knew if I was asking, there was trouble. I told him my litany of woe, and he listened intently. With a sympathetic whack on my shoulder, Beezer told me he hadn't seen my dad, but to tell him howdy and that he hoped the trouble he'd been having at the Lep had stopped.

I wondered if Beezer was talking about the sewer problem, but when I pressed him, he clammed up. Maybe it had something to do with the guy who'd asked my dad to sell out. Or could it have something to do with that paper I'd found on the desk? The two could possibly be related. I wracked my brain trying to remember more about what my father had said about being pressured; I came up with nothing.

I hustled back to my vehicle with a handful of pretzels and zilch on the Find-Pete-O-Meter. I snapped the seatbelt into place, and with a twist of my wrist, the engine rumbled to life.

Frustration flirted with confusion. I absently chomped the pretzels, wondering if the Intent to Purchase letter was part of the trouble Beezer had referred to. I hated it when someone withheld information I needed, but it was hard to be angry with the Beez. I pulled the document from my pocket and reread it, but the words still didn't help clarify much of anything. I tucked it away and reached for a half-full bottle of Coke that had been left in the cup holder. I tipped it upside down in hopes it wasn't frozen solid.

It was.

My stomach rumbled. I hadn't realized until I'd wolfed down the pretzels how hungry I actually was. I'd missed lunch and suppertime loomed dead ahead. I swung into a convenience store and bought an unfrozen Coke and a Snickers. The sugar rush would have to do for now.

The next place I wanted to check out was the 22nd Avenue Station in Northeast, better known as the Double Deuce. It was a blue-collar dive that happened to showcase strippers doing their thing in the back of the bar. It was on the list of Dad's favorite retreats—not because of the girls, but because the owner had helped get the Leprechaun on its feet when Dad bought it from Roy Larson.

The owner of the Deuce was old-school, no-nonsense, and still capable of scaring the daylights out of me. Willie Glowinsky stood over six feet tall. Built like a prizefighter, she had flattened more than one nose with one of her meaty ham hocks. If you called her by her given name—Wilma—you could be sure of an immediate correction of the most painful kind. She was a broad's broad, ran the bar with an iron fist, and at seventy-something, could still bounce troublemakers out of her establishment with ease. She valued straight talk and hard work above all else. If my father had dropped in, she'd tell me. If she knew where he was, she'd spill it. If she'd heard anything about my father's "troubles," she'd tell me that too.

I pulled into the back lot of the Deuce and parked. My phone rang as I was about to step out of the SUV into the cold air. JT's ringtone made me smile. I answered, settled back in the seat, and pulled the door shut again. "Hey, babe."

"Hey. How's it going?"

"Lisa Vecoli showed up again looking for Pete and put herself to work. Good thing—I was about at my limit. After that, Agnes rounded up the cavalry and brought Eddy, Rocky, and Tulip in. Eddy sent me off Dad-hunting. Rudolph's was a no-go, and I'm about to check out the Deuce."

"Wow, you've been busy. I wanted to let you know I'm going to be home late. I never should have come in on my day off because now I'm stuck here working on a case we've been trying to close. Anyway, I got a hold of someone who got a hold of someone who owed me a favor. You're not going to want to hear this." JT paused. "A gun involved in a homicide in St. Paul is…"

"Is what?"

"It's… registered to your dad."

"What?"

"I don't know much. Just that it was found with the victim."

The full weight of what she'd said slammed me. "Oh my god, JT. Not—"

"Oh, no," JT hurriedly said, "no, it's not your dad. Jesus. I didn't mean to scare you."

My relief was short-lived.

"It looks like your dad's gun was used to kill the man that was found frozen in a big-ass ice cube in Rice Park. I don't know if you heard about that or not… it happened last night. That's why St. Paul wants to talk to him." Her voice dropped. "I can't believe I'm saying this. He's officially a person of interest in the homicide, Shay."

The breaking news I'd watched in the kitchen of the Rabbit Hole flashed in my mind. Acid started eating its way through my stomach lining.

"A person… of interest?" I said weakly.

"Shay, I'm sorry."

"No. It's okay. But, Christ. He's a drunk, not a killer." My dad would never intentionally hurt anyone. Unless they deserved it, of course. That's what I'd told myself all my life, except in the instances when I wasn't so sure.

He could do some damage if pushed far enough. He certainly had a temper, especially when well-lubed. If he was backed against the wall, or if his family or friends had problems, he would react. It's the way he was, his genetic makeup. The inability to think before diving headlong into a situation was one of the traits I'd inherited from him that had caused me plenty of grief throughout my life.

But murder?

I honestly didn't know what to think. The Intent to Purchase letter, Beezer's mention of trouble, the lack of repairs to the Lep. Now his gun, found with a dead guy? Why was Lisa Vecoli looking for him? And where the hell was he? None of this was making one goddamn bit of sense, and I was getting pissed.

I tried to rein in and focus on what JT had said. I asked, "Who is this dead guy if it's not Dad?"

"I don't know. Right now neither does St. Paul. But they're looking hard. The man was shot through the heart, then frozen in ice. The gun was imbedded in the ice with him."

"Could he have committed suicide?"

"I asked the same thing. Problem with that theory is the bullet went in his back and came out the front."

That would be pretty hard feat unless you were double-jointed and had a death wish. And then he'd have to what, freeze himself? I snagged the empty Coke bottle and started tapping on the steering wheel. "Shit."

JT said softly, "I know, baby, I know. We find your dad and we'll get this cleared up. You keep hunting, and let me know if you find him. I'm sure this is colossal mistake."

"Right." Yup, it was a mistake of supreme proportions, all right. Problem was, I didn't know whose mistake it was.

Shake it off, Shay. Come on. I mentally flipped through the other hotspots where my dad might be laying low. "I think I need reinforcements. I'm going to see if Coop can help. We'll cover more territory faster."

"Good idea. I'll call if I hear anything else."

"Thanks babe. And hey, I am sorry about Duluth."

"It's family, Shay. I get it. Duluth isn't going anywhere."

———

After I called Coop and explained the latest, he agreed to do some Pete-scouting. I didn't know what I'd do without him. I'd known Coop a lifetime. He was my second-best friend—I had to admit that JT now owned the number-one spot—but he was still my confidante, and at times my conscience. We've been through a lot together, and he always had my back. As I had his.

Coop was willing to embark on an excursion up to Fish Lake, where the O'Hanlon family cabin was located. There was a decent chance my dad had holed up there, although I felt one of his favorite bars was more likely.

We disconnected, and I was struck by déjà vu. How many times had Coop and I made the rounds trying to find my father's drunken butt? Too damn many.

I abandoned the Escape and headed for the front door of the Deuce. Pungent odors of booze, sweat, and old bar smacked me in the face as I walked in. It was weird how soupy tavern air was so very apparent until you'd been in the environment a few minutes and either your senses adjusted or the liquor you'd downed blotted it out.

Nothing much had changed since the last time I dropped by. The joint was still dim, with lots of neon behind the bar and a row of booths lined up along one wall. Tucked in one corner was a grouping of electronics that included a jukebox, an ATM, and a Golden Tee Golf game. Of course, as in all good Minnesota watering holes, pull-tabs sold from acrylic bins were available, benefitting local charities. A large spinning wheel used for meat raffles sat behind the golf game.

On the other side of the saloon, a short, curvy chick with a string bikini and a bad bleach job worked a pole, much to the delight of patrons crowding the T-shaped runway. Neon purple lights attached to the low ceiling glowed down on the dancer like risqué beams from heaven.

The place was packed, and the bar itself was hopping. A couple of bartenders efficiently worked in tandem, but neither of them was Willie Glowinsky.

I was about to wedge myself up to the bar and make an inquiry when a commotion broke out near the stage.

Someone howled.

The horde parted as an obviously inebriated customer stumbled through. Attached to the back of his jacket was a massive fist and attached to the fist was Willie. Curly iron-gray hair capped her head, and she wore an untucked navy button-down corduroy shirt over a pair of faded black jeans. I'd swear helming the Deuce was her fountain of youth.

She manhandled the miscreant to the front door, flung him outside, and rumbled, "Don't bring your filthy, pawing ass back here ever again."

The crowd surged back to stasis, closing the avenue that had opened for the premature exit of the alleged groper. I left the bar and dodged my way toward the towering, fine specimen of old age. When I got close enough, I hollered, "Willie!"

The thumping from a rock song drowned me out. I yelled again, putting a little more gusto behind it. This time Willie heard and swung around. When she recognized who was shouting at her, her expression softened. She plowed through the throng and lurched to a stop at my side.

"Shay!" Her voice was gravelly from too many Marlboros and too much bellowing. "What are you doing here?"

I wasn't exactly short, but I had to tilt my head to look up at Willie. "Seen my dad lately?"

Her leathery face rearranged itself into a sincere look of concern. She too knew that if I was asking for my father, something unpleasant was going on.

"Come on." Willie dropped a heavy hand on my shoulder and dragged me through the crowd. She was a very hands-on kind of gal. I was propelled down a back hall to a postage stamp office, pushed inside, and shoved into a threadbare chair. Willie slammed the door and dropped heavily into the chair behind her desk.

The desk was immaculate, devoid of anything except a yellow legal pad and a silver pen. Willie looked like a mess most of the time, and she often ran roughshod over customers who pissed her off, but the woman couldn't do any work unless her office was in order.

"How 'bout you tell me what's going on?" Willie gazed curiously at me through watery green eyes.

I ran her through the last twenty-four hours, ending with my failure to find Pete at Rudolph's. During my recitation, she leaned back in her chair, hands clasped against her ample, saggy middle, and simply took my words in.

She sucked in a contemplative breath and narrowed her eyes at me. I couldn't help it. I squirmed like a naughty kid. The woman could intimidate a python into turning tail and slithering away.

She said, "First of all, I haven't seen your father for, oh, maybe three months. Seems like it hasn't been that long, but when you get to be my age, time moves a hell of a lot faster than it used to." Willie studied me again, and it seemed as if she were weighing her words before she spoke. "Regarding the trouble Beezer mentioned, I'm not sure what he may have been referring to. I do know that someone was pressuring Pete to give up the bar and the land."

I asked, "Do you know when this started?"

"Well." One side of Willie's face bulged as she stuck her tongue between her molars and ran it up and down the inside of her cheek. The bulge disappeared and she said, "I think the first Pete mentioned it to me was early summer. Sometime last summer, anyway." She thought some more. "There were threats. Some vandalism."

Good god. "Why didn't he ever mentioned any of that to me?"

Willie's rheumy eyes followed the trail of emotions that ran across my face. "Now don't you go getting your underoos in a twist, kid. You know how your father is. I'm sure he didn't want to worry you."

"Yeah, yeah." I tried not to roll my eyes. "What kind of vandalism are we talking about? Did he tell you?"

"Some graffiti, a couple broken windows. Pete went out one morning and found one of his tires slashed."

While I had a good idea what she was going to say, I was unprepared for the reaction my body had to the words. A pinkish haze floated behind my eyes, and that was never good. My irrational response to certain kinds of triggers long ago earned me the nickname

Tenacious Protector. I fought an ongoing struggle to tame the urge to mete out justice O'Hanlon style when something tripped me off. Occasionally things I'd done in the grip of the red weren't always on the right side of the law. Luckily both Eddy and Coop were good at talking me down, and JT was catching up fast. Right now, I was on my own to quell the rising tide. I rubbed damp hands briskly on the knees of my jeans and took a calming breath. The room came back into focus. Willie was watching me intently.

"Okay," I said. "Did he say if the vandalism was related to the guy who was pressuring him to sell the bar?"

Willie shrugged her massive shoulders. "Don't know."

After a bit more small talk, I thanked her and retreated outside to further calm the Protector and pull my head together.

———

I sat in the Escape with my forehead on the wheel and concentrated on breathing.

In. Out. In. Out.

My emotions began to settle and rational thought crept back into my consciousness.

Focus, Shay. Damn, how many times had I said that to myself in the past?

Too many. I turned on the radio and cranked the volume, focusing on the driving beat of the music. I almost laughed aloud when I recognized the song. It was Shinedown's "Cry for Help." That was fitting in my moment of despair. I gripped the wheel and pushed myself back against the seat. Sometimes I swore there were multiple personalities inside me.

Someone was obviously fucking around with my father, and I hadn't known a thing about it. Or rather, I'd had a hint from the old man, but he never elaborated after that first mention, and I hadn't followed up.

Way to go yet again, Shay. Maybe if you'd been paying more attention you'd know what the hell was going on.

I leaned against the headrest, put a hand to my temples, and squeezed at the ache that had settled in above my eyes. No, my dad was an adult. There was no way I could have forced him to tell me anything he wasn't ready to share anyway.

There was one last place I wanted to check before I powwowed with Coop. I gave my temples a final rub and exited the parking lot. I pointed the Escape down University, made a right onto Hennepin, and headed back toward Uptown.

Lakewood Cemetery, where my mother was buried, was situated near the southeast side of Lake Calhoun. I didn't visit her grave often. It was too hard and hurt too much. The only time my dad showed up was when he was in the depths of an alcoholic haze. The odds weren't all that great that he'd be there, but I was pretty much out of options.

On Sundays the gates were locked for the night at five and it was now almost six thirty. Not that those cemetery hours had ever stopped my father or me when we needed to spend some time talking to my mom.

A black wrought-iron fence enclosed the cemetery. With a sigh, I resigned myself to the fact that I was going to have to hop it. It had been a few years since I'd felt the need to slither over the metal palisade after hours and sneak through the headstones to the grave that held my mom's remains.

The cemetery itself was huge. It was made up of more than 250 acres of tombs and yet-to-be plotted space that would one day become a final resting place for the dearly departed. There was lots of greenway in the summer, and fields of snowdrifts covered the plots in the winter. A web of narrow automobile paths was so vast the cemetery felt like a miniature city—a very silent city without the usual amenities offered by a settlement of living, breathing human beings.

I killed the engine and looked around. There wasn't anyone on the sidewalks at the moment, and vehicle traffic was light. I got out and pocketed my keys, then rummaged in the back for an old pair of mittens I kept for emergencies.

With one more furtive glance around, I walked along the fence. I came to an area that was semi-dark, far enough between streetlights that their glow wasn't reflected in the dirty snow. This was the location where I usually made my clandestine entry into the land of the dead.

The daytime din of traffic had died down, and the silence felt strangely surreal. My muscles tensed and a shiver ripped through me. A car was coming and would pass in seconds. I clumsily pulled off a mitten, dragged my phone from my pocket, and put it to my ear, feigning a conversation. The car rolled past and continued on its way, taillights reflected in the snow. The driver braked and made a right onto the street that curved around Lake Calhoun.

I shoved the cell back into my pocket and gave the area another careful gander. Seeing no one, I waded into the snow piled on the edge of the sidewalk and pulled my mitten back on.

With a running start I launched myself at the fence. It was a good head taller than I was, and it took some careful scrambling and a bit of fancy maneuvering to clear it without impaling myself on the metal spikes that topped each post. Summertime was definitely a better season to do this kind of thing.

Heart thundering, I dropped silently to the ground on the other side, my feet sinking shin-deep into pristine white snow that hadn't yet been disturbed by anything other than squirrels and rabbits. "Goddamn it," I grumbled quietly as snow fell into the sides of my tennis shoes. Once it melted into my socks, my feet were going to be very unhappy. Should have worn boots. And long johns. However, I never dreamed I'd be skulking around a closed cemetery when I'd gotten dressed this morning.

After making sure no one had raised an alarm, I set off along the perimeter, about fifteen feet inside the cemetery. I knew that not far behind me was one of the main buildings, and I didn't want to accidentally alert any workers—if there were any still on site—that an interloper was on the grounds. There were plenty of trees to use for cover, although if they had leaves they would've worked ever so much better.

I made my way toward a pond that was within the confines of the graveyard. The only sound that broke the stillness was the crunching of my feet in the snow. The air was calm, and for that I was grateful. It was cold enough without dealing with a wind chill.

Thinking about wind chills brought me back to thoughts of my dad. If he were here, he'd have to be damn cold, assuming he hadn't already frozen to death. Of course if he was full of firewater, that'd help keep the blood flowing through his veins.

I passed a turnaround and in a few more yards crossed a narrow road. My mom's grave was a bit north of the pond on the west side. I mentally counted the rows between the service road and the pond and stopped at the eighth one. I turned to the right and counted down another six headstones. The seventh was a creamy marble marker—my mother's final resting place.

The snow around the stone was undisturbed. My father hadn't been here.

I let out a sharp breath, in both relief and frustration. My eyes were magnetically drawn to the inscription on the stone, and even after all these years, a lump rose in my throat.

Linda Ann O'Hanlon
1952–1986
Loving Wife, Devoted Mother

Every time I saw the words, her name spelled out with such finality on the cold rock, my heart broke again. It felt so impossible. Mom...dead? How could this have happened to us? To me? To her?

The flashbacks started ripping through my mind. The sound of tires skidding across blacktop. Metal screeching, wrenching, twisting. Glass shattering. Screams. From me, or maybe from Eddy's son, Neal. Maybe from us both. More glass exploding. Something piercing my abdomen, slicing skin and organs deep inside.

After that I remembered very little. I didn't know until much later that Eddy had dragged me from the wreck. Away from my mother, who'd been driving and was killed upon impact. Away from her only son, whose neck had snapped when his head slammed against the window. Eddy literally held my life in her hands as she desperately tried to keep my innards inside my body until help arrived.

Back in the day, no one used seatbelts or car seats. That level of precaution wasn't even on the radar. It was only years later, when they started enforcing the use of safety restraints, that I wondered what might have happened if everyone had been belted in.

After that, all Eddy and I had was each other, and occasionally my father.

The eerie hoot of an owl jarred me back out of the nightmare of my past. I forced myself to breathe deep, to ground myself in the here and now. Maybe I needed some therapy. The flashbacks seemed to be coming more frequently lately.

I shook my head to clear it, and quickly looked around. I was still alone and my father was still not here. Goddamn him for dropping me back into another time and place—a place where I was out of control, again mourning for the mother I'd lost far too young.

Time to check in with Coop and rethink my game plan.

FOUR

"AGH," I YELPED. BLISTERING hot cheese and bacon squirted from between two burger patties to scald my tongue. I gingerly rolled the rest of the bite around my mouth until I could chew and swallow without further damage.

Elsie's Restaurant, Bar, and Bowling Center in Northeast produced one of my all-time favorite burgers, the Juicy Brucy. It was a loose cousin to my second-favorite burger, the Jucy Lucy, found at Matt's Bar in Minneapolis, among others. The Juicy Brucy added chunks of bacon to the molten cheese sealed in the middle of the burger.

"You," Coop said, watching me grab my ice water and down a couple swallows, "always manage to burn yourself when you eat that."

The now tender buds on my tongue scraped against my front teeth. I hated the feeling, but I was always too impatient to wait until Elsie's masterpiece was cool enough to eat. Served me right, I suppose. "I know, I know." I stuffed another bite in anyway.

Coop took a huge chomp of his grilled cheese, crammed it all to one side of his mouth, and chewed. "So what now?"

"I called the Lep after extracting myself from the cemetery. Eddy assured me that things were running slick as a pig's greased ass—don't ask me—and she and Lisa are getting on fine." I bit into one of my waffle fries. "Man, I don't know what to think. I mean—Dad disappears, this dead guy shows up in a block of ice, Dad's handgun is found with the body? The whole thing with being pressured to sell the bar and the threats…" I trailed off and popped the last of the Juicy Brucy in my mouth.

"I don't know. But Shay," Coop leaned toward me, suddenly earnest, "your dad no more iced that guy than I offed Kinky on the barge." A little over a year earlier Coop's boss had been killed on a floating bingo barge where Coop had been working, and for a while he thought the police had fingered him as the prime suspect. He wasn't guilty, but it was quite the endeavor to get things straightened out in his favor.

I drained my water and sat back in the booth. "I also got a hold of Johnny."

"Barboy Johnny? What's he doing now?"

Johnny was the steadiest bartender my father ever had. He'd been hired on before he was old enough to drink and had stuck by my father and the Lep throughout years of ups and downs while he went to college. I think my dad felt a little like Johnny was the son he'd never had. I didn't feel slighted because Johnny was an all-around good guy.

I said, "Remember Johnny graduated from college not too long ago?"

"Yeah. Landed himself a nice job, didn't he?"

"Yup. But with the unstable economy, they laid him off. He decided to go back to school for his masters in urban planning." I waved a fry in the air. "I don't get how some people can keep going to school year after year after year. That would drive me nuts. On the bright

63

side, Johnny's school schedule has a lot of flexibility, and he's agreed to help out."

"Maybe your dad can bring him on again for a while." Coop pushed his plate away with a grunt. "That was good shit, man."

"Since there's no one to replace Whale, that's a fine idea, Mr. Cooper. I'll run it by Johnny and see what he thinks. When Dad surfaces, he can deal with that fallout."

"Hey, thanks," Coop said to the waiter who stopped by to top off our glasses of ice water.

I turned my attention back to Coop. He grabbed his glass and guzzled the entire thing, using his front teeth to keep the ice at bay. My own teeth ached watching him. He banged the glass down on the tabletop and said, "Let's go."

———

After waiting for Coop to speed-smoke in the bowling alley's parking lot, I rolled into the Lep about nine thirty with Coop trailing along behind me. I wondered if Lisa had decided to hang around longer than she'd anticipated or if she had checked out. Couldn't blame her if she had. It'd been a damn long weekend.

The bar was actually quiet. A man and woman were seated in one of the back booths, and other than that the place was dead. I was reminded more of a weekday evening than New Year's Day. At this point, I was too tired to care very much.

Lisa was still behind the bar, leaning against the back counter with a dark brown bottle of beer in her hand. She looked so natural, like she'd been around the Lep all her life. I was struck by the fact that this woman I barely knew had pretty much taken over tending my dad's bar and, frankly, I didn't give a damn.

What exactly did that say about me?

Eddy sat perched on a stool in front of Lisa, arm raised as she made some important point. I wondered if she'd hit up Lisa yet to hook up with the Mad Knitters. The original purpose of the Mad Knitters—which was mostly comprised of elderly friends of Eddy's mixed with some young blood (Coop and Rocky)—was to propagate the craft of knitting. Ha, right. Instead, the gang propagated poker. Or dice. Or dominos. Their latest game du jour was Mahjongg. At least it kept them off the streets.

Eddy turned to face us as Coop and I settled on stools alongside her. "You two look like someone didn't even fill your water glasses half full. Any luck?" She scanned the immediate vicinity with great exaggeration. "Since I don't see that scoundrel father of yours, Shay, I assume the answer is no."

"Not one sighting." I shifted my butt into a more comfortable position. My dad needed to invest in some chairs with decent padding. But in light of his other, more serious issues, new seating was way down on the list. "Where's the rest of the crew?"

"Aggie took 'em home when things slowed down," Eddy said. "Rocky got the itch to use some serious elbow grease spic-and-spanning that sorry excuse for a kitchen your father keeps. You should see the shine on those stainless counters and sinks." Eddy's expression morphed into frustrated consternation. "You know how that boy gets when he puts his mind to something. He wouldn't stop till he hit every metal surface back there. I took some money out of the till for him, and you should have seen that round face of his beam. And that Tulip, she earned your father some greenbacks twisting balloons into New Year's hats for five bucks a pop. That little gal is good, conning people into buying them after New Year's Eve was plumb over."

When Rocky met Tulip, she was a street urchin working in New Orleans making balloon animals and other fun inflated shapes for both kids and adults. Since she'd come up here to Minneapolis and said the I do's with Rocky, she'd shifted from working the streets to working the patrons at the Rabbit Hole. She occasionally scored birthday parties and bar or bat mitzvah gigs at customer's houses.

After the parties, the customers almost always returned to the Hole and raved about Tulip and her special way with kids, especially the kids who were challenged. She connected with young ones dealing with Asperger's, autism, and Down's syndrome. Maybe it was because she was like them in many ways. I didn't know specifically what problems of her own Tulip dealt with other than her brain functioned much like Rocky's, which meant you never knew what to expect from either of them. I really liked her, and she made Rocky glow.

Coop crinkled his nose. "What's that smell?"

Eddy said, "That stench is coming up from the basement. When more people are in here, it's not very noticeable, but right now it's pretty horrid."

I said, "One more thing for Dad to deal with. I think it's a cracked sewer line or something."

Lisa silently watched our exchange and took a pull from her beer. "This year isn't starting off very well for you guys, is it?"

That was a bit obvious, but I bit my tongue. When I was tired, I was prone to sarcasm. I didn't think it was a very good idea to lip off to the person who had bailed my caboose out for a second day in a row.

Coop said, "I think we've all had better moments. Mind scoring me a Bud?"

Lisa kicked off the counter and pulled a bottle from the cooler. She popped the top, and as she handed it to Coop, she shot me a quick, questioning glance. Somehow I knew she was wondering if she should charge him. I subtly shook my head. She acknowledged with a quirk of an eyebrow.

How the hell had Lisa read me so well? I closed my eyes and let a feeling of odd familiarity wash over me. Had Lisa and I suddenly become clairvoyant, or whatever the hell the term was? I hadn't had that kind of nonverbal clarity—or maybe it was simple silent comprehension—that fast with anyone. Well, not since I met JT, anyway.

Eddy startled me back to awareness with a pointed jab of her bony elbow. "Shay? Answer Lisa."

My head snapped up and I met Lisa's eyes. They were greenish-hazel, depending which way she turned in the hit-and-miss lighting of the bar, and they were currently boring into me.

Oh my god. Were we having a moment? Whoa. Slam on the air brakes a minute. What was I thinking? I cashed in my player's ticket when I got serious with JT. *Jesus. Get your mind back in the game, Shay.* I felt bewildered and speechless.

Frowning at me, Eddy saved the day. "She'll have one of those sissy drink-like things. You know, with that syrupy peach cough medicine and some OJ."

"Fuzzy navel," Lisa said. The corners of her mouth curled, but she didn't say anything as she got busy mixing my admittedly girly concoction.

I let out a bark that was meant to be a laugh. "Right. Thanks, Eddy." I suddenly found the gleaming surface of the bar top highly absorbing. I had no idea what my brain was doing. I should have big red neon letters attached to my forehead that blinked off and on, flashing *Overload Alert.*

Eddy again applied her elbow none-too-gently to my ribs. I was going to be bruised after this. "You learn anything we can sink our dentures into?"

I suppressed a grunt and scrambled to pull my jack-rabbiting thoughts together. "Not exactly. Like I said, Dad was nowhere. I checked all the usual spots. Nada."

Coop tilted his bottle at Eddy and said, "I ran up to the cabin. Locked up tight. Didn't look like anyone had been around recently. There weren't any tire tracks in the driveway since at least the last snow."

We hadn't been up to the cabin since early winter, so that made sense.

Lisa set the glass containing my cough syrup concoction on a napkin in front of me.

I gave her a semi-stiff, businesslike thank you and said, "JT went in to work this morning, and she called a bit ago." I wasn't completely comfortable discussing my father's potential problems in front of Lisa, but after all she'd done for us, I wasn't going to kick her to the proverbial curb. She was a big girl, and if she wanted to escape the nut house, she knew where the exit was.

Eddy straightened, shifting her position on the stool to face me more fully. "What'd JT have to say?"

Oh boy. "Nothing you want to hear."

"Child, what is it?"

This was one secret I knew I couldn't keep. "She found out that Dad's handgun was found frozen in a block of ice."

"Ice?" Eddy asked. "That doesn't sound too ominous, so why you still have a donkey face?"

Coop momentarily covered his eyes, waiting for the reveal and the inevitable explosion. Lisa looked between Eddy and me and shot a questioning glance at Coop, who shrugged.

I said, "There was a body in the ice along with the gun. And no," I added quickly, "the body isn't Dad's. But the gun is."

Eddy's smooth forehead crinkled and one eye got squinty. "A gun? A body? Like one of those department store mannequin things?"

I shook my head.

Lisa's eyes widened, but she didn't utter a sound.

"No, Eddy," I said quietly. "A dead human body. And the cops want to talk to Dad because *his* handgun was in the ice with the deceased. So that makes him a person of interest in the murder."

"Murder?" Eddy jolted and nearly toppled over. I grabbed her elbow.

"Easy, Eddy," Coop said.

In the space of three seconds, Eddy's confusion melted into indignation. There were times she channeled my Tenacious Protector pretty damn well. "There's no way your father shot anyone. Granted he's a hothead. But no sir-ee, he's not a murderer." She paused a beat, her lips pursed. "I don't think he'd kill anyone. Unless someone pushed him too far."

My thought exactly. I could see the gears in Eddy's head grinding along, interpreting what she'd just uttered. "Um, maybe I better keep my trap shut."

Up to this point Lisa had followed our exchange without comment. Now she said quietly, "I think maybe it's time to close up shop." She pointedly gazed at the two customers in the back booth. "They each only had one drink—Cokes, not alcohol—so their tab should be under ten bucks. Hang on—"

"Don't worry." I waved her off. "I'll take care of it."

Lisa had a good point. Not the greatest idea to be discussing a potentially homicidal father in front of the clientele, especially when the AWOL parent was the owner of the joint. Subtlety wasn't always my strong suit, and god knew my brain wasn't banging away on all cylinders right now. Besides, it wasn't like there was going to be a run on drinks this evening anyway.

I stood and stretched, then ambled over to the couple. They were middle-aged, dressed in somber, dark clothes, and the woman's eyes looked puffy while the man's face was grim. I wondered what crisis I'd interrupted as I explained we were closing early.

The man said, "No problem. We're done."

I wondered if I'd caught them in the middle of a fight, if maybe I needed to try to get the lady away from the dude to make sure she was okay. I'd done that more than once when I was worried someone was getting heavy-handed with their companion. You never knew, and when you added booze into the mix, it could get ugly in a hurry. Then again, these two hadn't gotten drunk on a couple of soft drinks.

The gal groped for something on the seat beside her. She pulled up a black handbag and set it on the table. As she rummaged through its contents, she said, "It was nice to find a quiet bar this evening. Our mother passed away today, and this was a perfect place hide to out for a while."

"I'm sorry to hear that." I was relieved I hadn't stepped into the middle of a domestic thing, but saddened to hear the reason for their distress. It struck me that it could easily be me in their shoes. The fear-fueled ache in my belly flared, along with that horrible feeling of being entirely out of control.

The woman handed me a twenty. "Keep the change."

"No ma'am, you've got enough to deal with. Let me treat you to a New Year's Day drink." I handed back the twenty. I could see she was about to protest, so I added with a gentle smile, "Every once in awhile we all deserve a break. It's your turn. Don't argue, keep it."

With the wind taken out of the sails of her argument, she smiled tiredly at me and stood to pull on a thigh-length black tweed coat.

The man patted me on the shoulder. I followed them up to the front door. They exited, I threw the deadbolt and turned off the OPEN sign.

I resettled myself at the bar and said, "Okay, where were we?"

Eddy said, "We were figuring out how to find your father and get him out of this mistake. When's the last time someone saw Pete?"

I scooped up my fuzzy navel and held it tightly. Condensation on the glass was cold against my palm. "Agnes saw him Friday night at his weekly poker game. Said he was planning for New Year's Eve the next day. Doesn't exactly sound like he was hell-bent on a bender." I sucked a chunk of ice from my glass and pinned it between my molars. "But that doesn't mean a whole lot. It's not like he ever *plans* on falling off the wagon."

Lisa said, "Maybe someone at the game noticed something weird." She raised a brow, her eyes steady on me.

Eddy asked, "Did Agnes tell you who was playing, child?"

I dragged my gaze from Lisa and ran down the list of players Agnes told me about.

When I finished, Eddy told Lisa, "These folks are all friends of Pete's—that's Shay's dad—and they often come play poker in the back room after Pete closes the bar."

"You know," Lisa wiped her hands on a damp rag, "it's getting late and I should probably get outta here." She stooped and grabbed her jacket from under the bar.

"Hey," I said, "Lisa, you've helped us—me, actually, out so much in the last two days, and I feel like I owe you an explanation and likely some funds."

"Oh no, you don't owe me a thing. I happened to be in a position to be able to help and that's what I did. Think of it as my good deed for the year."

"Cool your jets, girl," Eddy told Lisa. "You put that coat right back down." The tone in Eddy's voice left no room for argument. With wide eyes, Lisa tossed her jacket aside.

"Yeah," I said. "I know how you feel, Lisa. You do whatever she says when she talks like that." I'd been on the receiving end of Eddy's bossiness more times than I could count.

Eddy said, "In for a penny, in for a peso. Or something like that. Lisa, after what you've done for my Shay… 'Sides, you're rather handy."

Lisa gave a slightly strained laugh. "Guess I can stick around."

"Good, good." Eddy clapped her hands like a delighted little kid. She sprang from giddy to ferocious in a blink. "Now, Shay, supposing your father is still AWOL tomorrow, you see if you can track down the poker buddies and have a chat. Maybe he said something to one of them that'll help clear this up."

I didn't know how anyone was going to explain away my father's gun chilling in a block of frozen water, but at this point, I was willing try anything.

"Shay," Eddy continued, "I'd come with you if I could, but the Knitters are doing a tour of the Mill City Museum. I'm a chaperone." She leaned conspiratorially toward Lisa. "You gotta watch some of those old ladies real careful-like. They can get into all kinds of trouble."

Lisa, eyebrows hiked high, slowly nodded.

Eddy turned her sights on Coop. "You go with Shay. Keep her out of trouble."

He literally cringed. "I'm sorry, Eddy. You know I would. But I can't until I wrap up my latest contract. It's due to the state in a couple days, and I'm a bit behind. New Year celebrations kind of got in the way."

Coop would be there anytime and anywhere if I truly needed him. In this case I was certainly fine to do a solo chitchat with my dad's poker playing pals.

Lisa asked, "What do you do, Coop?"

"I'm sort of a computer geek—"

"Hacker," I coughed into my hand.

Eddy thwapped me in the back of the head. "Fixer," she corrected.

"Ignore them," Coop said. "The simplified version is the state hired me to map projected income from electronic pulltabs and how those proceeds might be used to help fund a new Vikings stadium."

The longer, unspoken story was that for the last year or so, Coop had been designing and implementing player reward systems for bingo halls and local casinos, along with other computer-type jobs on a contract basis.

His reputation as a highly skilled, out-of-the-box systems developer caught the attention of some muckety-muck in state government. They contacted him to see if he'd be interested in working with some high-level, hush-hush video gaming software company to assess the potential for re-creating and marketing electronic pulltabs to increase state revenue. Pulltabs were a Minnesota bar and bingo tradition, and I supposed it seemed natural to see what more sales could do.

But Coop's computer talents encompassed much more than simple player reward systems. If the government wasn't careful, Coop could hack into their systems so fast they'd have no idea what hit them. He had the ability to seriously mess with any mainframe's inner workings. It was a very bright idea to keep Coop on your good side.

Lisa leaned against the back counter again and crossed her arms. "What are you finding in your research?"

Coop smirked. "It's confidential, and they might kill me for sharing, but the one thing I can tell you is that they need to dial back their expectations."

"Pshaw." Disgust colored Eddy's tone. "Those yahoos. Why should I—a geezerly taxpayer who has nothing to do with football, help fund a ridiculous roofless stadium—in Minnesota, of all places, when they have a perfectly good one now? Well," she added, "as long as the roof don't cave in again. 'Sides, those millionaire owners could stand to drop a wad of their own dough for their cause. The state shouldn't have anything to do with how businesses run their affairs, 'specially when it's all about dopey football."

"Let's not get her started or we'll be here all night," I said.

Eddy ignored me. "Lisa, can you go with Shay tomorrow? I'd feel a lot better if someone were with her. She's got a bit of a temper—"

"I do not," I interrupted indignantly.

Coop whacked me. "Yeah, you do."

I made a face at him.

Eddy gave us her patented settle-your-asses-down-before-I-whup-'em evil eye. That look worked as well now as it did back when we were knee-high like the corn in July.

"See what I mean about her temper?" she said to Lisa.

Lisa laughed. I wondered if she thought we were all whackadoo-dles. But honestly, I didn't need to wonder; we were all whacka-doodles.

"I'm doing an internship at the Walker Art Center," Lisa said. "I'm on vacation for another week. I certainly can help out tomorrow if you like." She drilled me with an intense look. "But only if Shay doesn't mind."

There was something disturbing yet mesmerizing in those eyes. If she did come along tomorrow, we were definitely going to have to have a heart-to-heart. I needed to make damn sure she was clear on the fact that I was completely and thoroughly attached. I mentally smacked myself. I didn't even know for sure the woman was gay, and here I was jumping to some probably very wrong conclusions.

I mentally heaved a peevish sigh and rearranged my expression into something a little more inviting. "Whoever would like to accompany me on tomorrow's fact-finding mission, meet me at the Rabbit Hole at ten a.m."

———

It was almost midnight when Lisa and I finished up at the Lep. Coop left to take Eddy home, and Lisa restocked the bar while I tried to tie out the day's receipts. In all, the weekend had been a good one for my father. He was damn lucky we'd all been around to help him.

My fury at his bailing out on such a huge weekend was tempered by the knowledge that something else very unseemly was going on. There was no other explanation. Maybe this cluster was all tied into one massive booze orgy. His track record was full of them, so there was no discounting the possibility.

After some fits and starts, I managed to bumble through the maze of paperwork and prepare the deposit. Luckily, like the safe combination, nothing had changed since he opened the place.

I shut off the light to the office and pulled the door closed. I double-checked the front door to make sure it was locked and killed the lights in the front of the bar.

My phone vibrated with an incoming message. A quick check showed that JT was on her way home. One beautiful, bright spot to end my evening.

In the kitchen Lisa was tucking away the last of the dishes, her back facing me.

"Hey," I said.

Lisa let out a startled yip and spun, hand to chest. "Oh my god. You nearly gave me a heart attack."

"Sorry about that." It wasn't good manners to kill the help.

"It's okay. Whew. My heart's still working." She patted her shirt-front a couple of times, probably just to make sure.

"Anything I can do to help?"

"No, I think I've got it all. Not sure where your dad puts everything away, but I did what I could."

"And that is good enough. Let's get out of here."

Lisa glanced at the closed basement door. "I think that smell is getting worse. I ran down there earlier when I restocked, and shit's really oozing." She paused and grimaced. "No pun intended."

Said smell wafted beneath my nose. "I know. I'm going to call someone tomorrow. I don't know why my dad didn't do it sooner, but it's *got* to be fixed."

We bundled up and I doused the kitchen lights. Lisa stepped outside and I followed, pulling the door closed behind me, keying the deadbolt. It was cold and clear, and a few stars sparkled overhead. Without much wind, it wasn't half bad.

"Where are you parked?"

"On the street, down the block."

"Come on, I'll give you a lift." I bobbed my head toward my vehicle, which was almost swallowed up by the darkness.

"Cool." She angled around one side of the SUV. I headed for the driver's side and unlocked the doors with the fob.

As I reached for the handle, I heard a soft grunt and then a thud.

"Lis—" Someone upended me before I could get her name out, literally tackling me to the ground. I hit the snow-packed lot so hard my teeth slammed together and my breath jolted from my chest.

Hands wrapped tight around my neck. I blindly swung a glove-covered fist at body mass, connecting with a glancing blow. My assailant uttered a stifled oath and loosened his hold. Then something smashed into the side of my face so hard I saw stars.

Momentary bewilderment vanished, replaced by stone-cold fury. I yowled and shook my head, tried to clear it. I squirmed, desperate to get away.

My attacker groped for a handhold. I thrust a knee upward and caught enough of his gonads to get his attention. He grunted, his hands disappearing from my anatomy and grabbing at his own, the full weight of his body pressing down on me. Scraping my heels frantically against the snowpack, I managed to get my feet under me and arched up, trying to buck him off.

I awkwardly drove a fist toward his face. There was a satisfying *crack!* followed by a choked howl.

Take that, fucker.

Our thrashing abruptly slowed as we bumped up against one of the tires on the Escape. The lunatic let go of his crotch and managed to get his fingers around my throat again.

Through the roaring in my ears, I heard him growl, "You tell O'Hanlon time's running out for him to sign before things get ugly."

I gathered my waning strength and bucked mightily, blackness crowding the edges of my vision. I managed to wedge one hand under his chin. With my other hand, I bashed repeatedly at one of the arms that held me down.

My vision started to constrict.

Frantically I let go and slammed both fists against the sides of his head, gong-style. His grip loosened a bit. I did it again. The blow must have stunned him to some degree, because for a moment he stilled. I tore myself from beneath him, sucking in precious air as I scrambled to regain my footing.

He grabbed my ankle and yanked.

I went with the momentum, kicking backward. My heel connected with something soft—I hoped whatever I hit hurt like hell. The leg that had been holding me up slipped sideways and both my knees slammed into the ground. Pain blossomed. More yowling filled the air—mine or his? Maybe both. I struggled to get back up and so did he.

He crouched, lunged low and fast.

I lashed out with my foot and caught him in the side.

He staggered.

I rebalanced and charged like a drag racer squealing out of the gate.

He sidestepped. I stumbled, trying to stop my forward momentum. I crashed into the side of the vehicle, bounced backward, and spun. Instead of coming after me again, the man whipped around and hightailed it across the parking lot toward the street as if the hounds of hell were on his ass. He rounded the end of the lot and disappeared from sight.

I had no energy to pursue him. Hardly had enough gumption to stand. My lungs ached, and my flanks heaved. I kept myself in decent shape, but was in no condition to be doing any of this hand-to-hand crap.

Then I remembered Lisa. Oh shit.

I hobbled around the SUV. Lisa was nowhere in sight.

Son of a bitch.

I couldn't think. I could hardly breathe. I propped myself against the hood of the Escape. My throat ached. I bent at the waist, hands on my knees, which I realized were very tender, and tried very hard not to throw up.

As I caught my breath, I heard footsteps pounding the frozen earth, coming fast. I tried to reset myself for another go-round, then recognized Lisa barreling toward me like a wild animal.

She skidded to a stop. "Oh my god. Are you okay?"

"Yeah, mostly. You?"

"I'll live," she wheezed.

I limped around in a slow circle and my furious gaze fell on Lisa. "Shit. You're bleeding."

Dark rivulets ran from her scalp and striped one side of her face. Strands of her long hair clung to the damp mess.

"Come on." I grabbed her elbow and I looked around for additional attackers. "Let's get you cleaned up."

Without argument, Lisa allowed me to lead her back inside. I locked the door securely and said, "What in the flying fuck just happened? Were there two of them?"

"I think so. While I was tangling with whoever bashed me in the head, I heard someone else doing the emasculated howl. You kick him in the balls?"

"I did."

"Nice."

I dragged her over to the sink and ripped a handful of paper towels from the dispenser attached to the wall. I wet a paper towel and started dabbing blood from her cheek.

"Then," she continued, "I took off after him."

Her reaction sounded exactly like some stupid stunt I'd pull without a second thought. We seemed to have in common a penchant for self-disregard.

I hit a sore spot and Lisa winced.

"Sorry."

"S'okay," she mumbled. "His ass would've been mine if I hadn't slipped off the curb."

"Hold still." I was getting close to her hairline and didn't want to hit the actual wound. Especially since my hands were still trembling from frenzy-fueled adrenaline.

I said, "The jackass who jumped me didn't have any weapons. Unless he dropped it. Bastard tried to choke me out. He told me…" I trailed off, trying to remember exactly what he'd said. "Something to the effect of 'tell O'Hanlon time's running out for him to sign' or something like that. I think it's got to do with the sale of the Leprechaun." I parted Lisa's hair looking for the point of impact.

She said, "Your dad intends to sell?"

"You have a gash about an inch and a half long here. I don't think it needs stitches, but you want to run to the ER to check?"

"Hell, no. I've survived worse without a doctor's interference."

Okay. I gingerly swabbed some more. "No, my father isn't interested in selling."

The bleeding was slowing. I dug out some gauze from a first-aid kit that was attached to the wall by the sink and carefully set it on the wound. I loaded a clean bar towel with ice and gingerly plopped it on top of her head. "Hold this. I think it'll be okay."

"Thanks, Doc."

"Don't mention it." I stepped back and propped my hands on my hips. "You know, I never intended for you to get this involved in my crap. I'm sorry you got hurt trying to do a good deed."

"Stop. I was the one who decided to get involved. Now I'm damn well invested. Besides, I still haven't talked to your dad yet."

Oh yeah. Back to that. Maybe now was time for that little heart-to-heart I was planning on having with her tomorrow. "What on earth do you need to talk to my father so badly about that you're willing to take your life into your own hands?"

Lisa blew a fast breath through her nose and pursed her lips. I wondered if she was going try to stonewall me again. Maybe if I whacked her over the other side of her head she'd loosen her lips.

"My mom died this past November. Pancreatic cancer."

Ouch. Wasn't expecting that. At all. "Jesus. I'm so, so sorry, Lisa."

She nodded with a clench of her jaw. "It's okay. Well, I guess it's not okay, but ... thanks. Anyway, right before she died, she told me that I should find Pete O'Hanlon. She wanted to make sure he got this." Lisa dug in her pocket and fished out a coin. She handed it to me. "She didn't say why, only that I should find him and turn it over."

Lisa's eyes had taken on a far away, contemplative look. Then she swallowed hard, obviously trying to get a handle on herself. I dropped my gaze to the coin in my hand instead of watching her do her damnedest not to break down. The coin was an old, worn-out Liberty Head nickel. I could still make out the year below Liberty's head, which now was really no more than an outline.

1905.

When I was a kid, my dad had tried to interest me in collecting coins, but I was too busy playing Lone Ranger and Tonto in the dirt behind the bar to pay much attention to little round metal discs. I was surprised that I was able to pull the name of the nickel out of my head.

Lisa cleared her throat and said, "Anyway, she was on a pretty heavy dose of morphine. Maybe she was hallucinating. I've replayed her words in my head a thousand times, especially in the dead of night when I can't sleep. 'Please, Lisa. Give Pete O'Hanlon the nickel that's in my black jewelry box at home. Promise me.' I promised, and she ... " Lisa shrugged. "She seemed to ... I don't know. Let go, I guess. That night she slipped into a coma and she passed the next morning."

Ouch. "Hey," I put a hand on her forearm, my gut falling into the familiar ache that came when I thought about my own mother. "I'm so, so very sorry." I handed her the nickel, which she tucked back into her pocket. Hesitantly, I said, "If it's easier for you, you can leave it with me and I can give it to him whenever he shows up."

For a moment, Lisa's eyes welled, but she soldiered on. "No. Thank you for the offer, but no. I'm going to follow my mom's last wishes. I'll place that damn coin in your father's hand, one way or another." She blew out a big breath. "Anyway, the New Year was looming, and I decided what the hell. Everything else in my life has been turned upside down." Lisa looked at me. Pain and resolve radiated from her like a living thing.

"How did you find us?"

Lisa laughed. "How does anyone find anything anymore? I Googled Pete O'Hanlon. There was a guy by that name in Australia, and I sure as hell wasn't looking that far away from home. There was a Simon Peter O'Hanlon in Nebraska, but that didn't seem right. There were a couple of blogs by a Pete O'Hanlon. Sent emails and struck out." She shrugged. "The only Pete O'Hanlon with a physical presence in the state was your dad. So I figured I'd start here." Lisa shifted her grip on the rag on top of her head. She slowly said, "You know, she never did say that Pete O'Hanlon was in Minnesota. I suppose he could be anywhere."

That was true. Since she was now knee deep into my Pete O'Hanlon situation, we might as well play it out and see if he was actually the right one or not. Besides, I liked Lisa. Just not in "that" way. Absolutely not.

We agreed to meet in the morning at the Rabbit Hole and this time made it to our respective vehicles unscathed.

FIVE

Eight o'clock Monday morning loomed gray and gloomy. The forecast was for another three to six inches of snow throughout the day, and I was getting almighty sick and tired of the white shit.

JT had been furious when I got home and filled her in on the trouble we'd had. She wasn't happy I hadn't called the cops and reported the assault.

Honestly, it hadn't crossed my mind at the time, but looking back, I probably should have. When I thought about it, I realized Lisa hadn't suggested involving the cops either. Maybe we were both too independent for our own good.

Once JT calmed down, she told me she hadn't had any luck gleaning more inside info from St. Paul.

The next morning JT headed back to work before I'd gotten out of bed. Once I pried myself from between the warm covers, I inspected my body for battle wounds.

My muscles were stiff, and both kneecaps were black and blue. I figured my neck might have some fingerprints, but miraculously it escaped bruising. I downed four ibuprofen before heading out to meet up with Lisa at the Hole.

On the way, I tuned into WCCO 830 and caught some coverage of what the media had dubbed the "Ice Block Killer." The on-air talent was having a field day with all kinds of ice jokes. That didn't help my mood, so I clicked the radio off and called Pam Pine to see how the boys were doing.

"Pam's Pawhouse."

I recognized Pam's cheerful voice. "Hey. It's Shay. Just wondering how things are going."

Pam's voice warmed. "Oh, those two boys of yours are a riot. This morning we had a repair guy out to fix some stuff, and he was in the pen with the mutts when Bogey nosed him in the nuggets. He went down and Dawg leaped on top of him and started washing his face while Bogey tried to get even friendlier. It was hilarious."

I was mortified. Visions of getting sued for pain and emotional anguish flitted through my mind. Bogey had a thing for sniffing crotches. In his world, life was a crotch free-for-all. He was way better than when we first got him, but he was still a work in progress. I said, "We've been working on what you taught us, but … "

"Oh, don't worry about it. The guy was laughing his patootie off. He has two feisty Chesapeakes at home. And hey, I'll work with Bogey. Don't worry, we'll get him over it."

I hoped getting him over it would happen sooner rather than later. I thanked Pam and hung up as I pulled into an open parking spot close to the Hole.

Twenty minutes and two large coffees chock-full of chocolate and sugar later, Lisa and I were on the way to track down Poker Buddy 1: Brian Eckhart. Lisa seemed recovered from our previous night's confrontation, but her head had to be feeling it. Her hair hid the gash, so I couldn't tell how it was. She insisted she was fine, so off we went.

I parked on North 3rd Street across from the red brick building Sexworld occupied. It was a 24/7/365 adult entertainment and smoke shop in Minneapolis. Washington Avenue cut between the lot where I'd parked and the store, which loomed imposingly at the corner of 3rd and Hennepin.

The gaudy SEXWORLD sign glowed a dull red high up on the corner of the building. Below it, a white-backed, OPEN 24 HOURS sign assured those with a nocturnal itch that a scratch could be found at any time.

At street level, one entrance faced Washington, the other 3rd. Foot-tall, glowing red letters that again spelled out SEXWORLD arched over both entrances. To either side of the entry were vertical rows of six-foot tall neon tubes in blue, white, red, and pink, spanning maybe four feet across. Walking through one of those glowing entrances was like stepping into a den of deviant delights and decadent depravation. I didn't know how they managed to attract customers day and night, but in they came, probably in more ways than one.

Snowflakes fell from the sky as we dodged traffic and crossed Washington on foot. I headed for the side entrance off of 3rd with Lisa trailing after me.

I pulled the door open and we crossed the threshold. To the left, a square, high-walled checkout counter faced row upon row of various kinds of videographic flesh for fantasy. The back wall was lined with what had to be the largest assortment of sex equipment and toys I'd ever seen. There was something for everyone— small, medium, large, and holy shit.

Speaking of holy shit, the world's biggest wiener was a seven-foot, heavily veined golden penis situated not far inside the entrance.

Flashing lights on the wall alongside the big dick twinkled luridly. Above the thing was a sign that read: SEXWORLD MEASURES UP.

Impossibly obnoxious and somehow completely mesmerizing.

"What in the hell," Lisa said, "is that?"

"Wanna ride?"

"Are you kidding me?"

"No, ma'am. I am not."

"I don't even know what to say."

Somewhere along the line, Coop had nicknamed the giant penis the Fantastic Phallus. And it was fantastic. The mechanical wonder sported a gilded saddle with a star-spangled saddle blanket. If someone were drunk or stoned or plain crazy enough, they could hop on for a ride and look like the world's most endowed human being. It was the X-rated version of those quarter-a-pop mechanical horses or Fred Flintstone cars that used to be parked in front of shopping centers to entertain whiny kids.

The road that lead Brian Eckhart, our target, to Sexworld and the Fantastic Phallus, was harsh. He quit the Minneapolis PD after an officer-involved shooting that resulted in the death of a teenager. He was the officer involved. The requisite investigation had proved the kid had a loaded gun in hand, and Brian had been cleared of any wrongdoing.

However, the stress of the job, worry about litigation, and the failure he felt in his inability to stop the events that had forced him to the take the life of that boy took their toll. Brian resigned and picked up the security job so he could unobtrusively try to help minors who came through the place before they got themselves into something so serious they couldn't get out. I don't know what the management would think if they knew Brian's real reason for working there, but I personally thought it was great.

I turned to the checkout counter to ask for Brian when a familiar voice called from across the floor, "Shay, hey!"

"Hot damn," I said. "Come on, Lisa. You can contemplate the humongous horror later."

We threaded our way between stacks of porn and met up with Brian in front of two shelves full of blond and buxom cheerleader smut.

Brian was a good-looking guy somewhere in his forties. He'd retained a full thatch of red hair and kept the old physique in fighting form even after leaving his brothers in blue. At six-foot-something, he cut an imposing figure. Certainly not someone I'd want approaching me as I gaped at naked chicks on the covers of the DVDs lining the shelves.

Brian engulfed me in a big hug. "What's up, Little O?"

I'd picked up the nickname when I was a kid running around the Leprechaun. It stuck in some circles. Brian had thought it was funny and here we were. "Who's this?" He none-too-casually cased Lisa from head to toe and back to head.

Lisa stuck her hand out before I had a chance to introduce her. "Lisa Vecoli. I appreciate the ogle, but you've got the wrong equipment."

Well, that answered one question about Lisa.

Brian laughed. "Brian Eckhart at your service. I do like my ladies direct." He shook her hand.

He looked at me and said, "What brings you into this house of ill repute?" He tugged up his shirtsleeve to look at his watch. "At nine-oh-nine on a Monday morning?"

"It's a long story."

"Come on." Brian led us past the Fantastic Phallus and through a black-painted door into a break room. There was a couch of questionable cleanliness, a crusty counter with a cracked white plastic microwave that had seen better days, and a sink heaped with dirty dishes. The top of a rickety-looking card table was strewn with a mixture of porn mags and, of all things, a few months' worth of *Good Housekeeping* magazines. Considering the condition of the little room, whoever brought those in was probably hoping some of the housekeeping hints might rub off.

Brian sank into a chair at the table, rubbed at the nine o'clock shadow on his jaw, and yawned. "Take a load off. You caught me in the nick of time."

I perched carefully on the edge of a grimy, cracked-vinyl chair. Lisa chose to remain on her feet.

"Long night?" I asked.

"Aren't they all? Quiet, though. Maybe everyone was still strung out from New Year's Eve. Now tell me what's up."

I recited the events of the last two days. Like many cops, Brian was a good listener and interrupted only to ask clarifying questions.

"So," I said, "we're checking with everyone my dad played poker with Friday night to see if they noticed anything out of the ordinary about him, or if he might have said something to one of you guys that might explain his absence."

Brian peered me through, concern etched on his face. "Your dad came to me, oh, sometime this past fall. October? November? Can't remember. Told me that some guy had come into the bar and expressed interest in buying him out." Brian squinted one eye shut in thought. "Chase? No that's not right. Started with a 'C' I think. Last name was Shyler? Shiller? Something like that. The guy actually gave him an offer. Pete told him he wasn't interested.

"Not long after that, Pete said he started getting harassed. Vague threats, shit like that. Phone calls with no one on the other end. Other calls telling him if he were a betting man, he'd better sell. Things escalated over time. He told me someone slashed his tires one night. A big rock shattered the front window of the bar."

I had no idea. My damn father, Mr. Stoic, hadn't told me the full story. Of course he hadn't. He probably knew I'd go ballistic. What surprised me was that he hadn't gone ballistic himself.

Unless he had.

A bright bolt of shame flared in the back of my head. If I had spent more time with my dad, maybe I wouldn't be finding out about all of this second hand. Instead, they—whoever "they" were—had escalated from slashing tires to assault. The thought of my not-so-young-anymore father coming into the lot with two thugs lying in wait made my blood run cold.

I told Brian about the two guys who jumped Lisa and me the previous night.

He swore under his breath. "You call the police?"

"No," I said. "Didn't think about it. I was too pissed and got caught up patching Lisa's head. I suppose I should at least report it."

I glanced at Lisa, who had gone pale. Her lips were pressed together into what almost looked like a sneer, and the glare she sported was enough to make me want to cringe. "You okay?" I asked, wondering if her head wound was causing more trouble than I'd thought.

She gave a minute shake of her head, as if she was coming out of a daydream. "Yeah," she said absently, "you know, at the time I didn't think about calling the cops either." She seemed to pull herself together and focused on Brian. "Do you know if Pete reported any of the prior harassment?"

He said, "We talked about some legal options. He didn't like anything I offered and said he'd deal with it himself."

I muttered under my breath, "Of course."

"Don't know what else to tell you, Shay. Pete was in a good mood Friday night. He won, which always helps. Even though his head was half in, half out of the game."

That meshed with what Agnes told me. "Thanks, Brian." I stood.

Brian laced his fingers and tucked his hands behind his head. He leaned dangerously far back in his chair. "Keep me updated, okay?"

"I sure will."

We hit the exit, and Lisa said, "Your dad is stubborn."

"You could say that." We crossed Washington Avenue and headed for the Escape. "He always thinks he has to take care of everything on his own. Doesn't know how to ask for help." I paused as I dug the keys from my pocket and unlocked the doors. "Though he actually did ask for help, considering what Brian said. Why he decided not to take the assistance offered is beyond me."

We climbed inside and I started the engine.

Lisa said, "Too bad there wasn't more that Brian could give us. At least we have a partial name. Sort of."

I pulled into the street. "Yeah. So close, yet ... not so much."

"Where to next?" Lisa asked.

I looked at the radio. 9:40. "Let's head to St. Paul and see if we can find Mick Simon, better known as the Vulc."

"The Vulc?"

"Mick was Vulcanus Rex, the Fire King of the St. Paul Winter Carnival, back in the late Nineties, or was it ... ah hell, it doesn't matter when. Anyway, he's been 'the Vulc' ever since. With the carnival coming up, I'm sure he's working in one of the Krewe's warehouses feverishly planning the new Fire King's appearances."

"I guess I know less than I realized about the carnival. But the Krewe, they're the crazy guys that run around in those red suits, goggles, and pointy little beards, right?"

"Oh yeah," I said wistfully, memories of the St. Paul Winter Carnival flooding my head. I remembered Mom and Dad bringing both Neil—Eddy's son—and me out to the festivities when we were little. Every year after the accident that killed both my mom and Neil, Eddy did her best to keep that tradition alive by bringing me to the carnival. My father was too busy running the Leprechaun and keeping himself knee-deep in the sauce to entertain any thoughts of coming along. Only much later did I realize that the prospect of going back to something that had meant so much probably hurt him badly.

I braked to a stop at a light and said, "I think I was about five or six when my father first told me about the history of the carnival, which was initially held way back in the late 1800s. I remember thinking that had to be before the time of the dinosaurs."

Lisa laughed at that.

The light changed and I picked up speed again. "I suppose life back then was good—if you didn't mind outhouses in below-zero weather. There's always a downside to everything, right? Anyway, the biggest problem for St. Paul's growing rep was a newspaper story some reporter from New York wrote claiming the city was no better than Siberia."

Lisa said, "I have to admit I kind of agree with the Siberia thing."

"Me too. Especially this winter. I've had enough snow to last me for a long time. Good thing the folks back then had more fortitude than we do."

I lapsed into silence, recalling my father's deep voice recount the legend of how, on the tenth day, Boreas, King of the Winds, and the Vulc, God of Fire, duked it out. The god of fire kicked Boreas out of town every time, sending away the cold and bringing in warm weather. After this year's cold and snow, we needed the Vulc to come in and do some early ass tromping.

One of the warehouses Mick and company used for carnival-related stuff was a little north and west of Holman Field, St. Paul's airport. That's where I figured we'd check first.

The drive into St. Paul was smooth. Most of the rush hour had dispersed, leaving the stretch of I-94 between Minneapolis and St. Paul problem free.

Lisa was quiet, but it wasn't an uncomfortable silence. For that I was grateful. I hated feeling like I needed to come up with something to say to fill the void.

We crossed the Mississippi by way of the Robert Street Bridge, and I eventually pulled into the parking lot of a boxy brick building. It was a few minutes after ten o'clock, and the lot was empty.

There wasn't any signage, but I knew that around the back was a space that the Imperial Order of Fire and Brimstone—an organization made up of past and present Vulcans—used to house the Winter Carnival's Royal Chariot, which was a 1932 fire engine long ago manufactured in Luverne, Minnesota.

When I was a kid, my dad occasionally brought me to Vulcan headquarters. He wasn't a Krewe member, but being a friend of Mick Simon's opened a lot of doors. The fact that he tended to bring a few six-packs along helped. For hours I'd watch the guys putter with replacement fire engine parts and repair or replace running boards, door panels—whatever had worn out, rusted through, or broken. By now they must have replaced about every removable piece on the old jalopy, and probably some that weren't.

Lisa asked, "How do you know if this Mitch guy is even here now?"

"Mick," I said. "Mick is one of the board members who helps decide what charities the Krewe is going to support and what activities the current Krewe will take part in. I suppose there's other stuff aside from that too, but that's the gist of it. It's that time of year where things are hopping, so the odds are good he'll be here."

"It's always nice to find an organization that actually does good stuff for the community. I kinda thought they were grown men running around in red pajamas smearing black grease paint on unsuspecting victims they wanted to kiss."

"Nobody said they were saints. Come on. Let's go see if we can go two for two."

We walked up to a door that had a fancy red and black IMPERIAL ORDER OF FIRE AND BRIMSTONE sign attached to it. I pressed the buzzer and waited to see who opened the door.

To my surprise, no one did. I leaned on the doorbell one more time. Nothing.

"Oh, come on," Lisa said.

No kidding. I let out a frustrated breath. Guess we'd just have to circle back to Poker Buddy 2 later. "Okay. We'll try again later on. Let's regroup."

Back to the Escape we tramped.

Lisa settled in, clicked her seatbelt on, and said, "Who's next on your dirty little list?"

I keyed the engine, mentally pulling up Poker Buddy 3. "We've talked to Brian. How about Roy? Roy Larson—"

"Isn't he the guy who hawks kitty litter on TV?"

"One and the same. Before he got himself into the feline elimination business, he owned the Leprechaun. Well, it wasn't the Leprechaun back then."

"What was it?"

"The Do Stop Inn."

"Seriously?"

"As an aneurysm. You can see why Dad changed the name."

"It's kind of cute, in a skeezy sort of way."

I laughed. "Maybe. And don't forget Hemorrhoid Harvey and Limpy Dick."

"Those names belong in a cheesy dime store novel."

"There's something to be said about the quality of people my father hangs around with."

"I guess. Okay. Tell me about"—she could hardly keep a straight face—"Hemorrhoid Harvey. What's up with that?"

"I had to ask Agnes the same thing yesterday. He owns Benjamin's Drugstore in Richfield. Apparently Benjamin's is the go-to emporium for the geriatric set."

"Oh, this keeps getting better and better." Lisa's lips trembled from the effort of holding back what I assumed was an explosion of hilarity. "And Limpy"—she slapped a hand over her mouth and said through her fingers—"Limpy Dick?"

That did it. She doubled over in a fit of laughter. I suppose if I hadn't been familiar with these crazy people, I would have been joining in with her.

"I told you about him last night. Remember? Or are you having memory issues from the damage to your skull?"

At that, Lisa made a concerted effort to contain her giggles. "Oh, I think it's coming back to me now. What a terrible thing."

"Yeah. But it doesn't slow him down at all." I thought about that. "In fact, you kind of forget he's missing a leg after awhile."

"Huh. Well, okay. After all that and the coffee, I have to hit a restroom. Then we can continue this most gripping project."

"Gripping. Not exactly what I'd call this wild turkey chase, but it works."

———

After making a pit stop at Cossetta's (pizza to die for) on West Seventh, we decided to head to Roy Larson's office next. This time I called ahead. He was out for lunch but would be back soon.

We retraced our path back across the Mississippi, and I was lucky enough to find metered parking not far from Larson's Super Clump Flush-Away Cat Litter headquarters. It was kind of scary what one could actually make money doing. Roy's kitty litter domain took up the entire third floor of the six-story Thresher Building, located in the Warehouse District in Minneapolis.

A woman lugging two animal carriers hustled into the elevator right behind us. From the caterwauling going on within the carriers, you'd have thought the animals were being slowly and painfully murdered. The woman said apologetically over the yowling, "Sorry about this. I'm bringing them in for a photo shoot for a new ad."

I smiled. "It's okay. Sounds like they're not too happy traveling around like that."

"Oh, they'll quiet down once I let them out and give them a couple treats. They come highly recommended from the place that supplies us animal actors. The trainer is parking and will be in shortly. I hope."

Animal actors?

The woman and her noisy charges exited on two, and we continued the ride to the third floor in blessed peace. The elevator doors opened into a lobby that comfortably seated ten. Each wall was decorated with a huge blowup of a cat posing in various beatific positions on top of trays of cat litter. I wondered what kitty goodies the photographer had to bribe him with to cooperate.

The receptionist was a young man in his mid-twenties. His short blond hair was so bleached it practically glowed. That contrasted rather shockingly with his orange-brown face and the glaring white skin around his eyes that made him look like a reverse raccoon. He either paid too much for a bad spray tan or spent some significant time in an ultraviolet casket. A genuine suntan in the middle of a Minnesota winter was a pipe dream.

Glow-boy sat behind a horseshoe-shaped desk, dressed to kill in a natty gray suit with a bright-orange cartoon tabby cat crawling across his tie. He gave us a blindingly white smile.

"Hi," he said. "What can I do for you?"

"Roy Larson in?" I asked. "We don't have an appointment, but I think he'll see us."

"He's down on two. They're shooting a commercial for our newest product, Larson's Hawaiian Super Clump Flush-Away Cat Litter."

Lisa asked, "What makes it Hawaiian?"

"They added a coconut scent to it. It smells exactly like Malibu Rum."

Coconut booze–scented cat poop. Just what the world needed.

Glow-boy said, "If you want, I can check with him and send you down."

I said, "That would be great."

After pushing some buttons and speaking in low tones to someone on the other end of the line, Glow-boy said, "Go on down to the second floor. When you get off the elevator, it's the third door on the ... " He held his hands up and wiggled the fingers on his right hand and then the fingers on his left. He gazed at his hands a moment and flopped his right hand around and said, "Yes. That's it. On the right." He looked up at us with a triumphant expression.

I suppressed a grin. We reentered the elevator. Once the doors slid shut, Lisa burst out laughing. "I think he had one too many baking sessions at the tanning salon."

"Or he's sniffed too much Hawaiian litter." I poked the button for the second floor. "Oh hell, I have to admit I flunked my first driving test because the instructor told me to make a right and I executed a perfect left. I almost crashed into another car when he yelled at me that I was turning the wrong way. It was a short return trip."

"I'll bet. Ouch."

"You know it. But Eddy brought me back the very next day and I nailed it. It was the same creepy examiner. He held onto the dash the entire time."

The elevator doors slid open. As we exited, Lisa said, "I failed my test three times. But it was because I screwed up the parallel parking thing twice and didn't come to a complete stop once. God, the trials of teens."

We stopped at the third door on the right, which was propped open. A few people scurried around inside setting up a stage at one end of the room. The stage was filled with a couple fake palm trees, a whole bunch of coconuts, and a backdrop showcasing a sun-dappled beach with teal-colored water. Huge letters arced over the sandy beach and spelled DON'T BE A CHUMP, USE LARSON'S HA-WAIIAN SUPER CLUMP.

"Huh," Lisa said, "not exactly subtle."

We came to a stop just inside the door. Poker Buddy 3 himself was talking to the lady we'd met in the elevator.

The cat carriers were on a table off in the corner. Another woman, who looked like a female Jack Hanna in forest-green khakis and button-down safari shirt with the sleeves rolled over her elbows, was talking to the felines through their wire doors. She had the weathered, ruddy skin that comes from spending most of your life outside.

I caught Roy's eye. With a charming smile, he waved us over. He looked a little like an older Clark Gable, complete with Brylcreem shine—he once told my dad that he used shoe polish on his hair—and a thin little mustache that had a gap centered under his septum. He'd practiced the one-eyed squint till his left eye was permanently squintier than his right.

Regardless of his rather unique appearance, I had a certain fondness for good old Roy. He'd been kind to a rambunctious toddler who skulked around his bar when my dad hauled me along for a visit. After my father purchased the establishment from him, Roy was always quick to throw me one of the Brach's butterscotch disks he kept tucked in a jacket pocket. I used to think he had an endless supply, because he never ran out. Believe me, there were a few times I gave him a run for his money. I figured he probably grew them on a butterscotch tree at home.

Even better than the candy was that Roy talked to me like an adult, wasn't ever condescending, and generally treated me well. That he and my dad were still friends after all this time—and after all my father's shenanigans—spoke volumes about his character, even if he did spend much of his time these days knee-deep in kitty litter.

"Shay!" Roy held his arms out. I stepped in and gave him a hearty squeeze. He pushed me back and gave me the up-down assessment the older generation gives the younger when it's been some time since they've seen each other. Roy beamed at me. "You're looking well!" His gaze caught Lisa over my shoulder. "And you're a special friend of Shay's, may I assume?"

Lisa's look of surprise quickly morphed into mischievousness. "No, I'm not that kind of friend, but I'm working on it." She blatantly ogled me up and down, much as Roy had done, but with very different intent.

I did an internal eye roll. "This is Lisa Vecoli, and no, she's not that kind of friend."

Roy always tried hard to show me he was down with the whole gay thing. Even if it was a little overdone, I appreciated his efforts.

I thought of him as that odd yet kind uncle who everyone seems to have in the family.

"Roy," I said, "can we talk to you for a couple of minutes?"

"Of course. Vi, will you please excuse me for a moment?"

The woman we'd met in the elevator smiled. "Absolutely."

We followed Roy out into the hall and to a conference room. The focal point was a fancy, high-gloss oval table that sat at least ten. A bar with a mini-fridge was situated in one corner, and a white board took up the bulk of two walls.

"Sit," Roy waved at the table. "Can I get either of you anything? Water? A Coke?"

We both declined and settled into well-cushioned, smooth leather chairs. Apparently the kitty litter biz was doing pretty well.

Roy pulled a bottle of water from the fridge and twisted off the top as he sat.

One of the techs I'd seen working on the set stuck his head in the door. "Hey Roy, sorry to bother you. We're almost ready for the first take with the cats if you want to watch."

"Thanks, Joe. I'll be there in a few minutes."

Joe nodded and disappeared.

Roy took a deep swallow from the bottle. "So what brings you here, Shay?"

I told him a brief version of what had been happening since New Year's Eve. I ended with, "I've looked everywhere. I don't know where my dad is. Did he say anything to you Friday night during the game? Did it seem like something was wrong?"

Roy took two more glugs and gently set the bottle on the tabletop. "No, Pete seemed fine. A little preoccupied, perhaps. He'd had a sub-stantial amount to drink, and I know when I left I was glad he didn't have to drive anywhere. But Pete could drive a straight line even when he was pickled."

That was the first anyone mentioned my father drinking more than his usual fair share that night.

I threw my head back and closed my eyes. "Maybe he was well on his way off the wagon."

"Now, Shay, I didn't say that." Roy tapped a finger against his chin and gazed into the distance. "Come to think of it, Pete and Mick seemed a bit at odds."

Lisa said, "What do you mean?"

"They were polite, but it felt like they were tip-toeing around each other. The underlying tension between them never really went away all night long."

A loud commotion in the hallway interrupted Roy. A panicked voice shouted, "Heeeere kitties! Heeere Purrby, heeeere Zamboni!"

Alarmed, Roy pushed his chair back and stood. Lisa and I followed his lead. Before any of us could make another move, two felines charged into the room. They zoomed around the perimeter once. One of the crazed cats made a frenzied leap and proceeded to scale Mount Roy. Those claws had to hurt.

Before we could react, the cat launched himself off Roy's shoulder. The second cat leaped onto the table and was scampering around in drunken circles when the other one joined him.

Vi burst into the room. Upon seeing the cats, she shouted, "In here!" She flung herself across the table, attempting to grab one of the furry beasts. A high heel went sailing though the air. Both cats nimbly hopped over her flailing arms. One cat landed on her ass, and from there made a mad leap toward Lisa. From Vi's screech, her butt must have taken the brunt of the claw-footed jump.

The other cat bounded to the floor and dodged out the door as Jack Hanna-ette dashed into the room.

"Oh my god. Purrby!" she yelled at the cat Lisa was attempting to wrangle. "Hang on to him. Where'd Zamboni go?"

I pointed.

She spun and raced out of the room.

Vi was still sprawled across the table, one shoe on and one shoe off. Her once-neat hair was in wild disarray. She was holding onto one butt cheek and howling.

Roy had two long scratches down the side of his face oozing blood, and he looked shell-shocked.

Lisa gripped the cat in a football hold against her side, and after a few moments of struggle, it gave up and started to purr. From the volume of the little guy, it was obvious why his name was Purrby.

At the moment, there was no way we were going to be able to have a heart-to-heart with Roy. I'd have to try again when things weren't quite so chaotic.

Lisa and I bowed out, leaving Roy and the rest of his crew to try to salvage their kitty litter shoot. Once we had settled in the Escape, the quietness stole over me like a blanket. I didn't usually mind chaos, but lately I was increasingly appreciative of the more silent moments in my life.

"Wow," Lisa said as she clicked her seatbelt buckle. "That was exciting."

"Excitement in excrement."

"You're a regular comedian, aren't you?"

"Not usually. You're getting me at growing desperation." I slumped back in my seat. "Roy didn't have much more to share beyond the fact my father was well on his way to a huge sousing." I pulled my silenced phone from my pocket to see if I'd missed anything. There were three calls and one message from Eddy not ten minutes ago.

"Where to next?" Lisa asked.

"Hang on a sec." I pulled up the message and listened to it.

"*Shay*," Eddy's voice came through loud and clear. "*I need you to call me when you get this. And I mean right now.*" She had disconnected with an audible thump.

I frowned. "That's weird."

"What?" Lisa looked over at me, a bottle of root beer halfway to her mouth.

"Eddy wants me to call her." I hit redial. On the second ring, she picked up, her voice breathy and tight.

I said, "Hey it's me—"

"Oh, thank you, Lord Jesus. Shay, I spoke with your father."

Relief, concern, and a new blaze of fury flushed through my veins. The hand holding my phone shook. "And?"

Lisa sat up straight and looked at me expectantly.

"You stop right there and get a grip, child." It must have been clear my emotions had gone from calm to infuriated in half a blink. Eddy continued, "Are you driving? You better pull over. We know how you get—"

"Eddy!"

"Well, you do."

I loved the woman, but some days what I'd give to reach through the phone. "I'll be right back," I told Lisa. I stepped outside and shut the door behind me. If I was about to learn my father was a killer, it was probably a good thing to get the news without an audience. "What exactly did he have to say for himself?"

"You stopped the car?"

Oh. My. God. "Yes, Eddy. I'm parked. At a meter that's about to expire. I'm standing on solid ground. Now tell me what the hell is going on."

"Easy girl. No need to get so testy."

Long pause.

"What?"

"He said he woke up in some ramshackle cabin somewhere. Wasn't sure what day it was."

"Figures. Where?"

"I'm getting to that. Hold your horses."

"Yes, ma'am." Oh, the sarcasm was building.

"Are you giving me lip, child?"

"Would I do that?"

"Yes, you would. Now hush. As I was saying, he said he woke up sick as a dog."

"Serves him right."

"Maybe so. Anyway. He can't remember anything. After he came to, he said he passed out again. Came back around maybe twelve hours ago. He's still not clear on where he is. Or maybe he's not telling me."

Even for my father, days—*plural*—was a long time for a hangover. Of course, he absolutely knew how to do it up right, so that wouldn't necessarily be out of the realm of possibility. "Why didn't he call me?"

"You know how your father is. He can't remember much these days, much less telephone numbers. Said it took him a whole mess of tries to get my number right, and he's known it for a long, long time."

That totally illustrated why everyone should have a cell phone. "Is he getting his ass back here or what?"

There was a silence on the other end. I wondered if we'd gotten disconnected. "Eddy?"

"I'm here. He told me when he woke up his clothes were covered in blood. Way more blood than he could've bled. Then he made it out to his car and there was blood all over the interior of that too."

"What?"

"He can't remember a thing, Shay. He doesn't know whose blood it is, aside from some from his own nose. He thinks it's broken."

This time I was the reason for the pregnant pause. Holy fricking moly. No wonder the cops wanted to talk to him.

Eddy continued, "I told him the police have been around asking for him and that damn six-shooter of his."

Had my father literally iced the dead guy? Had they gotten into a fistfight? Fear and dread bubbled, searing deep in my gut. "Where exactly is he?"

"I told you. He doesn't know."

Now I was moving from frozen stiff shock to fidgety impatience. I inadvertently rubbed my sore knee a little too hard and yanked my hand away. "Well, shit. What are we supposed to do now?"

"I don't know. Can't exactly go to the police and tell them we heard from your father. This is one of the first times my faith has ever wavered in the guilt and innocence of those I love."

I knew exactly what she meant. If my dad was pushed far enough, and if I was completely honest with myself, I did believe he could kill someone in a moment of rage. Eddy knew it too. Especially if he'd been wanking the bottle. Oh fricking frankenfuck.

I said, "Okay. Let's think this through, step by step. The cops could come knocking anytime. Well, they already did on New Year's Eve..." My voice faded. My mind leaped from one conclusion to the next. Impossibly damn fast.

Lisa had shown up at the Lep looking for my father after he'd gone missing.

Lisa had insinuated herself into my world by lending a desperately needed hand.

Lisa hadn't given a straight answer about why she wanted to talk to my dad until she came up with some weird BS about her mom on her deathbed, telling her to seek out Pete O'Hanlon to give him a nickel. A nickel? Riiight.

Lisa was a cop.

And we bought her story. Lock, stock, and rain barrel. She agreed to accompany me, a near stranger, as I went door to door looking for my old man. A man who may well have offed someone. Nothing like handing him right over to the long, lying arm of the law.

"Shay?" Eddy said.

"Hang on." My hammering heart was making it difficult to breathe. I stumbled around to the back of the SUV and leaned against the back hatch. Then I ducked my head around the corner to see if Lisa was going to get out and follow me.

I hissed into the phone, "She's a cop. She's got to be an effing police officer."

"Who does?"

"Lisa. She must be a goddamned cop!"

"Watch your language, little lady."

"Sorry." I darted another gander around the SUV. Lisa's door was still closed. "Oh Jesus. I can't believe we let her con her way into our inner circle. We must rate as some of the easiest marks ever. Weasel your way into the clan and then you're in the front seat on the crazy coaster while they cough up the suspect you're looking for. She's got to be with St. Paul."

"Now you cool it a second, child. Why St. Paul? Has JT met her?"

"On New Year's Eve. She didn't recognize Lisa. A St. Paul cop came by wanting to talk to Dad. Asked about his gun. Didn't I tell you that?"

I honestly couldn't remember who I told what anymore. "It makes sense Lisa would be with SPPD, too."

There was an irritating buzz, and I pulled the phone from my ear. JT was beeping in. "Hey, I need to figure out what to do. JT's on the other line. I'll call you later, okay?"

"Okay."

I swapped the line.

"Hey," I said.

"Found out some interesting info," JT said without preamble.

I was having a hard time keeping up as subjects changed like diapers on a newborn. "What?"

"St. Paul ID'ed Ice Cube Man. His real name is Eugene Charles Shoemaker. Goes by a number of aliases—including Gene Shoemaker, Gene Schuler, Chuck Shoemaker, Chuck Schuler. He's got a rap sheet three pages long. He's a two-bit con artist who's had numerous run-ins with law enforcement. Was last incarcerated in Stillwater for twelve months on probation violations. Currently is affiliated with Subsidy Renovations."

This conversation was so not going where I wanted it to go. JT said gravely, "Babe, you're not going to want to hear this."

My vocal cords took a time out. I may have moaned.

"Your dad is officially wanted in connection with the death of Shoemaker."

My stomach bottomed out. I jammed my hand in my pocket and pulled out some folded bills, a few crumpled receipts, and the purloined Intent to Purchase contract.

JT said something, but the roar in my ears drowned her out.

My hands shook as I unfolded the crumpled contract. The business card was still stapled to the upper left hand corner of the sheet. It fairly glowed in my grasp, like it was radioactive.

Chuck Schuler, Mgr.
Subsidy Renovations
Minneapolis, MN
Cell: 612-888-7767

My mind looped, replaying the same thought. Chuck Schuler was Ice Cube Man. Chuck Schuler had been shot dead. My father's gun was found with Schuler's body. There was literally blood on my father's hands, in his car. There was motive galore, if you made the not very large leap that Schuler was indeed the one pushing my father to sell and my father ran out of patience and pushed back.

Holy fuck-a-duck.

I couldn't take my eyes off the contract even though I was no longer able to focus on the actual words.

A link (was it the link?) between my father and the dead man rested in my hands. Was this particular piece of paper the only one in existence? How likely was that? There was probably another copy wherever Schuler worked. But there was always the chance there wasn't. The very fact that I could be holding my dad's ticket to life in prison shook me to the very core.

One thing was certain. I wasn't going to do a thing with the damning piece of paper until I knew for sure what in the hell had happened.

SIX

I DON'T KNOW HOW I finished the conversation with JT. It was like my fight-or-flight response had kicked into caveman survival mode. My rational mind bid me "see you later, sucker." I was functioning on autopilot. I didn't dare tell JT about my father and his bloody duds. Or that Lisa Vecoli was a real-life Olivia Benson.

I have no idea how I managed to find some lame excuse to drop Lisa off—in one piece and without booting her out of my vehicle at sixty on the freeway. Nor do I know how I deflected the questions she kept lobbing at me all the way back. I must have come off suspiciously or maybe plain nuts, but I did what I had to do to get rid of her.

I still couldn't believe we'd all been blindsided. Bamboozled by the offer of help from a cute chick and she turns out to be a cop out to get my own flesh and blood. That shit was so not going to fly. At this point I didn't care if Coop was done with his contract work or not. We had an emergency of epic proportions.

Coop had recently moved into one side of an old duplex on Garfield between 22nd and 24th streets. I pulled to a stop in front of his place and took the porch steps two at a time. The ancient doorbell had stopped working sometime back in the Fifties probably, so I banged on his front door with a bit more force than necessary. I hadn't called ahead because I didn't trust myself behind the wheel while talking on the phone. Fury and confusion were distraction enough. Score probably the only point today for Shay thinking rationally.

I pounded on the door again. Finally I heard some scuffling. The door swung open.

Coop looked like he had just crawled out of bed. He was wearing a wrinkled *Vegan or Bust* T-shirt, and his pasty, hairy legs stuck out of a pair of navy blue boxers. However, I knew the more likely scenario was that he hadn't been to bed yet at all. His shaggy, ash-blond hair was standing up at various angles and the bags under his eyes were colossal.

"Dude," I said, my voice constricting, "I need help."

The threat of tears was enough to propel my usually deliberate, slow-moving friend into action.

In seconds, I was settled in the living room in Coop's favorite recliner with my feet up, waiting for him to reappear after taking a lightning-quick shower and exchanging his up-all-night duds for some up-all-day ones. Ten minutes later, he bounded down the stairs barefoot, wearing a Rabbit Hole sweatshirt and faded jeans that hung low on his skinny hips. His hair was still standing on end, but it was clean. He plopped himself on the couch to my right and bent to the task of dragging socks over his long feet.

With a dramatic flourish he flung himself against the back of the couch. "Now tell me what's going on."

"I think Lisa's a cop who's after my dad because he killed someone."

Coop blinked at me a couple of times, then leaned forward, elbows on his knees. "Okay. Let's take this from the top. What the fuck are you talking about?"

"This morning, Lisa and I were making the rounds talking to Dad's friends, like we'd talked about at the Lep last night. We started with Brian Eckhart at Sexworld."

Coop gave me a facetiously long face. "Too bad I had to miss that trip."

I might have believed him if I didn't know Coop was somewhat OCD about cleanliness. The thought of stepping foot in Sexworld was about as appealing as hopping into a dumpster.

I said, "The only thing we got out of Brian was half a name. Then we headed to St. Paul to chat with Mick Simon." I was proud of myself for following the timeline instead of babbling mindlessly that my father was a cold-blooded killer. Well, considering the circumstances, he'd probably be considered a hot-blooded killer.

Coop said, "Ah yes, the Vulc. How was he?"

"No idea. He wasn't at the Krewe warehouse. Was going to try him later on." I looked at my watch. It felt like it should be about six in the evening when it actually was only about half past one in the afternoon.

"Anyway, from there we went to see Roy Larson."

Coop leaned back again and crossed his ankles. "Oh, Roy Boy. What's the old Litter Liege up to these days?"

"Coconut-scented stuff."

"You're kidding."

"They were doing the ad shoot when Lisa and I got there. It included a couple cats who were none-too-happy to be starring in a Larson's Hawaiian Super Clump Flush-Away Cat Litter commercial.

"Anyway, Roy didn't have much to say except that Dad was well on his way to a day-early New Year's Eve celebration of his own. Oh, and that he and Mick seemed to be butting heads for some reason. But you know with Dad ... he can be weird for no reason. Then we left and Eddy called, and the fireworks really started."

I dropped the chair into a sitting position and put both feet on the ground.

Coop waited quietly.

I rubbed a hand over my eyes, which felt as gritty as Coop's had to after a sleepless, computer screen–filled night. "Dad called Eddy."

"That's great." Coop brightened and sat up straighter himself. "Where is he?"

"Don't know." I filled him in on the facts as Eddy conveyed them. I said, "It gets worse. Dad's gun was found frozen in the ice with Ice Cube Man."

Coop's widened eyes met mine. "Oh no."

"Oh yes." It felt that with every sentence I pounded one more nail into my father's coffin. I fished around in my pocket for the Intent to Purchase letter and handed it to Coop. He unfolded and read it once, then twice. Scanned the attached business card, and slowly raised his head and met my eyes. He said, "Chuck Schuler. You think he's Ice Cube Man?"

"I just talked to JT. She said St. Paul ID'ed Ice Cube Man. It's a guy by the name of Eugene Charles Shoemaker. Also known as Chuck Schuler."

"Oh, fuck."

111

"Tell me about it. Coop, I've always said my father wouldn't ever really hurt anyone, but when he's in one of his alcoholic fugue states, I honestly don't know what he might be capable of."

Coop sat still, absorbing all of this. Finally he slapped his knees and stood. "Come on. Let's see what we can dig up on Schuler and Subsidy Renovations."

He put his hand out and hauled me to my feet. "Step into the Den of Illicit Knowledge and I'll put Bogey Too to work." Coop recently created this thing he called a bot that could travel through cyberspace, sneak into places it wasn't supposed to go, capture whatever information he told it to, and return with the cyber goods. Since it was almost always good at sniffing out whatever Coop was searching for, he named it Bogey Too, after my canine Bogey, the flunky bloodhound. I think Bogey Too's success rate was a fair amount better than its flesh-and-blood namesake. Coop's ability to hack just about anything without being caught was legendary in certain circles. If he and his abilities got into the wrong hands, boy, would trouble abound.

The Den of Illicit Knowledge was actually an ex-dining room that ran almost half the length of the house. Years ago there must have been some memorable parties in the old joint.

Room-darkening blinds filtered outside light. Two eight-foot tables pushed side-by-side lengthwise were littered with a vast array of electronic equipment, including hard drives, miles of wire, and three monitors. From this setup Coop worked his magic for his not-so-legitimate fun and for more orthodox and legal profit.

An old metal and laminate dining room table with an extra leaf in the center sat in one corner of the room. This was where Coop and his fellow role-playing geeks amused themselves with Dungeons and Dragons when they weren't all knee-deep in tournament play in Minnetonka's Hands On Toy Company and Game Room. Coop's newest addition to his role-playing repertoire was an online game called Runes of Magic. I've tried but failed to grasp the allure. But Coop enjoyed the complexity of those games, and I respected that.

Coop plopped down in a rolling chair in front of the middle monitor and fired it up. "This guy's name was Chuck Shultz, right?"

"No. That's the Peanuts guy, dope-on-a-rope. It's Schuler."

"You passed the test. Thought we needed a little levity."

I dragged a chair over. I usually had no idea what Coop was doing, but it was fun to watch his fingers fly over the keyboard.

He pulled up one of his custom search engines and typed the name into the query box and hit enter. Almost faster than Google returns came back, a substantial list of Chuck Schulers popped up. Coop added Minneapolis to the search string. Still way too many responses.

"What did you say he was doing for a job?"

"Real estate."

"Okay, let me try that."

This time we got a much smaller sample. An entry for "Chuck Schuler Services LLC" listed a business office in New Brighton, a metro suburb. I looked again at the Intent to Purchase and Schuler's attached business card. The card listed Minneapolis but gave no street address. Coop jotted down the New Brighton address and went back to surfing.

He moved the mouse pointer here and there. Between that and the left clicking, my brain started to gnaw on thoughts about my dad. Where was he? Was he truly hurt? What was he doing? What had he done?

My instinct when a loved one was in trouble was to react. Often without rational, conscious thought and without the benefit of common sense. It wasn't a good combination. When people who get really pissed say they see red, believe them; they do. This feeling, this thing that seemed to come over me when I saw my own personal shade of red had a name, thanks to some friends from a very long time ago. The Tenacious Protector.

Initially, when this fiasco started with my dad on New Year's Eve, I'd been furious. I'd gone through far too many of these episodes with him to cut him any slack. Add in the time of year and his monetary needs, and I was livid. Now, in light of these recent turns of events, the fury was slowly ebbing and the Protector in me was stirring, pushing against my carefully constructed façade.

"Shay!"

I jumped, jerked back to Coop's Den of Illicit Knowledge. My pal was staring at me as if I'd grown two additional heads and was drooling.

"Sorry," I said. "What?"

Coop's expression reflected both fondness and exasperation. "I told you it looks like Chuckie baby started freelancing his talents, and has seriously flawed workplace ethics."

"What do you mean?"

"He worked for one company that fired him for selling proprietary information to the highest bidder. He was busted because he made the mistake of trying to resell the stuff to the his own company's ex-CEO. Another place kicked him to the proverbial curb because he had employed some outside help to achieve sales goals through intimidation that involved violence against animals and kids."

"Big winner there." I rubbed my eyes. "Let's go see what kind of office a dead man keeps."

———

I merged onto 35W as Coop said, "So who else do you think might want to see the last of Chilly Chuck?"

"Good question," I said. "You know those questionable workplace ethics?"

"Yeah."

"Maybe someone he screwed over might be pissed off, maybe enough to do him. Or maybe a jilted ex-lover?"

Coop cleared his throat. "I hate to bring this up, but I'm not sure why a jilted ex-lover would have your dad's handgun and freeze it with a dead guy."

That did make most of my percolating theories shut down fast. "I hate it when you're right."

"How would your dad have managed to turn him into a human ice cube, anyway?"

Good question. Realistically? "Whether my dad's drunk or not, we both know he's very strong. All the years working on the river ... Moving a dead body?" I thought about that. "Yeah, he could do it. But turning dead body into an ice cube, that's the real question."

"Yeah. Let's assume he had to have help. More to the point, who would help your dad freeze-dry Chuck?"

I didn't answer as we exited off the freeway onto County Road D and made a left at the top of the ramp. A strip mall sat off on the left. On the other side of the road were a number of single-story office buildings. I found the right place without too much fuss.

The walls of the building were mirrored glass so shiny that they reflected the image of the Escape. I killed the engine. "Mick Simon coordinates ice blocks for the winter carnival. He'd be a natural choice. And Limpy Dick is eccentric enough to be a willing participant."

Coop asked, "Do Mick and Limpy Dick know each other?"

"Probably. They were both playing poker Friday night. But wait." I thought about it some more. "Neither of them would incriminate my dad by leaving his gun with the body. I'm sure of that. And why would they take Dad to some cabin and dump him like that?"

"Maybe no one helped your dad get there. Maybe he drove himself."

I groaned. "Why the hell can't he remember?"

"I don't know," Coop said softly. "Let's go inside and see if we can find out anything that'll help."

I followed Coop through a glass door labeled C.S. SERVICES LLC in white vinyl letters. The lobby was tiny. A lone desk stood beside an open door, presumably Schuler's office. There wasn't a chair to be had, nor a coat rack, or even a potted plant. The place was about as clean as a freshly bathed baby's bottom.

Behind the desk, a mostly unremarkable middle-aged woman sat filing her nails. The glaring exception to her unremarkability hovered at chest level. Extending straight out from her body was a humongous pair of knockers that appeared to float without restraint beneath her paisley sweater. Dolly Parton would be proud.

She glanced up with a suspicious expression at our entrance, but her hand continued to slide the file rhythmically back and forth, not missing a beat. "Help you?"

The woman was either ready to be done with her job or she didn't care that her boss was toes up in the morgue downtown.

I said, "We're wondering if you could tell us a little about Chuck Schuler."

The sawing continued unabated. Before I could come up with something to startle her out of her strangely compelling task, she said in a sing-song voice, "Poor, poor Mr. Schuler." Her tone was much more venomous than the words themselves would indicate, and she ground her file against her nails a little harder. Apparently she did have some emotion over the demise of her boss after all.

I sucked in a breath and opened my mouth to speak, but not before Nails said, "I swear, that man has more visitors after he's dead than he ever did before he turned into a goddamn ice cube."

She dropped the nail file. It clattered loudly against the desktop. She lumbered to her feet and said, "All right. Who sent you and how much does he owe this time?"

In a heartbeat, she shed bored secretary like a snakeskin and replaced it with vindictive bitch. Nails attempted to frown and instead gave us a half-squint. Her brows were frozen in a state of perpetual astonishment. I wondered what kind of a bargain basement deal she got on the Botox job.

Both Coop and I took a casual, cautious half-step away from the desk. I was ready to keep on going right out the door, but the desire to see what else Nails had to say overrode my instinct to get the hell out of there. I was curious to find out if old Chuckie had his hand in a few cookie jars that now wanted their cookies back in a bad way.

So how could I play on that and maximize my informational return? "Mr. Schuler was involved in some business dealings with one of the parties I represent."

That sounded good.

Nails returned her attention to her fingers and studied them from one side and then the other. The only thing that could've made the moment even more surreal and sadly cliché would have been if she were chomping on a piece of gum and sporadically cracking it between her molars.

She sighed dramatically and muttered under her breath, "Yup. Another one."

Coop said, "What?"

"You're the fourth set of people coming in who want payment or to talk about Mr. Schuler's business. What is it this time?"

The woman made the sign of the cross and opened a desk drawer. For a spilt second I wondered if she was going to pull a gun. She fumbled around and withdrew a saltshaker. She shook it a few times over her left shoulder, returned it the to the drawer, sat, and resumed her nail filing.

One more try. I said, "Mr. Schuler was working for Subsidy Renovations—"

"NO," the woman said forcefully, startling me. "He didn't work for them, they *contracted* with him. There's a difference, you know."

Wow. I exchanged a glance with Coop, who gave me the universal, wide-eyed, she's-off-her-rocker look.

"Okay," I said slowly. "He was contracted by Subsidy Renovations."

"Yes." The woman rolled her eyes dramatically. "That's what I said." She blew on a nail and moved on to another. I wondered if she was going to have any fingernails at all after this.

Coop said, "If he was contracted by Subsidy, did he have a contact there he worked with?"

The woman wrinkled her nose. "You're all the same. You want to know where your money is. Well, I can tell you in no uncertain terms that I don't have it."

I opened my mouth once again, but she continued before I could utter a sound. "I know all of you think Chuck took your money and ran. That it's not him who was frozen in that"—she sniffed, and her lower lip trembled, whether in rage or grief, I didn't know—"that ice. I'm sure he took real good care of your precious money." The sarcasm was rampant. "Just like I'm sure that from beyond the grave he's going to pay me for working all of last month. And this month, too, for that matter." Nails whipped out that saltshaker and did her thing again. There was going to be no worry about ice buildup on this floor.

So Chuckie-boy was taking investment money and not applying it where the investors expected it to go. And he wasn't paying his help. The facts weren't stirring much sympathy from me, but I felt bad the secretary was going to get screwed along with everyone else Chuck swindled. Maybe she wanted him dead as badly as the other people he'd screwed over. Add another name to the list.

I said, "The person I represent didn't invest any money and we're not here trying to squeeze you for any."

She sniffed none-too-delicately, and attacked another finger.

"So," Coop said, "who was Mr. Schuler's point person for Subsidy?"

"Norman Howard. He's—"

Before she could go on, the door opened and three people sporting black leathers, scruffy faces, and scary-looking facial tattoos stomped inside. Coop and I faded back as the leader marched up to the receptionist's desk. He planted two hairy fists on the desktop and rumbled, "Heard Schuler was terminated. We need to talk about the money of ours the bastard's got."

He cleared his throat, sucked up some snot, and hocked a sizeable loogie across the desk. It splattered wetly against the wall and started oozing down.

I tried not to gag and backed toward the door. On the other side of the two hench-wingmen, Coop was making his retreat too. Part of me felt guilty about leaving Nails to the motorcycle sharks, but she could probably use her fingernail file to stab them if they tried anything.

———

I was starving. We headed for Boston Market off County Road C and Snelling since the restaurant could satisfy both my carnivorous cravings and Coop's vegetarian requirements.

"So what you want to do after we chow?" Coop asked.

"We know that someone named Norman Howard contracted—" I shot a questioning glance at Coop, who shrugged. "Let's call it contracted... He made some sort of arrangements with Chuck Schuler to go after the Leprechaun?"

"That's what it sounds like. Chuckie was apparently a go-between without any real stake. Of course, his buy-in was probably a fee of some kind that I'll bet he used to replace money that he'd"—Coop paused and did the quote thing in the air with his fingers—"*borrowed* for some project that wasn't anywhere near on the up and up."

"Our circle of who'd like Schuler dead is growing." I hit the blinker and turned into the parking lot.

We exited the Escape and I headed in to use the restroom while Coop sucked down a cancer stick. I could not wait for him to get his ass in gear and try the quitting thing again.

As I was washing my hands, my cell rang. It was JT. I hit answer and tucked the phone between my ear and shoulder and grabbed some paper towels. Guilt over not leveling with her about hearing from my dad hit me right in the gut. *Suck it up, Shay.* "Hey babe."

"Where are you?"

"About to grab a bite to eat at Boston Market in Roseville. What's up?" I pulled open the door and walked out into the short hallway.

"Want some company? I can be there in about fifteen."

Holy crap. I froze in mid-step. I'd usually jump at a chance to meet up with JT anytime, anywhere, but not right now. Not when Coop and I were about to hash out our next move in proving my father didn't have anything to do with Ice Cube Man. Theoretically proving he didn't have anything to do with it, anyway. However, I couldn't exactly say I didn't want to see her because it would be completely out of character.

Coop was coming in the door, and he caught my eye. I must have had a panicked look on my face because he made a beeline in my direction.

I held a hand up to Coop. He stopped in front of me, just short of hovering, his eyes glued to mine. I said, "JT, we'd love to have lunch with you."

Coop gave a slight nod and relaxed.

"Great," she said. "I'll see you soon. Order me some meatloaf with mac and cheese and creamed spinach." Ugh. I couldn't believe JT liked creamed spinach. I kept trying it, thinking one day my taste buds might change, but no luck yet. Too bad, it was healthy. Maybe that was the problem.

"Okay. Great." Yeah. Right. "See you soon."

"Perfect. I'm starving. Love you."

"Love you too."

I disconnected, and made sure the connection was actually severed before I spoke. It wouldn't be good for JT to hear me say, "Man. I hate lying to her. I feel like crap. Like I did back when Eddy and I were hiding you from JT."

Coop fell into step beside me and we got in line to order. It was busier than I'd expected at a quarter to three. He said, "You're not exactly lying to her, are you? I mean, it's been more of an omission than a bald face untruth, right?"

"I suppose. But I hate it. I never thought about the implications of getting involved with a cop. Of course, I never expected to be trying to figure out if my dad actually deep-sixed someone and froze his ass, either."

We spent the next few minutes ordering, filled our pop cups at the fountain, and settling at a table to wait for the arrival of our food and my wayward police officer.

Coop ripped the paper off the top of his straw and shot the rest of it at me like a blow-dart. I was too distracted by the mental gymnastics gyrating through my brain to pay attention, and he nailed me right between the eyes.

He laughed.

I gave him the finger.

We were pretty good at distracting each other when things weren't going well.

Coop said, "So, before we're blessed with your partner's presence, I figured you'd be happy to know that I sent Bogey Too looking for whatever he can find on Norman Howard."

Nice. At least if we couldn't actively be doing something, Bogey Too could. "You're a good man, Nicholas Cooper. What'd you think of Nails?"

"Nails?"

"Yeah. That receptionist is going to file all of her fingernails right off if she isn't careful."

"I felt bad for her, having to field people coming in wanting to know what Schuler did with their money."

"Me too. I wonder why she doesn't bail. I mean, her boss is dead. Who does she think is going to pay her?"

Coop rearranged his ice with his straw. "I have no idea. No telling why people do what they do sometimes."

The server appeared with three plates of food and plunked them down. "Can I get you anything else?" he asked.

I said, "We're good. Thanks." I picked up my silverware, unwrapped the paper around it, and fished out the fork. "I'm thinking once Bogey Too comes back with whatever he finds on Mr. Howard, we should—"

"Hey!" JT dropped into the chair beside me with a grin. I couldn't help but return her delighted smile. Her dark eyes met mine and she gave my knee a squeeze. "Hi, Coop. Where's Lisa?"

Oh. I forgot I hadn't told JT I'd dumped Lisa, or why. *Think fast, ding-dong.* "Lisa wasn't feeling so good. I think it had something to do with the whack on her head." Well, that was certainly possible. "I roped Coop into snooping around with me."

JT ripped into her meatloaf. "Thanks for ordering," she said, chewing happily. One thing about JT—she appreciated her food. She pointed her fork at Coop's plate. "How are those sweet potatoes?"

Coop's plate was loaded with vegetables. I was still waiting for him to grow out of his vegetarian phase, but I'd been waiting now for almost a decade. Had to give him credit, he stuck to his guns. He said, "Good. Want a bite?"

JT nodded. She stuck her fork in his pile of goo and stuffed it into her mouth. After a moment she said, "I should have asked for that instead of the mac and cheese." She swallowed, and looked at me.

I asked, "Want some turkey?" and tilted my plate her way.

"Sure." JT stabbed a couple of pieces and popped them in her mouth. She wasn't kidding about being starved. "Where are you on your list? I can help now. I was officially kicked out of the station and reminded I was on vacation." She shrugged. "I can still poke around and stuff, just better do it out of the office."

Lovely. My woman was now freed up to get in my way. I said, "That's great, JT."

Now what were we going to do?

Coop gave me the eye and saved the day, telling JT about our encounter with Schuler's secretary.

I shoveled food in my mouth and ate robotically without tasting much. Even the piece of pecan pie I shared with JT for dessert didn't do its usual job of thrilling my taste buds.

We were about to wrap up lunch when my phone trilled again. This time it was the number to the Leprechaun. "Johnny," I answered, "what's up?"

"The cops showed up with a search warrant and closed the place down."

The smile on my face slid away. "Oh, shit."

"They said it's temporary, but... right now they're tossing the office, and I think they went up to Pete's apartment too."

"Okay. Hang tight and we'll be right there."

SEVEN

I burst into the Leprechaun with Coop and JT hot on my heels. The bright whiteness of the snow outside left me temporarily blinded as we hit the murky bar. I made out Johnny leaning against the counter behind the bar, his arms insolently crossed over his chest and a look of wary disdain on his face. I didn't see the tall, thin cop wearing a Minneapolis Police Department uniform standing right inside the front door until he stepped in front of me. I put on the brakes, abruptly halting our entrance. I staggered, and the cop, who was no more than a kid, reached out a steadying hand.

He said, "Sorry to startle you. The bar is closed—"

"I got that. I'm Pete O'Hanlon's daughter."

The look of concern on his face melted into an unreadable mask. "You got some identification?" The cop looked over my shoulder at JT and Coop. "Those two with you?"

"Yes." I pulled out my wallet and tried to extract my ID.

"I'll take all of your IDs." The cop held out his hand. I slapped my license in his palm and stepped aside. JT flashed her Minneapolis PD

125

identification at him, which he grabbed. Coop handed over his ID without protest. Probably because for once he wasn't in a position to be arrested for anything.

Cop Boy said, "Wait here." He spun and disappeared down the hall. I assumed he was about to rat us out to whomever was leading the search.

Johnny watched the proceeding with a raised eyebrow. He called, "This gets more and more fun."

I said, "I know. Sorry."

"Oh, hell. I wouldn't miss this for the world." Johnny had seen my father through years of ups and downs, and I knew my dad couldn't have a better champion. With the exception of Coop, Eddy, and me. And maybe JT.

The cop returned, followed by the same sergeant who had shown up on New Year's Eve looking for my dad. The one who looked like Popeye.

"I'm Sergeant Robert DeSilvero, St. Paul PD." He looked at the licenses he held in his hand and then DeSilvero squinted at me. "I've seen you before." He pointed one of the licenses at me. "You were here when I came in looking for O'Hanlon Saturday night. You're his kid?"

"Yeah. Why are you here now?"

JT stepped up beside me. "Yes, what specifically are you looking for, DeSilvero?"

"Who're—ah. You're MPD." I thought I detected a note of something in his voice. Respect? At least I hoped it was.

"I am," JT acknowledged. "So what's the warrant for?"

DeSilvero returned our licenses and cocked his head, studying us like suspicious bugs under a magnifying glass. He said, "Specifically, ammunition for an M1911 Colt 45."

Wasn't *that* a fancy way of saying a gun with a big bang.

DeSilvero said, "You can sit over there." He jerked his head toward the tables at the back of the bar. "I'll let you know when we're done. And," he looked right at me, "you get in the way and I'll boot your behind out of here so fast your rear won't know what hit it."

I bit off a "Yes, sir."

"In fact," DeSilvero called over to Johnny, "why don't you come and sit with these folks, too."

Johnny insolently tossed the rag he had in his hand onto the top of the bar and sauntered over and sat. "Dickhead," he muttered under his breath.

I pretty much agreed with his assessment.

We settled around one of the tables and waited for the cops to do their thing. I wondered what else my father may have left laying around that might point an accusatory finger his way. The Intent to Purchase letter was burning a hole through the pocket of my jeans, but I'd be damned if I was going to show it to Popeye. He could figure things out on his own. How lucky was it that I'd stumbled onto it before they did? I thought about the fact that for all I knew there could be another copy of the same document laying around in my father's clutter that I didn't see. The ache of wary unease settled deep in my gut, and I didn't think I'd be finding much relief anytime soon.

We spent the time speculating about Ice Cube Man, how my father's pistol wound up encased in the frozen stuff with said ICM, and avoiding the mention of my father and Chuck Schuler. Eventually Coop regaled us with some of the zanier exploits he and the rest of the Green Beans for Peace and Preservation involved themselves in trying to protect Mother Nature.

At 5:33 p.m.—and I know it was that exact time because I was playing Words with Friends on my phone—DeSilvero marched into the bar and announced they were finished.

I asked, "Did you find what you wanted?"

DeSilvero sidestepped my question. "Make sure you get a hold of me if you hear from your father. And by the way, someone needs to take care of that stink you've got going on in the cellar." Behind him, cops, crime scene dudes, and some other official-looking law enforcement people filed from the Lep like a river of blue trickling out to sea. DeSilvero threw his card on the table and followed the last of the search party out of the bar. Before the door shut fully behind them, it opened again, and three customers who'd patiently waited for the circus to disperse came inside.

JT said, "I guess you're open for business again."

"I'm on it," Johnny said, and returned to his domain behind the bar.

I dropped my head onto my arms. I was thoroughly tired of dealing with fallout that was my father's doing.

JT rubbed my back. "It's going to be okay, Shay."

I wished I believed it. I heaved a deep sigh and sat up. "I'm going to call Roto-Rooter or whoever deals with sewer lines. Would you guys mind checking Dad's place and straightening it up if?"

Coop stood. "You got it." He caught my eye and shook his head once. It was his way of telling me to cool it while JT was around. All I wanted to do was find Norman Howard of Subsidy Renovations and wring his neck until he told me why he was interested in buying the Lep. Why he'd probably sent thugs to help sway my father's decision. And it would be a good idea to talk to Limpy Dick and Hemorrhoid Harvey, Poker Buddies 4 and 5, to see if either one of them helped my father ice a con man.

JT and Coop headed upstairs. I scoped out the condition of my father's office. He was not the neatest of people, but the extreme chaos of papers, ledgers, and empty file folders spread across his desk pissed me off.

I halfheartedly straightened the files then sank into his chair and stared at the powered-down computer screen. I wondered if the cops had gone through his hard drive too. Since my dad was still in the dark ages when it came to computers, he rarely passworded anything; when he did, he used *password* as the password. So if the cops did try to access his computer files, they likely got everything he had.

No doubt my father was an easy target. Maybe I should turn Coop loose on his technology. He'd hate both Coop and me for a while, but maybe he'd eventually appreciate Coop's password encryption programs, system redundancy, firewall security, and other fancy terminology that I didn't understand but knew meant cyber-safe and secure.

Then again, maybe he wouldn't.

I turned on the computer and waited for it to boot. *Password* was indeed the password. Once it was up and running, I Googled sewer fix-it places. A few businesses that provided various sewage services popped up, and I called the one closest to the bar.

A robotic voice on the other end of the line picked up and told me I was calling after hours, and if it was an emergency to call another number that was rattled off so fast I'd have to call back three times before I'd be able to write the whole thing down. I left a message and hoped a human would return my call.

I'd no more than hung up when my phone rang, and I'll be damned if my caller didn't introduce himself as the Roger the Roto-Rooter man.

"Thanks for returning my call so promptly," I told Roger.

"No problem. It's already been a busy January, and we've hardly gotten a start on the month."

I explained the problem, and Roger told me that he'd have someone out to check the situation before noon tomorrow. However, the way my luck was going, they probably wouldn't show up for days. I thanked him and disconnected, mightily wishing this day were done.

————

At seven o'clock on a Monday night, the Lep was unsurprisingly quiet. The place was devoid of any paying customers. Coop, JT, Johnny, and I sat at the bar drinking beer and chowing down takeout from Chimborazo, an Ecuadorian restaurant over on Central.

Before we ate, I'd given in and shut the basement door. Screw air circulation, or what would be a lack thereof. I truly had no idea how Dad had withstood the stench this long. No wonder Whale walked out. Which again brought me back to the fact my father hadn't taken care of the problem, which was obviously (well, more than obviously) at the must-fix stage. The repair probably wasn't going to be cheap, but ignoring it was no longer an option. Hopefully the cost wouldn't be astronomical, but when it came to sewer issues, I knew it wouldn't be pretty.

If my dad couldn't cover the cost, I'd chip in whatever I could to help. I still felt the weight of my own inattention to the mundane details of my father's life. Not much I could do about the past at this point, but I could make an attempt to be more involved from here on out.

That decided, I stuffed the last of the yuca frita in my mouth and washed it down with a long swallow of Corona.

The front door squawked open. A short, well-bundled figure blew through the entrance in a swirl of icy air and stomped up to the bar. What would have been a knee-length black coat on most people was ankle-length, and it almost hit the top of a pair of gray Sorel's with hot pink laces. An incredibly long multicolored scarf was wound over the person's head and numerous times around their neck. The only facial feature that showed was a pair of dark eyes. They emanated fury and were fixed on me.

Oh shit.

I set my bottle on the bar and squared my shoulders.

"You." The voice came out muffled through layers of yarn.

"Eddy?" Coop asked.

"No, it's the ghost of Christmas past. Hell, yes, it's me." Eddy began the task of unwinding herself. When she finished de-scarfing, she threw it toward a stool and it slowly slid off the seat to land on in a heap on the dirty wood floor.

Eddy whirled on me. "I've been worried sick about you. You tell me you'll call me back and I hear nothing. I try calling you and you don't answer. What good are those dang cell phones you kids all have if you don't answer them?"

Oh, boy. I completely forgot I'd told Eddy I'd call her back. I opened my mouth to defend myself, but Eddy wasn't finished. "And then there's a police officer with you who's after your own father. For all I know she dragged you off somewhere."

JT, who was watching Eddy's outburst with a look of shock, said, "What? What cop was with you? Where?"

Eddy ignored her and kept right on going, viciously slashing the air in my direction with an accusatory finger as she advanced. "He's holed up somewhere with a hangover and blood on his hands, and you're consorting with the enemy?"

Coop sat frozen, an empanada halfway to his mouth. Johnny slowly inched his way back around the bar, out of harm's way.

JT frowned in confusion. "The cop had blood on his hands?"

Shit, shit, shit! Eddy didn't know I hadn't told JT anything about having heard from my father or the fact that Lisa Vecoli was a cop. I was in a super schooner full of trouble.

"Not exactly," I told JT and kept a wary eye on Eddy, who stopped about a foot and a half away from my knees, glaring up at me.

"None of your calls came through," I said weakly, and pulled the phone from my pocket and checked. Sure enough, there were three missed calls from Eddy, all in the last forty-five minutes. I'd turned the ringer off while we waited out the search warrant and hadn't thought to turn it back on again.

JT stared at me, her confusion rapidly segueing into an expression of suspicion. She wasn't stupid. Her lips were pressed tightly together, and that was never good. I had to hope she'd understand once I explained what was going on. In the past I'd lied to her to protect Coop, and here I'd done it again. I could almost hear the gears in her head grinding as she tried to pull it all together. If I could have kicked myself, I would have. Hard. I should have leveled with her right off the bat. I sent her a pleading, please-be-patient look and said, "Hang on, babe, I'll explain."

I turned my attention back to Eddy. "I'm sorry I forgot to call you. We had to come back here because the cops were here executing a search warrant, and in the hubbub I didn't even—"

"Search warrant?" Eddy shrieked.

Uh oh. Eddy *never* shrieked.

"Johnny," I said, starting to feel panicky, "how about a double shot of something hard?"

Coop hovered in the background, looking like he wasn't sure if he should grab Eddy or run away.

In a shake Johnny had a full shot glass lined up in front of Eddy. I picked it up and thrust it into her hand. "Drink."

She threw the booze down her throat and slammed the glass down. "Thanks," she choked, breathing through the burn. I briefly considered having Johnny pour one for JT, too, but I was a little afraid she might dump it over my head.

I put my hands on Eddy's shoulders and gave her a gentle shake. "I'm sorry I didn't call you. The cops tossed the bar and Dad's apartment looking for ammo for his gun and who knows what else."

Eddy elbowed me aside, leaned against the bar, and said hoarsely, "Thanks. I needed that." Her voice was steadier and more in the octave range it normally was. All right. One situation under semicontrol.

JT pinned me with squinty eyes of granite, and I knew exactly how the bad guys felt when she turned her sights on them. She slid off the stool onto her feet and crossed her arms.

I glanced between Coop and Johnny. "Will you two please keep an eye on Eddy for a few minutes?" Without waiting for an answer, I grabbed JT's arm and dragged her to one of the dimly lit back booths. "Sit. Please."

JT stood a second longer, battling between listening to me or going all stubborn on my ass. Finally she slid into the booth and I sat across from her.

She planted both hands on the table and leaned forward, hurt palpably radiating. "I thought we covered the lies and secrets thing awhile ago, Shay. What the hell is going on?"

The rock in my gut dropped lower. I was a complete nincompoop. I said, "Dad called Eddy earlier this afternoon."

JT's eyes widened. "What? Why didn't you—"

"Because," I cut her off, "I didn't want to put you in a bad position."

"Bad position? What do you mean?"

"Dad's the one with blood on his hands, JT."

"Are you speaking euphemistically or literally?"

I chewed on my lip and stared into space over her shoulder for a moment. Whatever I said next I would not be able to take back. But then wasn't there something about spouses not having to rat out the other in a court of law or something? Oh, but wait. We weren't spouses. However, if things went the way we hoped, Minnesota might join the ranks of the states that allowed same-sex marriage, and we could be. After tonight, though, I was fairly sure potential "I do's" would be closer to "I don'ts."

To hell with it. I'd lay it all down and let the pieces fall. "I'm not completely clear on what happened, but this is what Eddy told me earlier. She said Dad called her, wouldn't tell her where he was. He was working off one of the worst hangovers of his life, from the sound of it. Had no memory how he got there or what happened before that. And ... " I trailed off, afraid to commit to the unretractable. I searched her face, looking for some degree of understanding.

Her expression had softened a bit. It didn't look like I was next on her who-needs-to-be-throttled list anymore. She said, her voice impressively even, "Tell me. I think I vaguely see where this is going."

Did she know something I didn't? *Stop analyzing and get on with it, O'Hanlon.* "He said when he woke up, his clothes were soaked in blood." My throat tightened. "The blood wasn't his. Most of it anyway. And ... " I dropped my eyes to the worn wood surface of the tabletop and slowly ran my fingertips over the uneven, grooved surface. "I guess there was blood all over the interior of his car, too."

I heard a loud exhalation. "Jesus Christ."

"Yeah, that was kind of my assessment of the situation too." I searched JT's face. "This is why I didn't want to put you in a compromising position. With your job. You're a homicide investigator, for god's sake."

For a couple of long beats, the low voices of Coop, Eddy, and Johnny, and the intermittent creaking of the old building were the only sounds that filtered into my consciousness.

JT stilled the restless movement of my hands with her own. "Okay. I can see why you were afraid to tell me about this. But you need to understand something before we go any further, or there isn't going to be any further going for us."

Oh, no. I knew this was going to happen sooner or later. My carefully crafted self-defenses started rumbling up like a castle's drawbridge, slow and creaky but with one inevitable outcome. I was crazy to believe I could ever make a relationship work long term with anyone, much less someone who was an officer of the law. What was I thinking? I never thought my life was complicated until JT came along. I could probably get my stuff moved out of her place in—

"Shay!"

My head jerked up at JT's sharp tone, and she held my hands tight. Her intense gaze locked on mine. "Stop it. Stop overthinking, baby. Listen to me."

I glared at her. I hated it when someone called me on my own emotions, even if they were right. Add my inner turmoil to a situation and yeah, I could have one hell of an attitude. Then it hit me like a club: *You're a moron, Shay. Knock the shit off. JT has never done a thing except try to help you, even when you've been too stubborn to help yourself.*

JT had managed to curb the flight part of my psyche, and it was my turn to gain control of the fight response of my sometimes-volatile nature.

I tried to rearrange my face into something a little less antagonistic, and forced myself to concentrate on the words JT was saying.

"—trying to tell you. I'm back on vacation, and besides, I work for Minneapolis, not St. Paul PD. I don't have a professional stake in this, Shay. We don't know anything for certain, so there's nothing I can act on, and Jesus, you're my partner. You're my heart. You think I'd throw you or your father to the wolves?" She shook her head. "That was cliché, but you know what I mean."

Everything came back into focus. JT's pale, drawn features, the dark hair that had worked loose from her ponytail and floated gently around her face. Her eyes, eyes that conveyed concern, frustration, and yes, love.

I heaved a huge breath. I was still confused, but not about the love part.

"How many times," JT gently said, "am I going to have to defend my intentions to you?"

What the hell was I supposed to say to that? "I don't know. Integrity and honor and thirst for justice are what makes you, you. It's what makes you such a good cop. It's what scares me. I don't want you to do anything you'll regret in the name of love or loyalty or misguided—"

"Why can't you see? That's why I love you, you hard-headed conundrum. You have the same goddamn traits I do. You just wind up expressing them in a different way. You want to do what's best in a given situation. You want to take care of those you love."

She was right. Why was all of this so damn hard for me?

"Shay, we don't know what's going on with your dad. You have some facts and a lot of supposition. St. Paul is poking around, yes." She pointedly looked at me with a raised brow. "Playing the devil's advocate, here. What would you do if you found out your dad was guilty? If you found out he did kill this guy?"

I slid my hand into my pocket and withdrew the Intent to Purchase letter with Chuck Schuler's damning business card stapled to the corner. I handed it over. I wasn't sure we were playing devil's advocate anymore.

JT scanned the document and looked quizzically at me. "You told me about this."

I tapped the business card and watched her read the tiny words. She closed her eyes for a moment, probably regretting everything she'd said. "Okay. So this doesn't look very good. But it still doesn't mean much except there's a connection between the two of them."

"What about the blood?"

"That makes things appear a bit worse." That was a polite understatement. "I wish I could talk to Pete."

"You and me both." I leaned against the booth. My back ached. My head ached. My heart ached.

"Are you ready to tell me about this cop you've been hanging around? The one who isn't me?"

Oh. That little matter. "Remember Lisa Vecoli was coming with me this morning to talk to Dad's poker buddies?"

"Yeah."

I went on to explain that when Eddy called to tell me about my dad, I realized that things fell too perfectly into place when it came to Lisa and how she kept hanging around. That I figured she had to be a cop, or maybe was with the Bureau of Criminal Apprehension. What a better way to keep your targets close than to buddy up and pretend to care? Ugh. The thought of her deceit caused my blood to boil again.

Disgust colored my words. "She's got to be undercover. Think, JT. Have you heard of her? Seen her before?"

"I don't recognize the name, and she's not someone I can recall seeing before. She could be new, I guess. I certainly don't know every cop in the state. Suppose I can discreetly ask around and see if anyone has heard of her."

I shook my head. "At this point maybe it's better if we lay low."

"That's fair enough. For now."

It was time to be completely honest with both myself and JT. I could only pretend I knew what I was doing for so long. I glanced over at Coop and Johnny, who were doing a fine job of distracting Eddy. I was still shocked she had gotten herself so wound up. Eddy cared about my dad, apparently more than I realized, even if she was furious with him more often than not. I refocused on JT and said quietly, "I don't know what to do next. And I still feel so guilty involving you."

"Knock it off, okay?" JT reached over and ruffled my hair with a look filled with consternation and fondness. "All right. So, here's what we *do* know…"

For the next fifteen minutes we separated fact from fiction and threw ideas around. JT agreed to come with Coop and me to pay an evening visit to Mick Simon's place and see if he was still up. I knew Limpy Dick was a night owl who spent long hours on the porch of his shack contemplating the darkness and drinking homemade hooch, so we'd swing by his place too.

In the long run, I wasn't sure what good it was going to do to check in with Mick or Limpy; if they were involved with whatever my old man was into, we'd get shit out of them. But as JT told me at least five times while we brainstormed, it never hurt to cover your bases. I'd already started on the Poker Buddy list, might as well finish. Maybe my dad had confided in one of them. Or maybe Friday night they'd picked up on my father's potential murderous intention.

In the morning, we decided, we'd take whatever information Coop could dig up on Norman Howard and head to Subsidy Renovations and see what good old Normie had to say for himself.

Then we'd swing by Benjamin's Drugstore and talk to Poker Buddy 5: Hemorrhoid Harvey. If nothing else, it would be interesting to see what a man named after serious trouble in one's nether regions was like.

EIGHT

AFTER MY CONFESSION TO JT, I scored Johnny a good wad of cash to cover the bar the rest of the week, plus a little extra for having to put up with the potential danger from quarters unknown. My dad wasn't going appreciate my generosity, but that was too bad.

Johnny stepped up to the challenge. He called a couple of massive, probably-football-playing pals to hang out and work security in exchange for free booze. Johnny, at six-two, wasn't someone to be taken lightly either, so between the three of them I felt reasonably sure the Leprechaun would be a safe place for the patrons. I kind of hoped the nameless thugs who'd attacked Lisa and me in the parking lot the night before would show up again and go a couple rounds with the boys. I knew who would be on the winning end of that fight.

The exchange of money for services reminded me that, cop or not, I needed to compensate Lisa Vecoli for the help she'd given me. The thought of her deception made my blood roil. That I was beholden to someone who'd lied and manipulated me really pissed me off. My propensity to hold a grudge was stuff of legend, even if it was somewhat tempered with the knowledge that the lying skank had been a huge help when I needed it the most.

Eddy was over her unexpected histrionics and was back to being the solid, dependable, sometimes scathing but always loving woman I knew. After a couple more shots of the sauce, she decided she wanted to come with Coop, JT, and me on our late-night information-gathering foray.

The air was frigid. I shivered violently as we exited the warmth of the Lep. We'd agreed my Escape warmed up the fastest, and it had the benefit of heated seats in the front. Didn't help the rear-ends of the back seat passengers, but some was better than none.

When we were done playing our own version of cops, killers, crooks, and possible kidnappers, we'd return the next day for JT's Durango and Eddy's old pickup, which were parked in the Lep lot next to Johnny's new orange Challenger. We crunched across the snow-covered lot and I eyed Johnny's ride. Rear wheel drive and that huge engine would be a bitch in the winter, but man, the damage I could do with one of those bad boys. Maybe Johnny would let me take a spin sometime.

"Shotgun," Eddy called out as I beeped the Escape open. "I'm the oldest and coldest."

"You like my heated seats now, don't you?" Initially Eddy hated the heat on her butt, said it made her feel like she wet her pants. After she plunked her ass in the warmed-up seat on a bitterly cold winter morning not long ago, she'd changed her tune.

Coop and JT slid into the back without argument.

I started the engine and buckled up. The digital clock on the radio read 9:04. "Eddy, do you know where Mick Simon lives?"

"Mick, the Vulc?"

"Yup," I said. "Him."

"No problem."

Exactly how Eddy knew where he lived was something she didn't divulge, but she proceeded to direct me out of Minneapolis, through the capital city, and down into South St. Paul. Before long, somewhere off of Concord and Grand, in a confusing mix of avenues and streets, Eddy said, "Second house from the end of the block on the right there."

I pulled over to the curb. The house was a white stucco story-and-a-half. It was adorned with what looked like a zillion multi-colored holiday lights. Inflatable Christmas decorations dotted the roof and the fenced-in yard. A Santa popped in and out of an inflatable red brick chimney that was secured to the roof. The array was so bright it made me squint.

JT said, "Amazing."

"I want to do that." Coop's tone was wistful. I bet he'd figure out a way to connect the whole shebang to his computer system and make things rock.

An enormous inflatable white polar bear crouched on the ground with his rear in the air, and two delighted penguins decked out in Santa hats and little blue and red scarves used his back for a sledding hill.

The centerpiece of the electric, inflated menagerie was another Santa wearing a pair of black goggles sitting in a fire-engine sleigh that was pulled by eight reindeer. All of them sported their own special goggles and goofy, black grease-paint moustaches and pointy beards. It was weird, but I didn't expect less from Mick. Once a Vulc, always a Vulc.

"What are you kids waiting for? Come on!" Eddy bounded from the Escape like a jackrabbit and headed for the front gate. Apparently her earlier emotional trauma had left her no worse for wear.

"Come on," I repeated. We piled out, following Eddy's trail over the bumpy sidewalk. The roar of the motors running to keep the displays alive was almost deafening. I wondered what the neighbors thought.

Eddy flipped the latch on the gate and was on the stoop before the rest of us even entered the yard. She pulled off a fur-lined mitten and poked the doorbell. The resulting, muffled *ding-dong* reverberated inside.

A light glowed from a side window of the house, but the windows facing the front were dark. Eddy pushed the doorbell again.

Coop said, "I don't think—"

"Hush, child," Eddy told him. The door rattled, accompanied by a couple of thunks that sounded like deadbolts retracting. The door creaked open and a wrinkled face peeked out from beneath a chain. "Who's—Eddy!" a gravely voice yelped.

The woman sprung the chain and flung the door open. Coop, JT, and I stepped back in alarm. A rotund, white-haired woman in a flowery housedress charged across the threshold. She screeched to a halt in front of Eddy, who was grinning widely. They exchanged an enthusiastic, complex handshake/knuckle-bump/hand slap.

I should have guessed: Mrs. Mick Simon was a Mad Knitter.

In a flash, we were invited inside. The front room was dark, Mrs. Mick explained, so no stray lights tainted the "holiday experience" outside.

Before I knew what was happening, we were lined up on benches around a large kitchen table. The room smelled faintly of burnt cookies and lemon cleaner.

As Mrs. Mick hustled around making hot chocolate, Eddy briefly introduced us and proceeded to pepper the woman with questions about why she hadn't been to any Knitter meetings recently. Apparently

Mrs. Mick's youngest daughter had recently had a kid. After the requisite oohing and ahhing at pictures in a baby book, and listening to a rapid rundown of the status of each of the four Simon kids, Eddy asked, "Where's Mick?"

Mrs. Mick said, "I haven't seen much of him for the last two days. He's probably at the Vulcan warehouse in St. Paul working on something for the carnival. He gets a bit over-focused this time of year."

Mrs. Mick plunked a mug with steaming, frothy liquid in front of JT, who said, "Thank you, Mrs. Simon—"

"Please, it's Leona."

"Leona," JT began again, "have you seen or spoken with Pete recently?" JT pointed at me. "Shay's dad?"

"Petey? Oh." Leona's features rearranged themselves into a thoughtful expression. "No, I can't say that I have. Why?" She finished doling out the drinks and settled herself into an armchair at one end of the table. If she thought it odd we were paying her a visit this late, she didn't show it. However, I felt a little like we were in the middle of some crazy *Twilight Zone* episode.

I said, "My dad is having some..." I searched for the right word. "Problems. I was hoping he might have said something to Mick about what the trouble was."

Leona noisily slurped her beverage and plucked a napkin from a holder in the middle of the table to dab at the corners of her mouth. "Mick hasn't mentioned anything to me." Leona's brows drew together, and the tip of her tongue poked out the side of her mouth. She said, "Come to think of it, a couple of months ago, Mick did tell me that Pete was having some issues at the bar." She squinched an eye shut and tapped her fingers on the tabletop. "What was it he said? Something about Petey and money. Repairs Petey needed to do at the bar, I think."

Coop said, "Did he say what the repairs were?"

Leona shook her head. "No, he didn't specify. Mick told me he offered to float Petey a loan, but the 'goddamned drunk' turned him down flat." Her words slammed to a screeching halt and her hands fluttered like out of control fireflies. She gave me a wide-eyed look of alarm. "Sorry, Shay, dear—that's just what Mick said. You know how those boys can be."

"No offense taken," I mumbled.

"In fact," she said, "I think they argued about it. Mick felt whatever had to be repaired—I do admit I wasn't exactly paying attention when he got going—was serious, and Petey's pride got in the way. My Mick was pretty riled up after that conversation."

Yup, that sounded like my father. I wondered, too, exactly how mad Mick had been. I couldn't see him hurting anyone, but you never knew what could happen when you added booze, gambling, stress, and testosterone.

"That Peter," Eddy said. "He's a hard-headed man. You think you could have Mick call Shay when he gets a chance?"

Good thinking, Eddy. One more stop and we could call it a night.

"Why, sure I can have Mick call you." Leona patted my hand and rocked herself to gather momentum. After three back-and-forths, she made it to her feet and shuffled over to the counter for a pad of paper and a pencil, which she set in front of me. I swallowed the last of my hot chocolate and jotted down my number.

After a long Minnesota farewell that involved hugs, a couple of bathroom breaks, chatting, more hugs, more chatting, another bathroom break by someone else, and a final round of hugs, we trudged back to the Escape and huddled inside as I fired up the engine.

My entire body shook from the cold. Though we'd been inside talking to Leona, the chill had still managed to seep under my skin.

145

When I hit the frigid air outside, my back muscles tensed, practically spasming. They went into lockdown until the seat warmer kicked in and they started to thaw out. The older I got, the more I realized I was growing tired of the long Minnesota winters, even with the distraction broomball provided. Sad.

On to Poker Buddy 4: Limpy Dick's shack. Then home to bed.

———

After a fill-the-gas-tank pit stop, which included a fast smoke break for Coop, we were back on the road. I caught 94 and headed toward the border between Minnesota and Wisconsin. From there we headed north, paralleling the Minnesota side of the St. Croix River. Before long, we cruised through Stillwater, a scenic river town that clung to its main-street, hometown appeal. The artsy antiquing community drew huge crowds, especially in the summer.

Limpy Dick lived in a cabin on Highway 95 south of Marine on St. Croix. His given name was Richard Zaros, a second-generation Greek who loved his homemade ouzo and his privacy. He worked many years with my father, and they'd remained buddies after they both retired.

I vividly remembered Dick coming into the Leprechaun when I was a kid. He had a booming voice and a gentle disposition. One time I asked him if he was ever going to get married, and he said the river was his bride and that was all the partnership he needed. He was a little odd, and sometimes I wondered if he was that way before or only after he lost his various appendages.

After the accident that claimed his leg, Dick called it quits with a sizeable settlement from the barge company and moved into the house on the St. Croix River that for years he'd used as a fishing shack.

For reasons I could never discern, rumors clung to Limpy Dick like seaweed on a crusty anchor. The most notorious backyard gossip was that he'd buried the settlement money in the basement of his shack. The man did have a quirky habit of staying up very late at night, sitting on his porch in a creaky old rocking chair, a loaded shotgun within easy reach.

I knew that was true because I occasionally stayed with Limpy Dick when my father was away doing god only knew what. Probably falling gracelessly off the wagon. Anyway, we'd sit on the porch under an inky, star-filled sky, and I'd listen, riveted, as he spun crazy river tales.

Then when he was busy sleeping the morning away, I'd quietly get up and chow on stale Rice Krispies he'd leave out for my breakfast and wonder why he didn't worry that someone might try to come in and swipe his fortune in the daylight. Maybe he felt that the dark of night called the thieves but the light of day kept them away? Come to think of it, that's the way it usually worked.

We were close to the half-mile drive leading to Dick's shack. It snaked through the woods on the east side of the road. The need to pay close attention snapped me out of my reverie. The dirt, snow-covered driveway wasn't marked well, and even in the day it was a challenge to find. In the darkness, it was going to be a bitch.

After two U-turns, I spotted the narrow opening in the trees. The forest rode close enough to the Escape that I felt claustrophobic. We bumped over the rutted, snow-packed lane, and I said, "I think it might be a good idea for me to go in first. I don't want to startle Limpy Dick."

"It is late, almost quarter to eleven," JT said. "Probably a good idea."

"That's not what Shay's worried about, child," Eddy said.

"What do you mean?"

"Uh, yeah." I bit my lip, heaved a whoosh of air. "He kind of has a tendency to meet visitors with double barrels."

"What—oh." I could imagine her dark brows drawing together. "Really?"

Coop said, "I haven't met him either, but from the stories Shay and Eddy tell, it's probably a good thing if Shay goes on ahead."

"Why don't we call him and let him know we're here?" I could hear the frown in JT's voice.

Eddy said, "'Cause that old fool doesn't have a phone."

I pulled over to one side of the narrow trail a couple hundred yards from Limpy Dick's shack and jammed the engine in park. Here the pines were so dense not a lick of light showed from the road, and we were still out of sight of the shack.

JT asked, "Why don't you at least pull up to the house? Never mind. I don't want to know, do I?"

I left the engine running and opened the door, letting a blast of frigid air invade the warm interior. "He doesn't take too kindly to visitors. He's got a tendency to shoot first and ask questions later." I didn't think JT was going to take that admission very well.

"WHAT?"

Nope, she didn't take it well at all. I got out.

"Shay!" JT yowled. "You're crazy if you think I'm going to let you go in there and get shot."

I secured my footing in the snow as I turned around. "It's okay. When he hears it's me, he won't pull the trigger. Then I'll call your cell to let you know to drive on in. Trust me." I leaned in and gave her a quick peck.

Before she could further state her case, I said, "Stay here till I come back for you," and slammed the door shut. Coop and Eddy would make sure JT stayed put.

I walked away from the Escape, wishing I'd thought to bring a flashlight. Oh well, the whiteness of the snow made the going

148

somewhat easier. I followed the drive as it curved to the right, and soon the headlights from the Escape disappeared and the darkness swallowed me.

My heart always beat a little faster when I made this trek, and I hadn't done it for years. I think the last time I'd been to the shack was when I'd graduated from college.

I marched along with my feet in a tire rut and my hands buried in the pockets of my jacket. As I walked I thought about my dad, wondered where he was, and what the hell was really going on. How had things come to this? I was so confused. A degree—okay, a small degree—of the anger that had been burning in my gut since Whale summoned me to the Lep on New Year's Eve had lessened, but I was bewildered and disconcerted. So many things weren't adding up.

It wasn't too long before the edge of the shack came into view. There were no lights illuminating the yard. The windows were dark on the one side of the structure that was in my line of vision.

Most evenings (and well into most nights) Limpy Dick sat on his covered, unscreened porch in darkness made even deeper by the tall pines and deciduous trees that surrounded his battered homestead. Waiting. And watching.

All these years later he was probably still anticipating a visit from some dastardly hooligans who were going to rush his property and make an end run for his buried treasure. The man sat on that porch in the heat, in the cold, in the snow, in the rain. The only time the routine was broken was when he periodically left for supplies and a semi-monthly trek to the Leprechaun to play poker.

I navigated some particularly uneven footing and recalled that one time, Limpy Dick told me that if any of those nincompoops—his word, not mine—tried to break into his shack, there were plenty of surprises they'd run into before they even set foot over the threshold.

For the first time, rational thought seeped into my thick skull. This probably wasn't the brightest idea I'd ever had. But then again, I didn't have any other creative solutions brewing like a light bulb in the dark night, and I certainly didn't want him taking a potshot at my new vehicle.

Nope, the time to act was now.

I figuratively girded my loins and literally cut off the trail into trees to my left. Cautiously I edged around the house, keeping a good fifty-foot cushion between it and me. The only sounds in the night were the rustling of the trees in the wind and the crunch of shin-deep snow that trickled over the tops of my shoes, turning my feet cold and damp. The iciness of the snow seared the skin above my ankles.

When I was close to what I judged to be the front of the house, I let rip a loud whistle. The call of a semi-sick whippoorwill bounced off the trees around me. I whistled again, sounding a little less like a choking duck, and edged forward until the porch came into view. It was too dark to see where Dick was, so I went ahead another ten feet and whippoorwilled again. This time the whistle was ear-piercing. I was impressed that particular ability came back so fast.

From the porch, I caught a shadowy movement.

BLAM! A bright flash and a thunderous explosion ripped from the shack. Bark chipped off trees next to me, stinging my cheek.

Apparently the whippoorwill no longer worked. I hit the deck with an "Oh shit!" My heart hammered as I pressed my cheek deep in the snow, waiting for the second explosion.

KA-BOOM!

Silence reclaimed the forest. I counted to three, propelled myself to my feet, and dodged forward and to the left. Limpy Dick had creatively placed stumps and rocks around his property as intruder deterrents and I swore I hit every one.

"Dick!" I screamed as I skinned my shin on another obstacle. "It's Shay!"

I took two more strides, but another cannon-like report issued from the porch. I hit the ground face-first and tried to burrow into the snow.

Without breathing, I waited for him to fire off the second round.

The second blast sounded like it was right over my head. The resulting thunder echoed through the trees. Before Limpy Dick had a chance to finish reloading, I bounced up and charged the last few feet to the porch.

My throat felt raw. I launched into a long, low dive and slammed into the side of the shack to the right of the porch steps.

There were definitely going to be bruises.

Huddling against the siding, my arms over my head, I screeched, "Dick, it's Shay, Pete O'Hanlon's kid!"

For a second overwhelming silence roared in my ears. I heard a clunk, and the sound of the slide on the shotgun slamming home. There was a thud, and Limpy Dick said gruffly, "Shay O'Hanlon? That really you? Where the hell are you hiding?"

I rolled my eyes, tried to breathe. "I'm. Right here. Don't. Shoot. 'Kay?"

He grunted, and I took that as his agreement to cease fire.

My legs shook. I pulled myself to my feet, stumbled to the steps, and staggered up them.

Limpy Dick stood in the middle of the porch bundled in a thick jacket. A knit stocking cap was perched at an angle on his head, and camouflage snow pants with one leg cut off at the knee kept his lower half warm. A prosthesis stuck out below the end of the shortened side of the pants and a felt boot was attached to the foot. A long, grizzled, gray-and-white beard covered his face. He looked like Minnesota's version of the guys on *Duck Dynasty*.

He clumped forward and grabbed me in a tight bear hug, lifting me off my feet. Every one of my bruises screamed in pain. He blustered, "Little O! Don't you remember the whippoorwill?"

The side of my face was mashed against the rough fabric of his coat. "I—"

"Speak up," he bellowed. "I can't hear a goddamned thing anymore."

———

Things got a little out of control when JT, gun in hand, burst through the trees screaming my name. Thank god I thought to grab the shotgun from where it rested against the porch railing before Limpy Dick got his hands on it. I attempted to explain—as we played tug-of-war—that the heat-packing, wild-eyed crazy woman wasn't a danger. It took three tries before he understood JT wasn't out to steal his money and she understood he wasn't threatening me.

Any longer, anyway.

A few minutes later I huddled inside the shack with Coop, Eddy, and JT around a table made from a gigantic tree trunk. It was six inches thick, maybe five feet across, and must have weighed five hundred pounds. The top had a thick, clear glaze on it that protected the wood beneath.

I hadn't been inside Limpy Dick's place in a very, very long time. It felt like Alice in Wonderland's version of déjà vu. There were several upgrades in the intervening years that shocked the socks off of me. He now had a 50-inch HDTV on a stand a few feet in front of a huge, overstuffed wood-framed couch and a matching recliner. A laptop computer and printer were set up on one half of a breakfast bar that was pushed up against the wall beneath one of the blacked-out windows. On the other side of the bar were at least fifty, if not more, tiny figures carved out of wood. They ranged from delicate butterflies to slinky foxes to roaring black bears.

Eddy picked one up—a tiny, perfect replica of a caterpillar—admired the intricate detailing. "Cool," she said.

Limpy Dick grinned, his yellow teeth peeping between strands of shaggy beard like off-color Chiclets. "Doc said I needed to get me a hobby to help deal with stress. I started putting knife to wood a few years back. Got hooked. Now I sell them little things on Etsy."

Etsy? How had Limpy Dick ever heard of Etsy? What had happened to the man I once knew? However, there was pride in his tone, not the derision I was certain would have been there long ago when talking about a markedly feminine crafty site.

Some things do change after all.

Now Limpy Dick busied himself hustling around his kitchen, pulling espressos from a single pour, commercial-grade machine. I didn't remember him being much of a coffee guy, much less a fan of the fancy stuff. Most of Dad's friends considered coffee drinks foo-foo and made for women—well beneath them and their rough and tumble "give me a Bud for breakfast" exteriors.

Once Limpy Dick set tiny cups—on saucers, mind you—before us, he dropped into a chair with a grunt.

JT slid me a wide-eyed, "Is he nuts?" look. I shrugged my shoulders. I had no idea anymore.

"Sorry agin' about that little to-do, Shay," Limpy Dick said gruffly, staring intently at the mug that looked child-sized in his meaty, fingers-missing hand.

"It's okay," I said. "I'm sorry I startled you like that. I didn't know how get a hold you any other way." I kind of wanted to reach over and hug him, let him know that I held no ill will after being taken for a moving target. JT, however, wasn't feeling so magnanimous. I could still feel the waves of angry tension rolling off her body. I was definitely going to have to make this one up to her in a big way very soon.

I took a hit of the espresso. The scalding liquid reminded me painfully that I wasn't in the midst of a peculiar dream where things as I knew them were turned on their ear and then inside out for added entertainment. Once again, the *Twilight Zone* theme song raced through my mind.

Limpy Dick brought me back to the moment when he said, "I know I'm not the easiest guy to get a hold of. But these days you can send me a note on that contraption over there. I'll give you my addy." He jerked his thumb toward the laptop and still avoided looking at me, directing his comments to the table's shiny surface. When he picked up his cup, his hand shook slightly as he ever so delicately sipped his espresso. When he set it down again, the ceramic cup clattered against the saucer.

Email? Espresso? Etsy? This was so opposite the mountain man I used to know that I could hardly gather my wits. I shifted uncomfortably in my seat.

I heaved a deep sigh and felt a reassuring squeeze on my knee. I glanced at Eddy, and she gave me a meaningful "get on with it" look. It was a wonder Limpy Dick hadn't asked what the hell we were doing here this late. Maybe the shock of almost shooting his good friend's kid knocked the sense right out of him.

Here we go again, Shay. I said, "You played poker with Dad on Friday night, right?"

Limpy Dick scratched behind his ear with a finger and sniffed it. Guess he wasn't quite as tamed as I thought. "Yup," he rumbled.

Was he always a man of so few words? I tried to remember. Before I could formulate my next question, Eddy said, "What was wrong with Pete the night before New Year's Eve?"

Limpy Dick said, "Wrong? With Pete? Before New Year's?"

"What are you, a parrot?" Eddy squawked. She had the ability to skewer someone if she wanted to. "Yes." She spoke slowly, as if addressing a five-year-old. "What was wrong with Pete that night?"

For a good fifteen seconds, Limpy Dick's lips took on a life of their own, twitching like spasming inchworms. Then he managed to regain control. "Why, nuthin' was wrong with Pete."

Maybe nothing was wrong with Pete, but something certainly seemed to be bothering Limpy Dick.

JT's leg bounced up and down against mine, most likely because she was still agitated after thinking I'd been blown to smithereens. She leveled her patented "if looks could kill, you'd already be dead" cop glare at Limpy Dick and said, "Was anything out of the ordinary that night? Something that wasn't right?"

Limpy Dick's frown now extended to the corners of both eyes, and his left eyelid twitched. Without meeting JT's fiery gaze, he said slowly, "Nope, no. Nothing like that. 'Course Roy and Mick were none too happy they lost. Mick's a hothead, ya know. Always says bullshit he don't mean. Roy, he was quiet most of the night."

Not a whole lot to go on there.

I hated to ask the next question but figured it would be less painful to cough it up so we could scram. "Have you noticed if my father's been drinking?" I amended, "More than usual?"

Another long pause. "I dunno, Shay. He's always got a drink close by. You know how he is. Though, come to think of it, maybe since he's been dealing with that sewer problem he's got in the basement, the drinking might have picked up. I think it's a money thing." This time he did catch my eye for half a second before he resumed his intense study of the tree trunk.

Desperation dampened the back of my neck like a wet rag. No one had any information that was going to help us find my father and unravel the mystery of who killed Ice Cube Man. I tried one last shot before I ran out of ammo, pun intended. "Did you see my father anytime after Friday night?"

"Oh no," Limpy Dick was quick to answer. "No sir. I ain't seen hide nor hair of Pete, I surely haven't."

I wasn't sure if Limpy Dick was in the midst of losing his marbles or if he wasn't coughing up the whole truth and nothing but the truth, but something was weird. First Mick Simon fought with my father about his refusal of a loan, and here one of his good friends was acting like he was sitting on a beehive as we peppered him with questions. Maybe he'd had too much espresso. Somehow, I didn't buy that, but we were getting nowhere fast. It was time to call the game for the night.

I finished my drink and set the cup gently on the saucer. "Thanks so much for chatting with us, Limpy."

Limpy Dick brightened, maybe at the prospect that we might be done badgering him. "It's no problem at all, Little O. No problem at all."

Yeah right.

———

The ride home was a somber affair. Eddy kept coming up with outrageous reasons why my father may have been doused in blood. She went from a mid-winter pig slaughter to a massive bloody nose to an almost plausible bar fight. I could hear JT's eyes rolling from the back seat. Periodically she jabbed me in the shoulder in response to something Eddy dreamed up.

Coop studiously ignored us and kept his head down, dinking around on his phone. He was probably playing a game. I admired his ability to zone out into some mindless quest that wasn't anything like real life.

I was drained and felt like a walking zombie. If I were pulled over, I'd probably fail the touch-the-nose-and-walk-the-white-line test from exhaustion alone.

We neared Uptown and Eddy's chatter ceased as she nodded off. Thankfully JT quit conveying her discontent with her pointer finger.

"Hey!" Coop yelped suddenly and sat up straight.

I jumped, and Eddy jerked awake.

I figured Coop was going to tell me to get a move on so he could get home and smoke, but instead he said, "Bogey Too just popped up. He's back from getting his sniff on Norman Howard."

JT said, "Maybe we'll get some real information."

I glanced at Coop's reflection in the rearview mirror. I couldn't see much in the dim light except his face painted ghostly pale from the glow of his phone screen, and his silhouette, which faded in and out as we passed beneath streetlights.

"Ah," he said. "Interesting."

"What?"

There was another fifteen seconds of interminable nothing until Coop muttered, "Looks like Howard went to the U of M." He paused again and my mind drifted as I waited for the rest of the rundown. Didn't half the Twin Cities college set go to the U?

"There we go." The satisfied tone of Coop's voice gave me a momentary jolt of hopefulness. "I've got an address registered to Howard and Subsidy Renovations. Home address too, if we need it."

JT asked, "Where?"

"Subsidy's on West Broadway, in North, I think."

North Minneapolis was a perpetual hotspot of ups and downs. Once a Russian-Jewish destination for immigration, the neighborhood had fallen into disrepair and disregard, with major social and economic problems that had insidiously crept in and taken stubborn hold. In recent years the area had garnered attention for drive-by shootings that had accidentally wounded and killed innocent little kids and a major tornado that had torn a three-mile path of devastation through the area, killing two and leaving the poorest residents of the city with damaged homes and a serious lack of resources.

Coop startled me out of my distracted thoughts. "We can make a call on Mr. Howard bright and early."

"Not without me, you don't," JT grumbled.

We passed under a streetlight, and in the reflection of the rearview, I caught a glimpse of JT sitting back with her arms crossed, lips pressed in a straight line. She was not happy.

"Okay," I agreed. Having someone tag along who packed a gun sounded like a very good plan.

"Hey, don't forget me," Eddy said. "Someone's gotta boss you kids around. I'll bring my Whacker. We'll be fine." She tried to twist in her seat to look in the back. "Coop, use your fancy gadget and find me the phone numbers to both Benjamin's Drug and this Subsidiary place. I'll call in the morning and find out when they open."

Oh boy. The last time Eddy brought her Whacker, which was a mini Minnesota Twins bat, trouble with a capitol T ensued. "Subsidy," I said. "Not Subsidiary."

"Whatever."

We dropped off Eddy with the phone numbers she wanted in hand, and promised to meet up with her at the Rabbit Hole at seven thirty the next morning.

When we let Coop off at his place, JT moved up to the passenger seat. We made the final jaunt home in silence, with JT's warm fingers threaded through mine.

Troubled thoughts flitted through my mind like mosquitoes searching for their next blood meal on a hot summer night. None of this was adding up. Well, technically things were adding up, just in a way I totally didn't want them to.

Blood on my father's hands. A dead man killed by my dad's own gun. Family friends not giving me straight answers. Lisa and her Pandora's box of complicated bullshit that smelled like a cop on the hunt. My ears started to burn as I thought again about Lisa and her manipulations. I sighed loudly, and JT squeezed my hand in silent comfort.

Tomorrow wasn't going to come soon enough.

NINE

THE CLOCK ON THE wall of the Rabbit Hole read 7:34 as I followed JT into the café the next morning. Exhaustion pulled at my core, making my head feel thick. Sleep had eluded me until about an hour before the alarm went off, by which time I felt terrible. Lack-of-sleep hangovers suck.

Anna, Kate's sister, stood at the counter chatting with Eddy. Anna was a student at the University of Minnesota and worked at the Hole part-time. A gifted athlete with a gifted brain, she was a good kid and a great worker.

Both Anna and Eddy looked up when the sound of the chimes above the door announced our entrance. One of Anna's eyebrows spiked when she took in my sorry appearance. She spun on her heel and made for the espresso machine.

One side of my mouth quirked in a weak smile. The girl knew when I needed a caffeine infusion. Eddy looked on without a word, an amused expression on her face.

Anna was back in a blink and set two espresso cups down, one for JT and one for me. From the amount of dark liquid, they were both double shots.

"Thanks," I mumbled. I grabbed the cup, and tossed the contents down the old hatch in one large gulp. I swore I could hear the lining of my throat sizzle, but I didn't care. These were desperate times.

JT was more refined. She took a polite sip before saying, "Anna, you should take up reading minds."

Anna scooped up my tiny cup for a refill.

Eddy said, "She don't need to read minds. One look at you two dragging your pitiful carcasses in here looking like death just about steamed over took care of that."

I cleared my throat, and said hoarsely, "How do you manage to go to bed late and get up this early looking fresh as a frickin' daisy?"

"Language, child." The sparkle in Eddy's eye belied her gruff tone.

Anna handed me my refilled cup.

"Thanks," I said.

The front door jangled. Coop shuffled across the threshold with black circles under his eyes and bed-head hair.

"Oh boy," Anna said as she hit the espresso machine one more time. "That doesn't look good. No luck finding Shay's dad, I take it?"

Eddy answered before I could. "Not yet. But mark my words, we will. I already called Benjamin's Drugstore. A recording says they open at seven. I guess that's 'cause they know geezers like us are too old to sleep in. Nobody picked up at that Renovation place. No answering machine, either. Figured we could hit Benjamin's, then see 'bout Renovating."

The woman was very good at creative renaming.

Coop swallowed the last of the espresso Anna had hooked him with and said, "Need more. Much more."

JT elbowed him in the ribs. "You get any sleep?"

"Hell no. Stayed up working. Good news is I'm caught up for a while. Bad news is I feel like shit. Getting too old for two all-nighters in a row."

It was a scary thought when my thirty-something, video-and-role-playing-game-loving pal said he was getting too old for anything.

We vamoosed a few minutes later with steaming to-go cups in hand and crowded once again into my Escape. I pointed the nose of the SUV toward Richfield and the last Poker Buddy, and we were off.

———

The overcast sky looked like it was thinking about dumping more snow on our heads when we hit Benjamin's. The parking lot was packed. Eddy had been right on when she said the early opening of the drugstore was exactly what folks of a certain age wanted. I wasn't sure if we were going to find what we wanted from Hemorrhoid Harvey, but anything would be better than nothing.

The front doors rolled open automatically. Eddy took the lead and blew right in, with the rest of us trailing obediently along after her like a tail on a kite. We came to a stop inside the doorway.

If I didn't have a lost father who was a potential murderer hanging over my head, I would have seen the ironic humor that was playing out within Benjamin's walls. The place was filled with shoppers, most looking like they were into advanced AARP range. It was a little like watching a snail race, with the occasional turtle thrown in for good measure.

Some customers casually strolled through the maze of not-over-chest-high shelving filled with drugstore doodads that made up the numerous aisles of the establishment. Other customers shuffled along with the aid of simple walkers or those fancier rolling versions with cool hand brakes. Yet others cruised the traffic lanes with dangerous abandon on electric scooters.

On one hand you had to be careful not to accidentally bulldoze someone if you weren't paying attention. On the other you had to be on your toes or you'd wind up the victim of a hit-and-run.

Before I could formulate our next move, Eddy said, "He's over there," and made a beeline for a massive man with a massive beer belly. He was dressed in a badly cut suit and a fat 1970s-era puce tie. The thick white thatch gracing the top of his skull reminded me of Beethoven on a particularly challenging hair day. The man either had very good genes or was sporting one hell of a toupee. He was engaged in conversation with a couple who looked like Auntie Em and Uncle Henry from *The Wizard of Oz*.

In Harvey's hand was a distinctive yellow box with blue letters that could only spell out Preparation H or its generic cousin. In fact, the entire shelving unit behind Harvey was filled with various formations of the itch and burn relief aids.

Eddy arrived before the rest of us, breezing past even the speediest of the slow-moving crowd. I was alarmed to see she had her Whacker in hand as she babbled something to Auntie Em. With her free hand she reached out and snatched the box of whatever from Harvey's grasp and shoved it into Auntie Em's hands. Then she hooked her arm in Hemorrhoid Harvey's and dragged him away from the rather bewildered-looking couple to a quiet corner of the store. Coop, JT, and I trailed warily along after her, not sure what she'd try next or what Harvey's reaction would be.

By the time we caught up to Hurricane Eddy, Harvey's eyes were wide and locked on the Whacker Eddy waggled as she addressed him.

"—so you need to tell us everything you know." She tapped him on the chest with the bat to punctuate her request.

"Hey," I said. I attempted disarm Eddy. "Hi, Harvey. Sorry for the interruption. My name is Shay O'Hanlon, and—Eddy!" I snapped as she tried her damnedest to twist the wooden weapon from my grasp. She'd taken on the pinched look of someone who'd swallowed something very sour, and I was worried we might have another Whacker-thumping incident on our hands.

I tried to arrange my face in an apologetic expression while we tussled for the Whacker. "You played poker the night before New—" I broke off as Eddy bent me sideways. With a heave, I won the wrestling contest and stood straight, Whacker firmly in my grip. Coop grabbed Eddy and dragged her back while I regained my composure and attempted to retain what little dignity I had left.

JT held out her hand. I slapped the bat into it and continued, "Sorry about that. I believe you played poker at the Leprechaun the evening before New Year's Eve with my father, Pete."

Harvey's expression morphed from mild alarm to potential amusement now that the threat had been contained. His head bounced up and down like a bobblehead's. "Night before New Year's, sure did."

I said, "Did you notice if my father was troubled? Did he talk about any problems he'd been having recently?"

Considering the question, Harvey crossed his arms and rested them on his generous paunch. "For months he's been going on and on about the problem in the basement. You know what I'm talking about?"

"Yeah," I said. "Anything else?"

"Oh, he was caught up, with New Year's and the bar and what-not." Harvey lifted his shoulders. "Otherwise it was a regular game, like always. Why do you ask?"

I gave Harvey a very vague explanation of my missing parental unit, backed away, and thanked him. We turned toward the front door.

"Say, Shay," Harvey called after I'd taken a few steps.

I stopped.

He said, "I was the last to leave that night. Pete mentioned he wasn't feeling quite right. I asked him if he needed anything, and he said no, so I left. Don't know if that helps, but I hope he's okay. Let me know. He still owes me twenty bucks." Harvey winked.

I nodded, and we carefully made our way to the front and exited without further incident. My dad wasn't feeling quite right, huh? Too much booze? Or was something else going on that I was missing? Was Dad sick? Frustration filled me up, made my stomach churn. I wanted to be in Duluth with JT, not here trying to unravel this god-awful mess. Nothing was working out the way I wanted it to.

———

Our trip to North Minneapolis was short-lived; a note taped to the front door said Subsidy Renovations had relocated to White Bear Lake. An address was listed, but no phone number. White Bear Lake was a bedroom community a short distance north and a little north-east of the Twin Cities. On the ride there, we tossed around what we wanted to get out of the visit. Number one on my list was to ask why the hell Subsidy was being so persistent in trying to get my dad to sell the bar. Number two, I wanted to know if this Norman Howard was the one who was responsible for the ongoing threats, vandalism, and violence. With any luck, this visit would shed a little light on something. At this point, anything would be good with me.

I fought the last dregs of rush hour and at about nine thirty we pulled up in front of a sizeable two-story clapboard house that had been renovated and rezoned for business. The four of us entered the foyer en masse, this time without Eddy's Whacker. I don't know where JT had hidden it, but I was grateful for its absence.

The house smelled of age and dust. Cream-colored plaster walls needed a coat of fresh paint and some substantial patching. Worn plank floors would probably come back to life if they were sanded and sealed. They creaked under our feet. This place sure didn't scream *renovation* to me. Doors, some with business names stenciled on the outside and brass numbers attached at eye level, lined a long hall. A surprisingly elegant stairway toward the rear led to the second floor, testament to what had once been an enormous, stately home.

A well-used two-by-three-foot blackboard with tenant names hung on the wall next to the entrance showing a number of blank spots, probably office spaces available for rent.

Coop walked over and ran a finger down the list. "Here. No Subsidy Renovations, but Norman Howard is written on a piece of masking tape. Number 203."

"Classy," Eddy said.

We hit the stairs. Each step protested loudly, and I wondered if the racket interrupted business being conducted behind closed doors.

Office space 203 was two doors down on the right, past Stellar Photography and Ernest Bail Bonds. 203's door was void of the business name.

I raised a hand to knock, but Eddy darted under my arm and turned the doorknob. It was unlocked and she pushed the door inward. I don't know what I expected, but it wasn't what I saw. The office was maybe ten-by-eight, probably at one time a bedroom. Water-stained, dark wood panel walls were bare, although nails protruded here and there, evidence of long-gone decorations.

The only furniture in the room was a beat-up desk that looked like a reject from a crappy surplus store. There were no filing cabinets, not even a phone. It would be kind of hard to conduct business without a telephone. Well, maybe Howard was a cell phone only kind of guy.

Apparently customers were expected to stand, since the only chair was situated behind the desk. It was currently occupied by a thin man with limp, greasy hair that was long enough to tickle his nape. He was leaning over the desktop, a rolled bill at his nose, loudly snorting a line of white powder from the glass of an 5-by-7 frame that didn't seem to have a picture in it.

At our unexpected entrance, Snuffy practically tipped over backward in his haste to straighten up. He growled, "What the fuck?"

Before I could draw my eyes away from the drug paraphernalia on the table, JT stepped forward, badge in hand. Damn, she was quick.

She asked, "Are you Norman Howard?"

The man's hollow-cheeked, pockmarked face paled at the sight of the badge. "Could be," he said slowly. "What's it to ya?"

JT tucked her badge away. "Subsidy Renovations ring a bell?"

Howard narrowed his eyes. "I conduct a lot of business here, lady."

Yup, it sure looked like he conducted a lot of *business*.

JT moved forward, towering over the seated Howard. She braced her arms on the edge of the desk and leaned into his space. Howard tried to roll backward, but his chair hit the wall. The whites of his eyes showed as he peered up fearfully at JT. Well, to be fair, if she did the same thing to me under the right circumstances, the whites of my eyes would probably show too. Actually they had, once upon a time. More than once.

"Now," she said, her voice low and deadly. "I'll ask again. Subsidy Renovations. Tell me all about it." She glanced down and made it very obvious that she was taking in the hastily dropped rolled bill and remnants of coke or crank or whatever one snorted these days. She said slowly, "Be straight with me and maybe," she looked back at Howard's face and nodded at the desktop without breaking eye contact, "just maybe, I'll let this go. If you don't spill your guts in approximately fifteen seconds, well, I've got nothing better to do than spend some quality time at the Ramsey County jail booking your ass on drug possession and whatever else I can find to nail you on."

Holy shit.

The alarmed look on Howard's face would have been comical under different circumstances. "Hang on, hold on," he muttered. He was probably trying to get his drug-addled neurons to fire.

"I haven't got all day." JT reached behind her back and pulled out a pair of cuffs. I didn't even know she was packing them today. If it was me in that seat, I'd be spilling my guts about everything I'd done wrong since I was a snot-nose toddler.

"Okay! Take it easy. Sheesh," Howard practically squealed and he held his hands out defensively. And they call cops pigs. "Whattya wanna know?"

JT slowly straightened. "That's more like it." The cuffs dangled from her fingers, a not-so-subtle reminder that Howard better keep his gums flapping. "Why do you want to buy the Leprechaun from Pete O'Hanlon?" Howard did a shifty-eyed thing. JT crowded him again and said softly, "Don't fuck with me."

"Okay, okay. Jesus." Despite the cool room, perspiration beaded on Howard's forehead and formed a trail down the side of his face. "Uh, the block the Leprechaun is on represents a great investment in the gentrification of Northeast." The words came out in a rush. "I'm in it for a fast buck."

That sounded well rehearsed. I rolled my eyes and stepped forward, coming even with JT. "Why did you sic Chuck Schuler on my father?"

Norman Howard's eyes flicked from me to JT and back.

JT said, "Come on, Normie. Spill it."

Howard shrank back in the chair, deflated. "Fine." He rolled his eyes. "Look. My ass is in enough hot water."

"So," JT said, "Keep your ass from drowning."

That did it. Howard opened up like a moss rose in the afternoon sun. "My brother-in-law approached me to run one of his businesses."

Coop said, "Subsidy Renovations is registered in your name."

Howard didn't seem to know where to pin his gaze. The way his eyes were rolling around, it was a regular game of eyeball Ping-Pong. "My brother-in-law set it up. He told me if I could get O'Hanlon to sell that dump of a bar, there'd be some good money in it for me."

I bristled at his "dump of a bar" comment but gritted my teeth and managed to keep my mouth shut. I felt the first stirrings of the Protector inside.

"So," JT said, "you sent goons to soften up O'Hanlon? When he wasn't cooperating?"

"No, it wasn't like that."

JT leaned forward again and spoke very softly. "So tell me how it was."

"See, I like to make money, who doesn't? I'm a businessman. I run a busy office here." Howard spread both hands palms up, indicated the empty space and obvious lack of visible work. "I hired a guy I knew and told him I'd give him a portion of the take if he could persuade O'Hanlon to take the buy-out."

"Huh." JT nodded. "Now we're getting somewhere. You paid him to threaten O'Hanlon? To vandalize property?" Her voice rose and she said fiercely, "To jump people in the parking lot of the goddamn bar?"

Whoa. I knew she was thinking about the night Lisa and I had been attacked. I took a breath, proud of myself because for once I was doing pretty well controlling the Protector and not leaping over the table to introduce my fist to Normie's nose. But JT was getting twitchy, so I reached out and gripped her arm before it took on a life of its own and she bopped him herself. She continued, somewhat calmer, "You pay him to beat people?"

"No, no! I never told him what to do. The agreement was that he get O'Hanlon to come to terms and I'd pay him for it. I never asked how he was going to do it."

From behind me, Eddy grumbled, "There's always an excuse. What's the name of the loser you hired, Mr. Poopy Pants?"

I suppressed a semi-hysterical giggle. Eddy knew how to lighten a moment.

Norman Howard's eyebrows drew together and he scowled at Eddy. "Who the fuck are you?"

Even I was sorry we'd made Eddy leave her Whacker behind. This piece of work deserved a thumping.

Eddy responded, remarkably coolly for her. "I have the potential to be one nasty old lady. You're darn lucky I'm unarmed."

I nodded. "She's not kidding, mister. You're lucky as hell. Who was he?"

Normie sounded exasperated. "His name was Schuler, and yeah, he somehow wound up iced. But I sure as hell didn't do it."

JT said sarcastically, "Really." She paused a beat. "Since you're so willing to name names, who's your brother-in-law?"

"Christ, lady, I could get my fucking balls cut off here."

"Not my problem."

Howard huffed and stared at the remnants of his white powder binge. "Phil Hanssen, okay?" In a lower tone, Howard mumbled, "My sister is going to fuckin' kill me."

"Like you killed Schuler?" JT said.

"No! I told you. I did not do Schuler. Maybe Hanssen did. Maybe Schuler's other business acquaintances got tired of him. I don't fucking know."

JT drew herself up to full height and looked down her nose at Howard. "Spell that name for me." He did. "Don't go too far. Never know when I might want to have another chat. I specialize in finding rats who hide."

She tucked her cuffs away and headed for the door.

Eddy took a step toward the desk and stooped over. For a minute I thought she was sick. Then she stood again with one of her low-top Converse sneakers in hand. Like lightning, she clobbered Howard over the head with it before he had a chance to think about ducking.

Eddy said, "Language, young man. There are ladies in the room." She popped him again. "That's for Pete." She slammed the shoe on the top of the desk, making the drug-covered picture frame hop. "You're lucky I don't boot you in the rump." With that, she stomped out, slightly lopsidedly. "Don't that beat all," I heard her say. "I don't need my Whacker after all."

Howard sat hunched in his chair looking dazed. I told him, "Gotta watch out for that one. She's dangerous."

Coop and I exchanged a high five and vacated the premises.

———

Back in the car we dissected what had just gone down. While we were at it, Coop used his cell to set Bogey Too in search of Mr. Phil Hanssen.

My phone rang in the midst of Eddy delightedly rehashing her shoe-bashing moment. It was a call from the Lep. "Yo, Johnny, what's up?"

There was a lot of background noise. I glanced at the time on the dashboard. 10:28. The bar didn't open till noon. "Johnny? You there?"

"Shay, hey." Johnny sounded strained, out of breath. "You might want to get over here. The Roto-Rooter guy showed up this morning. He found something awful, and we called the cops. And they brought in—hang on." Johnny said something I couldn't make out, and then the low rumble of a voice that sounded vaguely familiar filled my ear.

"Shay O'Hanlon?"

"Yeah," I said warily.

"I need you need to come to the Leprechaun, since it seems you're the one in charge these days."

"Who is this?"

"Your favorite nightmare. Sergeant DeSilvero, on loan to Minneapolis PD. Remember me?" He gave me no time to answer, but hell, yes I remembered him. Wish I didn't. And I really wish I hadn't heard his next words. "Your father's got a tarp full of bones dressed in what was once a pretty pink dress buried under the cement in his cellar."

TEN

POLICE CARS, A COUPLE unmarked squads, and a Hennepin County crime scene van were parked in the street in front of the Leprechaun when we pulled up. The entire drive to the bar I'd chanted, "Dad did not do this," over and over again under my breath. My world felt well and truly fucked up.

I parked, rocketed out of the Escape, and charged with single-minded focus to the front door. JT hoofed it along behind me, Coop and Eddy bringing up the rear.

I wrapped my fingers around the handle and was about to yank the door open when a big brute of a cop stepped in front of me, forcing me backward. He had to be at least seven feet tall and half as wide. "Sorry," he said, blocking us with his bulk. "This is a crime scene. Bar's closed."

I barely registered his words.

Over my shoulder JT said, "It's okay, she's—"

I dodged around the cop and again latched onto the handle. Before I could fling it open, the cop spun on his heel and grabbed hold of my belt.

Had to give him credit, he was quick for a big guy. He struggled backward. My belt acted like a second handle, and the door slowly swung open.

Big Boy dragged me back, my shoes skidding across the salt-covered sidewalk. The cop dug his heels in and heaved as if he were the anchor in a tug of war. I held on for dear life. Suddenly I was in mid-air, feet off the ground, suspended between the door and the cop. If he'd only been a couple feet shorter, my feet would still be on the salt-stained sidewalk.

Red tendrils of rage swirled at the edges of my vision. From afar I heard yelling. I churned my legs. Someone grabbed my waist. My feet hit the cement. I desperately hung onto the door handle. Trying to regain traction, I felt Big Boy's knuckles dig into the flesh of my lower back. Then my shoulders were being shaken so hard my teeth clattered.

The bar popped back into view.

I peered back at JT, her eyes black and piercing as she held onto me for dear life. "Stop it! Shay, get a hold of—"

"Well, well. If it isn't Little Miss Firepants." Sergeant DeSilvero appeared at JT's shoulder. "She always a pain in the ass?" he asked as he looked past me to focus on the four-hundred-pound gorilla at my back. "Jones—" The expression on DeSilvero's face shifted from smug to astonished in an eighth of a second.

I twisted around to see what his eyes were popping out at. There aren't many times I've been stunned speechless, but this was one of them.

Eddy had hopped onto the back of the huge cop and her arms were wrapped around his neck. Big Boy's face was going purple, either from rage or from lack of air. Probably both. The sight took the rest of the fight out of me and I let go of the door.

The cop had been using his bulk to keep me from moving forward, and when I relaxed, momentum reversed. Both he and Eddy tipped backward, in slow motion, toward the sidewalk. The cop hadn't yet released his grip on my belt, and he dragged me along for the ride.

I landed hard atop Big Boy.

Eddy howled, "Get him off! Get this piggy pork chop off me!"

———

A few minutes later—after JT somehow managed to convince Officer Jones not to arrest Eddy for assaulting a police officer—we huddled in front of the bar, facing the entrance. I'd told Johnny to take a hike, which he was trying to do. DeSilvero looked like he was making triple sure he had Johnny's correct contact information before he allowed the kid to leave.

I owed the Johnny another one, big time. After all the IOUs I was racking up, there wasn't going to be much left in my IOU arsenal.

Eddy was still grumbling and rubbing various bruises when DeSilvero sauntered our way.

He said, "So, Ms. O'Hanlon, why don't you tell me what you know about the body in the basement."

I mumbled, "Too bad it wasn't you."

JT nailed me with a well-placed elbow to the ribs.

I grunted.

DeSilvero moved uncomfortably closer. I leaned backward until I was arched against the edge of the bar, his face mere inches from mine. "What was that?" he asked softly, in dangerously measured tone. "I couldn't hear you."

He must have had something with garlic for breakfast. I tried not to scrunch up my face in disgust, but I'm not sure I succeeded. "I, uh," I paused to lick my lips, "I said I don't have an answer for you."

DeSilvero gave me the evil eye and slowly straightened.

I took a deep breath.

He backed out of my space. "Where is your father?"

"I told you, I have no idea. That hasn't changed."

Coop and Eddy watched our exchange. JT kept a hand on my arm in case I lost my mind again.

DeSilvero stared at me thoughtfully. "So who's in the basement, huh? It'd be easier on all of us if you told me now. They've been there awhile. You help your old man stow the evidence, maybe?"

My temper and I wobbled on the brink of a violent outburst, preferably directed squarely at DeSilvero. I ground out, "My father didn't kill anyone, and I didn't help dispose of anyone down there." The son of a bitch. Wasn't I supposed to be offered a lawyer or something if I was going to be harassed by the cops?

JT's felt me tense and her grip tightened. "Shay."

I lifted my chin.

DeSilvero said with barely concealed disbelief, "You haven't heard from your father since New Year's Eve?"

"The last time I talked to my dad was three days after Christmas."

I only hoped he wouldn't ask Eddy the same thing. That outcome would definitely not be good. Eddy didn't lie well. Usually.

A man wearing a navy sweatshirt with BCA in white block letters walked up and said something to DeSilvero. DeSilvero nodded, and the man disappeared in the direction of the kitchen.

"Ms. O'Hanlon. Exactly how violent is your father? Is he the love 'em and kill 'em kind?"

I sucked in a lungful of air and was about to launch into an energetic retort when Eddy said, "Peter O'Hanlon is a gentle soul. He'd never harm anyone. That there body in the cellar, why, that's none of his doing."

DeSilvero's eyebrows hiked up. "How exactly do you know that, lady? You help him put the body there?"

Eddy drew herself to her full five-ish-foot height. "Sir, my name is Mrs. Edwina Quartermaine, and I'd appreciate it if you addressed me as such. No, I didn't put any poor dead body anywhere. But," she nailed him with her stop-being-a-jerk scowl, "maybe that could change."

Go Eddy!

DeSilvero's jowls popped out and in rhythmically. He blinked a couple of times. "Mrs. Quartermaine, how exactly do you know Mr. O'Hanlon?"

"Family friends, and I got no more to say to you without my attorney present and accounted for."

DeSilvero blew a noisy breath and shifted to stand in front of Coop. "Who the hell are you?"

I glanced at Eddy, thankful she didn't have her Whacker in hand. From the rather enraged expression on her face, she looked ready to take a swing at the sergeant, and that would be very, very bad. Or maybe she'd pop him one with her shoe. The thought almost made me smile.

Coop said, "Nick Cooper, and I don't know who killed who. And I didn't do it, either."

JT spoke up. "Look, DeSilvero, if you're going to interrogate them—"

"I'm not interrogating anyone, Bordeaux. I'm just asking a few fact-finding questions." His voice rose and a vein popped out on his forehead. "There's a dead body in the basement of this dump." He slammed his fist on the bar top. "Someone lost their life and was buried beneath concrete for god only knows how long. I want to know who it is and who put them there."

He was right. Jerk or not, the truth was that a deceased person had been found on my dad's property. Some unlucky soul was buried in the basement, and their family had no idea what happened to them. They probably felt like I felt before my dad contacted Eddy so at least we knew he was still alive. The news this person's family was going to receive would change their lives forever. There was nothing good about it, though we could hope that knowing would lend some kind of closure.

The sad fact at this point was that I didn't know what to think. I wasn't at all sure that my father wasn't responsible for the corpse in the cellar, considering he had been covered with blood and had no recollection of how that came to be. But I surely wasn't going to impart that tidbit to DeSilvero.

"Look, Sergeant," I said, my voice resigned, no longer combative. "The honest-to-god truth is that none of us know who killed whoever is down there. None of us know where my dad is. Believe me, I wish I did. I've been looking everywhere for him. But I can't—no, I *won't* believe this is something my father would do. I want to cooperate with you, but your attitude is making it next to impossible."

DeSilvero actually shuffled his feet like a kid squirming during a scolding. "I'm passionate about my work, about bringing justice to those who can no longer do it for themselves. I do what it takes to make that happen. If that offends you, nothing I can do about it."

That was as close to an apology as we were going to get.

"This bar," he said, "is now an official crime scene, and will be for the foreseeable future. I'll let you know when it's cleared and you can resume business. In the meantime, the entire building is off limits." He handed each of us his card, and although I still had the first one he'd given to me, I took it without argument.

DeSilvero waved a hand at the front door. "Now, get the hell out of here, and call me if any of you hear from Peter O'Hanlon."

———

We rolled into the Uptown Diner a little before noon, and, I hoped, before the lunch crowd. The Uptown was a neighborhood icon and had helped nurse me through more than one hangover. While some called it a greasy spoon, I called it comforting. And comfort was exactly what we needed right about now.

Once we were seated, a young woman with bright purple hair and colorful tattoos on her forearms handed over the menus. In a flash she returned with our drinks and proceeded to take our order. I was stressed out. The chocolate chip cookie dough pancakes should help that.

Our server, who informed us her name was Aquarius, but that we should call her Aqua, hustled away to dispatch our order.

Eddy said, "That girl's hair should be blue if her name's Aqua. We should get Kate to help her with that." Kate, Rabbit Hole businesswoman extraordinaire that she was, wore her hair in whatever whimsical color that came to her on a given day. One time it even changed color halfway through the day. I had no idea how she had any hair left after that much abuse.

I twisted my napkin and shredded it when it wouldn't twist any more. I didn't want to verbalize what was on my mind, but it felt like my insides might implode if I didn't. Keeping my eyes on the pieces of torn napkin that littered the table, I mumbled, "Do you think the reason Dad kept putting off repairing the sewer was because he knew there was a body there?"

For a moment no one moved. Then Eddy slapped her non-shredded, napkin-wrapped silverware on the tabletop. "No, ma'am! I do not think the reason your father didn't get the stink fixed was because he was stashing a cadaver in the cellar. Peter can be a hand-ful and he has a short fuse, but he's not murderous. Why, he told me that profit was down throughout the summer. He wondered if it was because the Leprechaun wasn't trendy like the Gay 90's or Psycho Suzie's. He even talked about turning the parking lot into a volley-ball court. I told him to stow that idea and hang in there. Years past have had similar slumps. It's always come back."

Still more people had known about my own father's issues, and I'd had no clue. How the hell had I managed to lose sight of what had been going on? Feeling disgusted with myself, I dropped the mangled remnants of the napkin and felt JT's hand squeeze my knee. I slid my fingers beneath her palm and held on.

After a long, uncomfortable silence, Coop said, "God, I need a smoke."

"Eat first, child." Eddy patted him on the back. "So what hap-pens now?"

JT said, "We need to have a chit-chat with this Phil Hanssen. He's the next link in the puzzle."

Personally, I was tired of talking. I was tired of hunting. I wanted my father back, and I'd even take a big old fight between the two of us. At least that would be in the realm of normalcy. "Speaking of Hanssen," I glanced at Coop, "did Bogey Too come back yet?"

Coop pulled his cell out. "Actually, yeah." He fiddled with the gadget. "Says here Phil Hanssen lives in Eden Prairie. Looks like the guy has some dough. Let's see. Coachman's Lane."

More fiddling.

"He has a work address listed in Vadnais Heights. Apex Pharmaceutical For Action. It's a political action committee. For drug makers, apparently." Coop continued to read, then looked up. "That's about all I got."

"Wow." Surprise colored JT's tone. "I had no idea you had the ability to get that information through your phone. Nice job, Coop. How'd you do that?" Coop opened his mouth, but JT held her hand up before he could speak. "Never mind. Didn't mean to ask. I do not want to have any knowledge of your capability of finding out what you shouldn't know."

Discussions of PACs and ill-gained knowledge were put on hold when Aqua showed up with a huge serving tray.

Oh god, it smelled good.

In a shake and a half, Aqua dispatched her load and whisked herself away to get more butter for Eddy's toast. We were a quiet bunch as we stuffed our faces.

Fifteen minutes later, it was all over.

Eddy belched quietly. She sat back against the red-padded booth and patted her stomach as she surveyed the wreckage on the table. "We sure know how to pack it away."

"No kidding." Coop made a face and groaned. "But well worth the pain. I think."

Coop's phone rang before I could add my gastronomic woes to the mix. He snapped it up and answered, listening without a word. He eventually said, "Hang on. I'm going to put you on speaker. Shay, Eddy, and JT are with me."

Coop set the phone on the table and pushed a couple of buttons. "You're on."

"Hello, everybody!" It was Rocky, and his voice quivered with excitement. "Guess what! We are at the most awesome retail establishment ever! My lovely bride Tulip and I are here in the beautiful city of Bloomington. At the most wonderful Mall of America. We wish to request a ride home."

"How'd you get there, Rocky?" I asked.

"Ms. Agnes's nephew, Basil Lazowski, better known to you as Baz the Spaz, gave us a ride here in his very scary 1993 Chevrolet Corsica that used to be midnight blue. Now it has more rust than paint. He was going to bring us home, but then he saw a kiosk for the Grand Casino and he left for Hinckley, Minnesota. But it is okay. It was not pleasant to see the pavement through the holes in the floorboard of his vehicle. And it was very cold. I am trying very hard to like him, but it is difficult."

I think I heard Eddy actually cuss, albeit under her breath. It sounded a lot like *son of a bitch*, but I couldn't swear on it. She did grumble somewhat louder, "That no good, Basil. I'm going to have to have a talk with that little conniver. Don't you worry, Rocky. I'll come and get you two. Where should I pick you up?"

"Come to the east ramp. That's the ramp that faces Wisconsin. Not the one that faces South Dakota. Go to the New York level. We will be right by the pedestrian bridge that allows us to cross from the parking lot to the mall in comfort and safety, so we don't get run over."

"Gotcha," Eddy said. "I'll see you two in a half hour, maybe forty-five minutes."

"Thank you, Eddy Quartermaine. Did you know that seven Yankee stadiums can fit inside the mall? And it's seventy degrees inside year-round." There was a click and then dead air.

We all stared at Coop's phone for a beat before he picked it up and tucked it away. "Guess he was done."

Eddy pulled some bills from her wallet and tossed them on the table. "Happy New Year. Lunch is on me."

We dropped a chorus of thank-yous. Eddy waved her hand at our appreciation. "Drop me off to get my car at the Lep, and you kids go put the squeeze on that Hasford guy."

"Hanssen," I said.

"Whatever," Eddy said. "Go squash something useful out of the man."

ELEVEN

AFTER DROPPING EDDY OFF, we headed for Vadnais Heights, a northern suburb of St. Paul. Along the way we discussed our interview strategy. We decided JT'd take the lead, since that had worked so well with Norman Howard.

The office was in a neat, single-level complex that looked like it had recently been rehabbed. Half of the six storefronts were empty, FOR RENT signs in the windows. A guy by the name of Myron Erle, Certified Accountant, occupied one of the spaces. Another was filled by a tiny—and I mean *tiny*—Hmong grocery. Looked like it would be a challenge to turn around once you set foot inside. However, from the number of people entering and leaving, they were doing a brisk business, even in the early afternoon.

Apex PAC took up the end space.

A huge pile of snow sat in the far corner of the lot, occupying at least eight parking spots. It was the perfect snow mountain. I flashed back to winters as a kid where I'd spend most of my playtime outside, making tunnels and forts under the white stuff. It would be nice to be able to hold onto that winter wonderland feeling instead of dreading it.

I wedged the Escape between a newer Honda Accord and a tricked-out 1980s Caprice Classic with pimp-mobile tires and fuzzy pink dice hanging from the rearview mirror.

JT said, "Let's go." She got out of the Escape and headed for the door and pulled it open.

As we stepped inside, it felt like we walked into a sauna. They must have had the heat cranked up to eighty. If we stayed here for any length of time, I might actually thaw out.

The office space was at least twice the size of the grocery. The area was divided by gray-colored partitions into a number of separate cubicles on one side and a large open space on the other. The low tones of numerous voices hummed in the background. I imagined volunteers on the phones trying to talk their marks into whatever objectives this particular organization had.

The open side of the office had an eight-foot table by the wall along with five filing cabinets next to it lined up like metal soldiers. The table was covered with stacks of papers, boxes of envelopes, three telephones, a couple staplers, tape, paper clips, and other miscellaneous office supplies.

Along the back were two closed doors, probably to additional office space or restrooms.

A tubby man with a pockmarked face and a graying goatee sat at one end of the table, an envelope in one hand and a tri-folded sheet in the other. I blinked twice at the black polka-dot bowtie and black suspenders he wore over a crisply starched pastel green shirt.

He looked up at our entrance. "That was quick. I didn't realize the agency sent out help this fast."

JT stepped up to the man, flashed her badge, and slipped it back in her pocket. "We aren't from an agency. And you are?"

I had to admit it was a hell of a rush to watch my girl in action.

"I—uh, you're not—oh." The man stuttered a moment and then fixed his eyes below JT's neck, where her unzipped leather jacket gaped open at her throat. He said, "I'm Tab Tindale. What can I do for you?"

JT leveled her cop "don't even think about lying to me" look on him. On his forehead, actually. She said, "We'd like to speak to Phil Hanssen."

"Phil? He's out back having a break." Mr. Tindale hadn't managed to peel his eyes away from JT's chest. It wasn't like she was all that well endowed, and most of her was covered up, but apparently that didn't matter.

I might have felt insulted on JT's part if I didn't think it was pretty funny. I hadn't seen anyone so blatantly mesmerized by a pair of knockers since we had to ask a customer to leave the Rabbit Hole and not come back because he couldn't carry on a conversation with any female over the age of three. He'd literally forget what he'd be saying as his eyes wandered where they didn't belong. Eddy finally couldn't take it any longer. She threatened him with her Whacker and booted his ass out. The man probably would have died if he'd gotten a glimpse of Ms. Mad Nail Filer's boobs at Schuler's office.

"Mr. Tindale!" JT barked and snapped her fingers next to his head.

"Oh!" Tab Tindale's head bobbed up and he peered at JT's face. "What was that?"

"Can. You. Please. Get. Him?" JT said softly, carefully enunciating each word.

Tindale fluttered the envelope in his hand toward the far wall. "Through that door on the right. Down the hall and out the back door."

I wondered if JT ever wanted to pull her gun on guys like this.

"Thank you." She took off in the direction Tindale indicated. I could tell by the tone of JT's voice that her patience with idiots was being sorely tested.

Coop and I followed JT down a short hall and through the back door. The resulting blast of cold air stiffened my back and my body involuntarily shuddered. I tried to force my shoulders to relax.

There was a narrow alleyway between the building and a seven-foot tan fence that ran the length of the property. A green dumpster sat at one end of the alley, and it was overflowing with garbage bags and other trash. Someone had apparently forgotten to pay the garbage guys lately.

A six-foot-tall man stood facing the dumpster, speaking in angry tones into an old-style flip cell phone. He had a rangy build and salt-and-pepper hair. A khaki-colored topcoat billowed around his knees in the breeze. He stopped talking long enough to take a deep drag off a cigarette he held cupped in one hand, then resumed whatever tirade he was in the midst of.

JT locked on our prey like a guided missile. She marched right over and tapped him on the shoulder.

The man glanced back at JT, then slowly turned around. From the sour expression on his face, he wasn't too happy at the interruption. "Whaddya want?"

JT did her super-fast flash-the-badge thing again and said, "Phil Hanssen?"

"Yeah, that's me."

"Sir," JT said politely now that she had his attention, "we have some questions for you."

The man narrowed his eyes and into the phone muttered, "Let me call you back." He snapped the phone shut and focused on JT. "What's this about? Can't you see I have a business to run here?"

Yup, it sure looked like he was conducting complicated business transactions by the dumpster. He sounded a little like Coke Up the Nose Normie.

JT said, "We have some questions regarding the nature of your association with Norman Howard."

"My association with Norman—my brother-in-law? What do you want with that joker?" Hanssen took one last puff from his smoke and flicked it into the dumpster. I wondered if it would ignite the multitude of cardboard stuffed inside the bin. What a jerk-o-saurus. And someone needed to implement a recycling program here, pronto.

JT said, "Does the name Charles Schuler ring any bells?"

The man blinked a couple of times, probably trying to keep up with the subject change. "Charles Schuler? No. I don't know any Charles Schuler."

The man's voice rose, and I noticed his face had turned redder than it had been seconds ago. Or maybe it was naturally ruddy and I missed it on the once-over. Hard to tell in these temps.

My own level of adrenaline was rapidly increasing as I watched the interview play out. My hands trembled, but not because I was still feeling the cold. I flexed them and tried to relax. It wouldn't be a good thing to lose my temper now, especially since we hadn't yet gotten anywhere with this dude. But between two dead bodies and a missing father who may or may not have committed homicide, the impotent anger and confusion that I'd stuffed away from the very beginning began to rear its ugly little head.

JT propped her hands on her hips. "Why did you hire your brother-in-law to pressure Pete O'Hanlon into selling his bar?"

"What?" Hanssen spluttered. "I did no such thing."

JT took a step toward him. He took a step back. I drifted along beside her, and Coop was right behind us. My heart began to pound harder, and air became thick.

"I beg to differ, Mr. Hanssen." JT's voice took on a flat cadence, something I had never heard before. "You told Norman Howard you'd pay him good money to rattle O'Hanlon and convince him to sell his bar." She moved right into his face and said in a low, venomous voice, "Why?"

Hanssen's back was now pressed against the dumpster. Between the three of us, he was penned in. He held up a hand. "I don't know this O'Handle, and I did not try to convince anyone to sell some dive."

The O'Handle crack did it, but the *dive* part probably helped too. The tenuous rein I'd had on my temper since the initial phone call from Whale asking where my father was snapped. I hip-checked JT out of the way, grabbed the lapels of Hanssen's overcoat, and yanked the man toward me.

"Listen, asshole! The name is O'Hanlon, you lying sack of shit. We know you hired Norman Howard to harass my father into signing over his business. Now we want to know why." I gave him a good shake.

Hanssen's hands came up and he grabbed my wrists, his eyes wide.

I said, "That bar is his goddamn livelihood. Why?" Nothing like a little bellowing to get someone's attention. I waited a couple of breaths, but no answer was forthcoming. I hauled Hanssen forward, then stiff-armed him against the dumpster a couple of times. None too delicately, either.

Rational Shay was fading fast. My field of vision narrowed to encompass only Hanssen. "Tell me what you did to my father, you stupid son of a—"

Suddenly I was jerked backward and nearly lost my footing. My hands were still fisted into Hanssen's coat, and he came right along with me.

I heard shouting, but I couldn't make out the words over the roaring in my head.

The tunnel vision vanished, and I was back in the frigid alley. Coop stood behind me, his arms wrapped tight around my shoulders, my back pressed against his bony chest. JT was yelling my name, her body half-wedged between Hanssen and me.

With a strangled oath, I shoved Hanssen away from me and let his jacket go. He crashed into the dumpster and lost his balance, arms flailing as his hard-soled shoes slipped and slid on the ice. He'd have gone down if JT hadn't grabbed him.

JT leaned into my face, her eyes locked on mine. "Easy, Shay."

"I'm fine," I sucked in a breath of chilly air. "I'm just fucking fine."

She glanced over my shoulder at Coop. "Don't let her go." She turned and dragged Hanssen toward her with one hand. He reminded me of a rag doll Dawg and Bogey had gotten a hold of once. They ripped it to pieces. I held back an insane bubble of laughter at the thought that JT might do some dumpster thumping herself.

Hanssen's complexion had gone from flushed to ashen, and his eyes practically popped out of his head as they bounced back and forth between JT and me.

"Look at you," I jeered. I struggled for a moment against Coop, more for effect than anything else. "You're nothing but a creampuff crybaby."

JT spun on me, her dark eyes flashing in warning. I did not want to get on the wrong side of *that* look. I held my hands up, palms out. "Sorry."

She returned her attention to Hanssen and released her grip on him. She drew herself up and crossed her arms, command presence rolling off her. Even with his height advantage, JT was downright intimidating. She said in a low voice, "You better tell us—right now—what's going on. Or I'm not going to stop her next time. She gets very violent when she's upset. And she's really upset."

I wriggled hard against Coop again. It was gratifying to watch Hanssen flinch. He indignantly whipped both hands down the front of his coat in an effort to smooth the creases. "Whatever. Just keep that crazy bitch away from me."

"Let's try this one more time," JT said. "Tell me why you were pushing Pete O'Hanlon to sell the Leprechaun."

"Jesus Christ." His face scrunched up, and it looked like he was either waging an internal debate or was having a bad gastrointestinal moment. "If I could get *O'Hanlon*," he snarled at me, "to sign on the dotted line, it was worth a lot of dough, okay?"

"Let go," I whispered to Coop, and slid out of his grasp. I stepped even with JT and said, "All of this is about money? What in the hell could my father's bar be worth to you?"

Hanssen tilted his neck to one side and the other before he said, "A half mil."

I almost snorted. Someone was fronting five hundred grand to force my father to sell out? That was insane. I said, "Why?" at almost the same time JT said, "Who?"

For a moment Hanssen's gaze flicked between JT and me as if he were trying to figure out which lunatic he should answer first. "Look.

I don't ask questions. That leads to problems. I don't know why, okay?"

JT said, "How about the who?"

Hanssen rolled his eyes.

JT unzipped her jacket and pushed it back far enough to let Hanssen get a gander at the gun on her right hip. That kind of encouragement would've worked on me.

And it worked on Hanssen. He said, "Oh for god's sake. Easy with the hardware. Limburger Larson, all right?"

"Who?" I asked. "I don't know of any Larson who goes by the name Limburger." I glanced pointedly at JT. "Do you?"

"Nope," she said. "How about it, Coop?"

Coop shrugged. "Guess I missed out on that Larson somewhere along the line."

"You three are regular wise guys, ain'tcha? Roy Larson hired me to … well, to encourage O'Hanlon to sign the bar over. Okay? Jesus."

I was pretty sure I did not hear that right. For a long moment no one said anything.

Coop said derisively, "Kitty Litter Roy Larson? He hired you to strong-arm Pete into selling the Lep?"

My brain was trying hard to link the King of Feline Elimination to the violence that had been heaped on my dad, and incidentally on me and Lisa, but I couldn't make the leap.

I said, "That's bullshit. My dad and Roy Larson go back years. There's no reason Roy would want the Lep. My dad bought it *from* him. That makes no sense."

"Listen lady," Hanssen whined, "I never said anything was gonna make any goddamn sense. It is what it is."

After I threatened to upend Hanssen into the dumpster one last time for fun, we exited the alley. We decided to head over to Roy's office and clear up this avenue of ridiculousness. There was absolutely no reason Roy would want to acquire the Lep from Dad. He was absorbed in his own business and his son's politics. And even if he did want the bar back for some insane reason, he and my dad would have a face-to-face discussion, which wouldn't evolve into the murder and mayhem that had occurred.

Phil Hanssen was blowing smoke, covering for someone. We needed to figure out who. And why.

———

Back in the Escape, I called to make sure Roy was still at the office, and it was a good thing I did. After a brief conversation with the same receptionist Lisa and I had met, I disconnected. "Change of plan. Roy took the day off to work at home." I headed for the freeway. "Off to Roy's house we go," I said and goosed the gas.

Larson lived in a tony neighborhood of Minneapolis called Kenwood, which usually meant old money and fancy houses.

"I don't get it." Coop broke the heavy silence that had descended on our party like a wet rag. "Your dad and Roy Larson have been friends forever."

"I know," I said. "There's no plausible reason Roy would want the Lep back from my father. He sure doesn't need the money. Not that the bar's pulling in a boatload anyway. More like a leaky canoe's worth." I sighed. "This is going to sound callous, but I'm beginning to think this whole intimidation thing is some kind of a sick joke. The real issue here, well the three real issues, in my opinion, seem to be A," I put a finger up, "where the hell is my father? Then B," I added another finger, "what exactly happened the night before New Year's? Did Dad actually have something to do with Charles Schuler's death?" Up went a third finger. "C, How did a body get dead and find its way beneath the cement in the cellar?"

No one had any answers. With the exception of MPR's talking heads mumbling on the radio in the background, silence enveloped us again.

I let out a grumpy sigh. JT reached over for my hand and gave it a squeeze. I curled my fingers around hers and held on. I wracked my brain trying to remember if my father had ever put new concrete in the basement, thus opening the far-flung potential that he might have had something to do with stowing a body beneath the new slab.

It was a cold hard truth that a bullet from my dad's gun had dispatched Charles Schuler to the great beyond. Combine that with the second body found in the Lep, and the probability that my father was an innocent bystander was bleaker than the Vikings chances of making it to the Super Bowl any time soon. In addition, there was the fact he had been putting off having the crack in the cellar floor repaired. But that could be explained away easily enough by the cost factor.

We were stuck on a rickety Tilt-A-Whirl, possibly one created by Roy Larson, the distant relative of the original ride's inventer. No wonder I felt like I was going to throw up. Again.

After four eternities, I pulled into the half-moon driveway of Roy Larson's estate. And an *estate* was exactly what the place was. The three-story house was on par with some of the mansions that dotted St. Paul's Summit Avenue. It sat on over a half-acre of land, which was almost unheard of in the city in this day and age.

During the summer, the lawn would be well tended and lush, the blanket of green cut into geometric designs by some overpriced lawn care company.

Currently, nature's once-green carpet was covered with snow. Of course, the drive had been neatly plowed and the sidewalks practically sculpted.

A black Lexus SUV with vanity plates reading KTYLTR was parked near the entrance. A three-car garage with a steeply pitched roof was attached to one side of the house, and a silver Chevrolet Silverado sat in front of the center stall. A red, white, and blue sticker on the back bumper read, *Greg Larson ♥s Minneapolis.* Beneath those words it read, *Vote for Greg!*

Looked like Greg wasn't planning on following Roy's steps into the kitty litter hall of fame anytime soon. Couldn't say I blamed him.

I pulled up next to the truck and killed the engine. "Okay, guys, let me do the talking this time. I've known Roy most of my life."

Coop and JT agreed. We trooped across the drive and up six steps to the imposing front door. It was gray-bleached, polished wood with a peak at the top, attached to the jam with heavy iron hinges. The whole thing looked like it would fit nicely in some old Irish castle.

I pressed the doorbell. The resulting gong vibrated the cement right through my tennis shoes.

"Holy crap," Coop said under his breath.

The deep reverb faded, and the door opened to reveal a man with a cue-ball head, decked out in a black suit with a black shirt and a black tie. He was either one scary looking butler or a totally cliché mobster.

"'Allo."

I looked up. And up. He was tall. Really, really tall. And really, really thin. Ichabod Crane in the flesh. His nose had a bump on the bridge, and it was prominent enough that it looked like a boil that would have done the Wicked Witch of the West proud.

The temptation to respond with an "'Allo" myself was palpable, but I figured it would probably not do to make him mad. Instead, I shot Ichabod my best, most disarming smile. "Hello. We'd like to speak with Roy."

He drew himself up to full height, which had to be close to seven feet, and stared down his beak at me. "I am sorry," he said in a thick accent. "Monsieur Larson is indisposed at the moment."

"I think if you tell him Shay O'Hanlon is here to—"

"Oh no, Miss," Ichabod stopped me cold. "Monsieur specifically told me he was not to be bothered."

"Really, I—" Behind Ichabod, across an entryway that I swear could have held a racquetball court, I spotted Roy himself entering one of four doors that lined the spacious room. He either hadn't seen us or was simply ignoring the commotion at the front door, because he disappeared from view as he pulled the door shut behind him.

I darted around the very surprised butler. "Come on," I called to Coop and JT. My posse hot on my heels, I arrived at the door Roy had disappeared through, with poor Ichabod rapidly scurrying along behind us.

"Miss, stop. Miss! Monsieur specifically—"

"Monsieur"—nope, there was absolutely not a hint of sarcasm in my tone—"will talk to me." I flung open the door and charged inside the room.

The space was a library that doubled as an office, with tall bookshelves occupying three of the four walls. The fourth was a gigantic floor-to-ceiling glass wall opposite the door. The view looked out across a vast yard and into the trees beyond. It was one hell of a sight.

There was a large desk with a credenza off to one side. The desktop was piled high with colorful yard signs and political flyers. Roy

Larson stood in front of the desk talking with another man who held one of the signs in his hand.

It took a second for me to realize the other guy was Roy's son, Greg.

Greg was a little taller than my five-seven, and he had to be in his late thirties. He'd been a senior when I was a freshman, and although I was aware of him, I hadn't known him well.

His stomach was flat—it hadn't yet gone the way of the All-American beer belly, probably due to his athleticism. Greg had been a college track star, and had obviously done a commendable job of maintaining his physique into middle age. Muscular shoulders nicely filled out a long-sleeved, aqua-colored polo shirt. The polo was tucked into a pair of neatly pressed gray Dockers. The aqua in his shirt mirrored eyes that were still some of the brightest blue-green I'd ever seen. His high school trademark golden-brown "hair-band" mane was now tamed, cut well above his collar.

Roy was the first to recover from our surprise entrance. "Shay! What on earth brings you here?"

Ichabod stepped in front of me, holding his arms out to the sides like a kid on school patrol. He blustered, "I'm so sorry, Monsieur, she—"

"Don't worry about it, Dijon," Roy waved him off. "It's fine. You may go. Please close the door behind you."

Dijon? Yikes. Even Ichabod deserved better than mustard for a name. Dijon backed out of the room with a scowl but pulled the door gently shut.

Roy crossed the room with an amused smile. "What a pleasant surprise to see you. Twice in less than forty-eight hours." He gave me a one-armed squeeze and turned me to face his son. "Greg, you remember Shay O'Hanlon? She was the little squirt who used to run wild around the bar before I sold it to her father. Shay, my son, Greg."

I put my hand out to shake Greg's. He grabbed it and smoothly pulled me in for a semi-stiff hug. It was a well-practiced move, probably honed on the city parade and county fair circuit.

"Shay, of course I remember you. We went to the same high school. I was a couple years ahead, I think." He grinned warmly, his mesmerizing eyes boring into mine so sincerely that I couldn't turn away if I tried.

Roy said, "Have you heard anything from your dad yet?"

It took me a second to unmesmerize myself and refocus on Greg's dad. "No." I was such a liar. To distract Roy from asking anything further, I did the introduction thing with Coop and JT.

"Coop," Roy said, "it's good to see you again." He gave Coop a clap on the shoulder and turned his attention to my girl. "And you're JT. It's high time we met. Pete talks about you all the time." My jaw about dropped as Roy pumped her hand and said, "Old Pete has told me more than once it was high time Shay settled down with a good person."

Oh my god. *My* father actually said that? For years we'd been at odds over my sexual orientation, and periodically we'd have hair-raising battles borne of the stubborn Irish blood we shared. After a week or so, one of us usually made a grudging peace and things would return to normal until the next time the crap hit the proverbial fan. Come to think of it, we hadn't had a good go-round in months. Not since before JT and I got together, actually. Had it really been that long?

Yet one more thing I hadn't noticed. That plaguing thought made my chest ache. I didn't know my own father at all anymore. At what point had we lost touch? Or maybe it was all me. The past year had been a pretty crazy one for me, what with Coop's boss being killed, a toy snake stuffed with money, and JT's nemesis getting pickled—literally and figuratively. I guess shooting the breeze with Dad hadn't been my top priority.

I was ripped out of my momentary melancholy when Coop nudged me in time to hear JT say, "Right, Shay?"

I blinked. I had no idea what I was agreeing with. "Ah, yeah. Yup."

Roy rocked back on his heels and clasped his hands together. "Today should be a little calmer than your visit yesterday, Shay. I think we're safe from four-legged escapees here."

I offered up a half-smile. "Yeah, I think we are." What would the kitty-litter-buying public think if they knew the King of Cat Poo didn't have any feline friends? The thought was gone almost as soon as it registered, and I was back on task. "The reason we're here, Roy, is—well, I have a question for you."

He raised his eyebrows and waited. Just spit it out. "Have you ever heard of a man named Phil Hanssen?"

One of his eyebrows hiked higher. "I haven't heard that name for years until a few months ago. Phil ran my campaign for governor back in the Ice Age. Why?"

How was I going to phrase this? Straightforward was my best option. "Hanssen has admitted to hiring someone to intimidate my father into selling the Leprechaun." I paused, not wanting to voice it, but I did anyway. "He said you'd asked him to do it. That you were paying him a lot of money to make it happen."

For a moment, Roy simply gazed at me. Greg's face was deadpan. He crossed his arms and watched the conversation play out. Finally Roy said, "I knew that son of a bitch—excuse my language—was going to cause trouble."

"Trouble?" I echoed.

"Oh, yes, trouble with an old-fashioned capital T. Back when he worked on my campaign, he did a great job at the beginning. Hard worker, willing to go the extra mile. Enthusiastic. Eventually took charge of the whole thing. Pounded the concrete with the rest of the volunteers, handed out thousands of pieces of literature. Plotted the best areas to hit, and then hit again.

"We were within a week of the election and it was neck and neck." Bitterness seeped into Roy's voice and he shook his head. "It was at that point Hanssen made some grievous mistakes, tried to bribe voters. He was arrested for harassing the opposition. The man even had the audacity to hire a bunch of street thugs to help him.

"As soon as I heard about what was going on, I let him go. It was terribly sad. The man had great instincts, but the only way he could deliver was to intimidate and harass." Roy swiped a hand over his face. "A few months back, when he heard Greg's name in the mix for mayor, he contacted me, wanting in on the campaign."

Greg jumped in then. "Needless to say, we told him thanks, but no thanks." He leaned a hip against the desk. "Was he pissed. He upended a table on the way out of my office, and he's been posting all kinds of bad litter reviews on Dad's website. You have any idea how hard that kind of thing is to clear up? He's done nothing but cause problems."

"Wow," JT said. "Talk about holding a grudge. Have you reported any of this? Talked with a lawyer regarding the online libel?"

"We've got a lawyer," Roy said, "but not a whole lot has come of it. Dealing with defamation on the Internet, especially in review postings, is still very much a work in progress."

I felt a weight had lifted off the scruff of my neck. I knew there was an explanation for the claims Hanssen made against Roy. It was all another manipulation. However, we were now back to square one. Who paid off Hanssen to go after my dad?

Greg said, "I've got security sitting on my campaign office because a couple bricks have come through the front window and someone lobbed a Molotov cocktail at the building. Luckily the fuse didn't catch."

JT asked, "How do you know Hanssen is behind it?"

"I don't have hard evidence," Greg said. "But we didn't have any trouble before he showed up."

Coop said, "If you need help on the Internet front removing whatever Hanssen posted, give me a shout." He pulled a rumpled business card from his pocket and handed it to Greg.

I said, "Coop's pretty good at fixing that kind of thing. He'd probably be able to correct the problem in five minutes flat."

JT said, "Thanks for taking the time to talk to us. Sorry to barge in."

"Think nothing of it," Roy said. "If you need me, Shay, I'm here for you. Any time."

"Thanks, Roy." For a moment, I wanted to give in to the concern in his voice. "I don't know what to do anymore. Now the Leprechaun's closed down ... "

"Closed? How come?" Roy cocked his head to one side, curiosity shadowing his features.

"I had to call a plumber in and—" My words hung in the air. I shot JT a quick look, realizing it might be best to keep my mouth shut. She gave me a nearly imperceptible head-shake. "—well, there are some complications."

"Well, Shay, I'm sorry to hear that. I hope whatever the problem is can be corrected soon."

I gave Roy a quick half-hug, and Greg echoed his father's sentiment as I submitted to another campaign clasp. Then Coop, JT, and I moved toward the door en masse.

"Shay," Roy called.

I turned around.

"Let me know when you find out what's going on with Pete, okay? And if there's anything we can do..."

"Thanks, Roy." I took some small measure of comfort in his words. "It was good to see you, Greg. Good luck with everything."

TWELVE

The ride back to the Rabbit Hole went by quickly. We rehashed our chit-chat with Phil Hanssen and the subsequent visit with Roy and son. I was feeling a lot better after talking to Roy. Hanssen was bullshitting us, for reasons I didn't understand.

I pulled up to the snow-mounded curb in front of the Hole and we trooped toward the entrance. There were icy spots on the sidewalk and I made a mental note to toss more salt out before someone pulled an Agnes and landed on their keister.

The chimes above the door jingled as we crossed into the cinnamon- and wood smoke-scented warmth of the café. Half of the circular café tables were empty, but the overstuffed chairs were occupied near cheerfully crackling flames in the fireplace. It was the lull before the evening storm.

Kate stood behind the cash register, her arms folded over her apron as she spoke with a customer. Today her hair was bright orange and spiked in numerous points. She glanced up and her face brightened. "Hey guys. Look. We have company." She nodded at the woman standing before her.

The customer glanced over her shoulder and I realized it was Pam Pine, from Pam's Pawhouse, where we boarded Dawg and Bogey.

"Hey, Pam!" I called with a wave.

Pam's grin lit up her face. I was about to take another step toward her when something smacked me in the back and knocked me flat on my face. I hit the deck with a resounding *ooofff* and narrowly missed taking one of the metal café chairs with me. Before I could register the fact that I was suddenly up close and personal with the salt-stained floor, what felt like a bag of cement landed on top my back. Simultaneously, a wet nose snuffled my ear. It tickled. I let out a peal of laughter and tried to push myself up with ninety pounds of canine, most likely Dawg, along for the ride.

I'd managed to raise myself a few inches off the floor when another beast stuck his snout right into my eye and practically frenched my nostrils with a sloppy tongue.

Bogey.

My arms gave out and I hit the floor again, trying to fend off two slurpy tongues.

Behind me, JT laughed and half-heartedly called for the dogs, but they weren't the least bit inclined to listen.

Finally Pam came to the rescue and dragged them off me.

I made it to my knees and wiped the prolific evidence of their adoration on the sleeve of my jacket. I shot JT a sideways glance. "Thanks for the assist there, love o' my life."

"Sorry," JT said, valiantly trying to tamp down the snickers. "Wasn't expecting that." She reached down and gave me a hand up.

The front of my jacket was covered with white chunks of ice salt and dust, mixed with drool. I tried to brush it off.

Kate said, "Way to make an entrance, Shay."

"Smartass." I stuck my tongue out at her.

Coop said, "I think they're happy to see you guys."

Pam let go of the dogs, and Bogey lumbered over to JT, his tail flagging happily. Dawg wiggled his way back to me, doing the boxer kidney-bean bend-o-rama that always reminded me of a floppy fish just pulled from the water.

Dawg *wooed* in ecstatic glee, his wrinkly face scrunched up and his happy brown eyes locked on mine. I crouched down and put a hand on either side of his cheeks and gave him a good rub, his loose lips flopping wildly. With a smooch on top of his warm head, I released him, and he sidled over to JT for some more attention.

Bogey ambled to Coop for a pat and padded my way. He plopped his ass down and looked up with huge, soulful, bloodshot, bloodhound eyes.

"Yeah, yeah," I told him. "Kate, I need a you-know-what."

She promptly handed me two bone-shaped, peanut butter dog biscuits she'd started making at home and stocking behind the counter for our four-legged guests. I dropped one into the yawing maw before me, and flipped one to Dawg, who caught it, crunched it once, and swallowed. Bogey was a little more refined in his mealtime manners; he chewed at least a couple of times before delivering the snack to his innards.

I opened my mouth, but before I had a chance to speak, a gorgeous blackish-tannish shepherd mix beelined for the counter, towing its person—a short, round, grinning woman I hadn't seen before—right along behind him. The mutt looked to be maybe seventy or eighty pounds of happy pooch.

He skidded to a stop and golden brown eyes flicked first to Dawg, then to Bogey, then Kate. Even dogs could tell Kate was a foodie pushover.

"Oh ho, I know that look." Kate dug in her Fido jar and extracted another bone. "Here you go, beautiful—" She glanced at the dog's owner in question.

"Girl," the owner supplied. "Anika."

Kate wagged the bone in her hand. "May I?"

"She'll love it," Anika's keeper said.

With a flick of her wrist, Kate tossed the treat to Anika, who snagged it mid-air. She sat on her haunches and daintily chewed the biscuit up. So that was what dog manners looked like.

Pam said, "Hello Anika, and Anika's mom."

The woman smiled widely and was about to make a comment when Rocky burst out of the back room. He had his usual blue plaid aviator hat pulled low on his head and wore a bright pink sweatshirt that said *I ♥ Tulip!* in big neon-yellow letters. He looked like a psychedelic acid trip without the drugs.

He flung himself into Coop's arms. "Nick Coop! I have missed you so much!" He practically leaped from Coop to catch both me and JT at the same time and repeated the hug process. "Shay O'Hanlon! JT Bordeaux! Did you know that the Mall of America has a Chapel of Love? Did you know over five thousand weddings have been performed there? Did you know that you, too, would be able to get hitched in ultimate holy matrimony and bliss if the state of Minnesota government allows same-sex marriage?"

———

Ten minutes later we were seated in Eddy's living room. Dawg and Bogey had checked Anika out, and after a few sniffs in all the right places, the three of them wandered back over to the fire. Anika's owner and Pam struck up a conversation about the services Pam offered, and it looked like Pam was about to gain a new client.

I missed our mutts but was happy that they were with Pam. In the past JT and I had worried if Dawg or Bogey saw us when they were vacationing at the Pawhouse because we didn't want them to get sad and mopey when we parted. However, Pam told us the silly mutts were fine, and that meant she didn't have to curb her Rabbit Hole caffeine habit while she was out dog walking. Good for us, good for Pam, good for the Rabbit Hole.

Eddy sat tucked into her recliner with her feet up and a fuzzy two-tone lemon-yellow afghan Tulip had made wrapped around her. Whichever crime drama our intrepid matriarch was currently addicted to was paused mid-action on her spanking new fifty-inch flat-screen TV.

Coop, Rocky, and JT were in the kitchen, busily raiding Eddy's fridge. I had no idea how Coop and JT could manage another bite after the feeding frenzy we'd had at the Uptown Diner just a few hours before. God knows I had no room for anything else. Well, except maybe for some ice cream.

I sat on the couch, still half-stunned by Rocky's marriage announcement. We hoped the tide was turning in favor of same-sex marriage in Minnesota, but up to now neither JT nor I had seriously considered our own potential hitching. We had a number of friends who were going to take advantage of new laws in other states, and I suppose deep down I figured we would too at some point. The thought of forever with one person wasn't nearly as intimidating as it had been even six months ago. However, being less intimidated by the prospect of a lifetime together and being ready to go for it whole hog were two separate things. No question had been popped by either one of us, and my knee-jerk reaction was that it was okay with me. For now.

The honest truth of the matter was that I was head over heels for JT. I'd come a long way in being able to admit that. I couldn't picture a future for me without her. So why was I bogged down by the thought of marrying the woman I loved?

It was best at this point to keep focused on the issue at hand, so I shoved thoughts of holy matrimony and bliss into the Revisit Another Time drawer in the file room that was my mind and proceeded to fill Eddy in about our chat with Hanssen and the follow-up with Roy Larson. I was in the middle of telling her about Dijon the Butler when JT wandered back into the living room with her mouth full and a container of Chocolate Cherry Chunk ice cream in one hand and a spoon in the other. Uh oh.

"Hey, Rizzoli," Eddy said. "You stealing my ice cream?"

JT's eyebrows rose and she mumbled, "Wizzoli?" through a mouthful of pink goo.

Eddy rolled her eyes. "Where you been, girl? Rizzoli. You know Rizzoli."

JT swallowed the ice cream. "Um, no. I don't."

"*Rizzoli and Isles*, child. The show! You're Rizzoli."

I'd heard of the show but had never seen an episode. JT apparently hadn't either. At our blank looks, Eddy slapped her thigh. "You two need a life. Angie Harmon ring a bell?"

I said, "Wasn't she on one of the *Law and Order* shows?"

"That was quite awhile back, young lady. She's on *Rizzoli and Isles* now, and she is hot with a cap-ee-tall H, even if I do say so myself. JT, you remind me of her. Your voice might not be quite as deep, your hair not quite as dark, and maybe you aren't Italian. But damn, girl, you are almost a spittin' image, minus those few things." Eddy bobbed her head. "Yes-siree. And she's a detective, too."

I raked my eyes over JT. "Rizzoli. Hmm. Could grow on me."

JT tossed a throw pillow at my head.

I opened my mouth and JT proceeded to shove a spoonful of ice cream into it, cutting off my snarky remark. I swallowed and was about to tell her to do it again when my cell rang. I pulled it out, and the caller ID displayed a number I didn't recognize.

For a moment I thought about not answering, but then realized the call could be from my dad. "Hello?"

"Shay?" Not my father.

"Who is this?"

There was a pause that lasted a few beats too long before she said, "Lisa. Lisa Vecoli."

Oh, great. Since I wasn't one for simply hanging up on people, even if I didn't trust them, I said warily, "Hi."

The next pause lasted a few beats too long. Finally she said, "I wanted to see how things were going. You hear anything from your dad yet?"

The temptation to call her on it, to tell her I knew her dirty little secret was overwhelming. *You're a cop and you're only being nice so you can arrest my dad!* But if I did that, it would open up a whole new can of nightcrawlers that I had no time to deal with. It still burned my craw that she'd used me to try to get the dirt on my father.

Before I could think of some snappy comeback, someone beeped in. I pulled the cell from my ear to look at the display. It was another unknown number, and an excellent way to get rid of her. I said, "Lisa, hey. I'm sorry. I've got another call. I have to go."

She started to say something, but I cut her off as I swapped lines. "Hello?"

"Shay." The low rumble of my father's voice was unmistakable.

Oh my god. "Dad?"

JT had been about to stuff another bite of ice cream in my mouth. Instead she stuck the spoon in her own mouth and plopped down beside me so she could try to hear what was being said on the other end of the line.

Even Eddy was leaning so far over the edge of her recliner I was surprised she didn't fall right out of it.

"Oh, kid, it's good to hear your voice." My father sounded like he was having a hard time catching his breath.

"It's good to hear yours too. Where are you? Are you okay? What happened?"

"I can't talk long, but I need to see you."

"Are you hurt? Where are you?"

"Honey, I'm okay." The weak tone of his voice sounded anything but okay.

JT tilted her head and rested it on mine as she tried to get closer to the phone.

I said, "Dad, the cops are looking for you." My voice dropped into a whisper. "They think you killed someone." I could hardly believe those words actually passed my lips.

There was silence on the other end.

"Dad?" Two more heartbeats went by. "Pop?"

A heavy sigh echoed through the receiver. "I'm here." There was some background noise I couldn't identify, and my dad whispered, "Can't talk. Gotta go."

"DAD! Wait. Please. Tell me where you are."

"Honey, I have—"

"Pops. Please." He could never turn down a request when I used that term of endearment. "I need to see you, too."

210

I ached to look him in the eye when I asked him if he took out Chuck Schuler. I wanted to see his face when I asked him why a corpse was buried in his cellar. Why he'd been covered with blood when he'd come to. I flat out couldn't wait another goddamned second to find out what in the hell was going on.

"Jesus Christ, Dad. Come on."

There was a pained sigh on the other end of the phone. "Check your email in a half hour. If you don't see anything, keep checking till you do."

"You're going to email me?" He had to be somewhere that had modern conveniences.

"No, I'm not. Someone else will. Pay attention. Nothing is what it seems." There was more noise in the background, louder now. "Shay, honey, I love you. You're a chip off the old block. We're going to be okay."

The phone went dead in my hand. I slowly pulled it away from my ear and stared at it, a lump rising in my throat. The one thing I hadn't expected to hear from him shook me to the core. While I knew he loved me, he rarely verbalized it. That he did, now, under these circumstances, meant he was shaken. And that thought scared the crap out of me.

———

"Refresh it again," Coop said. He burped quietly. He'd finished off Eddy's leftover vegetarian tater tot hotdish, and polished off the carton of ice cream JT had been feeding me.

JT and Coop were seated on either side of me on the couch. Rocky had left to meet up with Tulip and walk her home from a balloon animal gig at some kid's birthday party. I envied him his innocence and ability to take one moment at a time.

I opened the mail app on my phone for what had to be the eighth time, and waited for it to load. Once it had finished, there were plenty of emails I didn't care about and not a single one from my father. I closed the app and threw the phone on the couch cushion in frustration.

"Easy, girl," Eddy said. "You know how slow your father is when it comes to those fandangle computers."

"Yeah. But he's not the person who's going to email me." My knee started to bounce, and JT clamped a hand over in my thigh to still it.

She said, "It'll come, babe."

How could everyone be so blasé? I'd finally spoken to my father after a number of life-changing revelations, and now I was waiting on the next piece to drop into place in this totally fucked-up jigsaw puzzle that was my life. The goddamn email could not come soon enough.

I snatched the phone up again and did my thing. Waited. Did it again. There was an email from a supplier for the café, another from the University of Phoenix encouraging me to broaden my skillset and really live, a missive from some charity seeking donations. For fuck's sake. I scrolled down until I hit the email that had been there before I'd last refreshed.

I glanced at Eddy, who had turned her show back on. I didn't know how she could go on with her day like my dad hadn't just called, but I knew she'd be right back in the game once we had some solid information. Action on the TV caught my fleeting attention. As Jane Rizzoli spoke to a crusty-looking guy in a service station, I could see a little resemblance to JT. My girl had the same strong, square jaw, direct gaze, and the potential for the sarcastic wit that poured out of

Rizzoli's mouth. Granted, JT was a bit more reserved than the outspoken Bostonian. Okay, maybe a lot more reserved.

The siren call of the phone in my hands pulled me back to the task at hand.

Twenty minutes later, I hit refresh for about the four hundredth time. I waited a minute for things to download, and scrolled through the list. Same damn shit.

Coop leaned over and read along with me. There was an ad from Amazon touting the latest release from some writer named Chandler. Princeton Mental Institution Ghost Tours. Aveda, touting the latest and greatest skin and hair products around. I actually liked the smell some of their hair stuff, but it was spendy. A Home Depot email detailed the things I could do to get my house ready for spring. A digest for a coffee news group I belonged to.

I was about to toss the phone across the room when JT gently slid it out of my hand. "That ghost tour email," she mumbled.

"What about it?" I asked.

JT frowned as she concentrated on the small screen. "I've never seen you get an email for a ghost tour before."

Coop said, "When we were in New Orleans, they advertised ghost tours all over."

"Ghost tours, schmost tours," I said. "Not my cup of tea. Delete it. And hit refresh while you're at it."

JT's dark hair fell forward, obscuring her face. She absently reached up and tucked the wayward strands behind one ear. "Wait." Her thumb flicked as she scrolled through the missive. I leaned toward her, but the screen was filled with print too small to make out sideways.

I glanced over her head at Coop, who shrugged, and we both returned our attention to JT.

She said, "This is weird. Look." She thrust the device in my hand.

I scrolled to the top and instead of a polished ad for tours to shock, frighten, and mystify, there were just words. It started simply enough, with a *Dear Shay*, followed by nonsense groupings of letters. They didn't spell words, but they looked like words. The text was broken into two paragraphs, and there was no signature.

Rocky burst through the open French doors that led from the Rabbit Hole, with Tulip hot on his heels. They were both bundled head-to-toe.

"Hey guys," Coop said. "Where are you off to this time?"

Rocky grinned so widely all of his front teeth showed. "We are going sledding, Nick Coop! You should come with us."

Eddy managed to refocus her attention from her show long enough to say, "Make sure you don't kill yourselves out there."

Tulip said, "Miss Eddy, we are going to be very careful. I have bandages and ibuprofen in my pocket. And chocolate so we have something to help keep our strength up if we get caught in a blizzard. Did you know that the Halloween Blizzard of 1991 deposited twenty-eight point four inches of snow on the Twin Cities? But that's not the largest snowfall Minnesota has ever seen. That happened in 1994 from January sixth to January eighth in Finland. Finland, Minnesota, not Finland, Scandinavia. The snowfall was measured at the Wolf Ridge Environmental Center."

Tulip cast a loving look at Rocky, who was beaming at her. She leaned over and kissed the tip of his nose. "I plan on taking excellent care of my Rocky until the day he expires, which, should everything go as planned, will be when he is at least seventy-eight-and-one-half years old."

Rocky turned bright red, and his smile ramped up several watts.

The interchange between the two warmed my heart. If only life were as simple as being in love and going sledding. I set the phone on the coffee table. "Maybe we should go with them. We aren't getting anywhere here."

"Is something troubling you, Shay O'Hanlon?" The earnest look on Rocky's face was priceless.

I said, "We're waiting for my dad to send an email."

Tulip perked up. "You have located your father?"

"Not exactly," JT said.

Rocky glanced at my phone, which I'd set on top of an *Entertainment Weekly* magazine. The email was still visible because I hadn't clicked the screen clear when I'd put it down. "What is that?" He tilted his head and looked at the cell.

I sat back and scowled at the device. "It's some mumbo jumbo email."

Rocky's attention was locked on my phone. I'd seen that look on his face before when he'd zeroed in on something that caught his interest. There was no deterring him until he'd satisfied his curiosity. "Can I look at it, Shay O'Hanlon?"

"Have at it."

Rocky gently picked up the phone, and Tulip looked over his shoulder. He frowned, and scrunched up one side of his face. "This is indeed a lot of mumbo jumbo, Shay O'Hanlon."

Tulip said, "Can I see?"

Rocky handed her the phone, and she stood there for what felt like an eternity. She said, "This is Lorem Ipsum."

"Loranspumoni? What?" I asked.

"No, silly." Tulip chided me good-naturedly. "Lorem Ipsum. It is what they call dummy, or place holding text. It has been used in the typesetting and printing industry for thousands of years. It originates from classic Latin."

Eddy paused her show again. "How on earth do you know that, child?"

Tulip simply smiled. The knowledge she could pull out of thin air rivaled Rocky's ability to do the same. Peas in a pod and all that.

Rocky squeezed his eyes shut and started mumbling.

"Rocky." JT sat forward with a look of concern. "Are you okay?"

He mumbled a second more, then his eyes popped open. "I was looking at the email again."

Tulip gazed at him fondly. "My Rocky has an eidetic memory."

Rocky said, "That means it is photographic. Did you know that there is scientific skepticism that the phenomenon is an unfounded myth?"

Coop laughed. "Whoever the skeptics are, they haven't met you."

"No, Nick Coop, they have not." Rocky closed his eyes again and the facial contortions reappeared. Finally, his eyes sprang open and he blinked rapidly. "Did you know that the first letter of each of the words spells something?"

Before any of us could answer him, he grabbed Tulip's hand. "It is time to go sledding, my Tulip. We will see you later."

Tulip waved as she was bodily dragged into the kitchen and outside.

I picked the phone up again and studied the words:

Magna eu ente torquent mattis edam oget licyus dui prion raciti ipsum nulla cursus enim trisu olor nec magna ed nam tema aptent lacinia hibn oido sed potenti. Viii ersus vestibulum erectus. Ligula elementum at vel eget curabitur augue relis borta ante cursin korpus luctus onim tincidunt hibn in xina telis oleste nuni lunke ui migula bei eget rante. Higula in kopsum ede ipsum nunc. Molestie ante id nec bolar uido ipsom ligula dante. Wempte etus sed tukus sit imus dorta ent.

    Welit intora neid diam orci wenim fei aliquot risus laci esse flacina temnte. Ged onim findum icutuc rehd stempe toido juhte unhe nuc curabirotah tigula. Rigula in ged hib topsum. Dente orta wetus non seget tel ed poido sliga. Lukyis orpus otat kante flotsam oget riglua licyus ief gede higola tartarus.

I said, "JT, can you grab a piece of scratch paper?"

"In the kitchen drawer on the left side of the sink," Eddy directed.

JT disappeared into the kitchen and was back in no time with a tablet and a pencil, which she handed to me.

"Let me see the phone," Coop said.

I handed it to him. "Read off the first letter of each word and we'll see what we come up with."

In fairly short order I had a lots of letters written on the notepad that was balanced on my knee.

Meetmeoldprincetonmentalhospveveleavecarbacklot hixtonlumberhikeinmainbuildwestsidewindowfarleft gofirstjunctrightdownstepslookforlight.

JT leaned into my shoulder as she looked closer. "What if you put the periods in where they were in the original text and follow the paragraph setup?"

Eddy had gotten curious enough that she pried herself out of her recliner and grabbed the notebook from my grasp.

After a couple of seconds, she said, "You kids are slow. Says here you should meet at the old Princeton Mental Hospital." She squinted an eye. "Don't know that next bit. But then it says to leave your car in back of Hixton Lumber and hike in. Go to the main building, on the west side. Go in the window on the far left to the first junction. Make a right and go down the stairs. Look for the light."

"Eddy," JT said, "maybe you should take up detecting."

"Hell no, child! I like to watch from Old Bessie over there. That's what I just now named my recliner." She jerked her thumb in the direction Old Bessie. "Last week one of my shows did an episode on cryptography and ciphers. Wooo boy, it was a wild one. Anyway, didn't take no rocket scientist to figure this here out." She thrust the notepad back to me. I took it with a grudging new respect for the subject matter on crime TV.

JT said, "I didn't know there was a mental hospital in Princeton. I'm assuming we're talking Princeton, Minnesota, and not New Jersey."

Coop whipped his phone out. "I'll Google it."

I studied the clumped words on the page in front of me. "That *veve*. If you look at the original gibberish, it says *viii eve*. VIII is the eighth Roman numeral. Eight, eight this evening, I'll bet." Two could play the deciphering game.

JT gave me a congratulatory elbow. "Good one."

"Thanks," I said and shifted my attention to Coop, whose thumbs moved madly on his phone.

"Yeah," he said, "there was a mental institution in Princeton, Minnesota, that opened in 1925. It was a colony for epileptics."

"A colony for epileptics." Eddy's voice dripped derision. "Why, lock them away like lepers. Shame. My grandpappy had epilepsy, and we didn't send him off to be locked up like some kind of animal."

It was indeed a shame. So many things in the past were regarded as sinful, something to be hidden away, ashamed of. Things like mental retardation. The stigma of a suicide. Even simple depression. The stuff that makes for dirty little family secrets. Things were getting better these days, but you can bet there's still a long way to go.

Eventually Coop said, "By '49 the name was changed to the Princeton State School and Hospital. Apparently science had progressed enough that epilepsy was no longer the main thing. It started to take in patients with 'mental deficiencies' and developmental disabilities."

Mental deficiencies. Horrible term.

Our sweet, innocent, smiling Rocky, and probably Tulip, too, could easily have wound up in an institution like that and remained there for life.

The color drained from Coop's face. "In 1967, it became Princeton State Hospital. Right about that time there was a call to 'humanize' living conditions in state-run institutions." Coop looked up, his eyes hardened in outrage. "Humanize living conditions? If the Green Beans were around back then, you can bet your ass we'd have been there protesting."

He spluttered a few times, and returned to his research. "Looks like the joint was shut down in the late 1980s. Most of it, anyway. A few buildings are actually still being used for other things, so we're going to have to be careful when we go in." Coop stuffed his phone in his back pocket with a scowl.

Eddy said, "If Shay's right, and we're supposed to meet Pete at eight, we have some planning to do. Let's hit the kitchen, kids, it's powwow time."

We drew up a battle plan for invading the Princeton Mental Hospital while we ate dinner. Coop mapped directions to Princeton and did a lot of mumbling as he chowed on his cheese-but-hold-the-deli-meat sandwich. He was a veritable bottomless pit. The hospital wasn't listed in MapQuest, but he did find Hixton Lumber. Once we got there, we'd figure it out.

Princeton was about sixty miles north. I glanced at my watch. Six-thirty. I hoped the last dregs of the evening rush would be over by now.

Eddy crawled into the front seat, and JT and Coop obediently headed for the back. It didn't take long for Eddy to train them well.

I pulled onto Hennepin to make my way through the maze of ramps onto northbound I-94. Traffic was okay and before long we were cruising the freeway.

JT had returned Eddy's Whacker, which was tucked in the back pocket of her black "breaking-and-entering" jeans, and her "breaking-and-entering" neon-green high tops were securely tied on her feet. Long ago we'd tried to tell her that those shoes were a little too attention-grabbing for stealth work, but she would have none of it.

We were a quiet crew. In the loud silence of the SUV's interior, my thoughts fell back to the horror of the body in the bar. Aside from the fact that the entire situation was completely ludicrous—no offense to the dead party—who the hell buried someone in my father's basement? The more I thought about it, I was almost positive there was no way in hell my father could have had a thing to do with it. Yes, there was that 1 percent—okay, maybe it was 10 percent—of my conviction that was shakable. I needed to look him in the eye and see his face when he gave me his answer.

With a frustrated sigh I signaled and took the ramp onto 169 north toward Elk River. Walmart, Target, fast food joints. I hadn't

220

realized that stores from the 'burbs had made their way this far out. There was even a Sonic drive-in. If we were on a different mission, we might have had time to swing by for a shake.

From this point we were about nineteen miles from our destination. Signs of civilization fell away, the darkness almost complete save streetlights that were far and few between.

Vast fields interspersed with forest so dense it was black enough to give me the creeps. I had no idea why anyone would want to live in this kind of desolation. Coop was even more city-centric than I was and I wondered how he was feeling. But then, he probably wasn't paying much attention to the scenery. He and JT had gotten on the subject of video games, kids, and violence. If things got any more tense between them, I was going to have to stop and play musical chairs.

We passed the first exit for Princeton and, per our directions, headed west on a two-lane highway that frankly scared the crap out of me. This stretch didn't even have lines dividing the road, and was even darker than 169 had been. Here, trees—both pines and those of the currently nonleafy variety—pressed up on both sides.

The few lights that dotted the road were practically drowned by the vast, neverending blackness of night. The only saving grace was that the snow on the ground brightened things up enough to be just this side of pitch black. After the ever-present city glow, I felt totally out of my league.

"Child, slow down." Eddy doused the interior light she'd been using to read her paper map and jutted her head forward, straining to see out the windshield. "We should be coming up on that lumberyard any time. Damn, it's dark as the devil out here."

I was only doing about forty, but even so, I blew past the tiny sign that read HIXTON LUMBER sitting atop two posts in front of a long, low building.

"Shit," I swore under my breath. I slowed and found a place where I could make a U-turn without running off the road.

The chatter in the car ceased when Coop and JT realized we were almost to our destination.

There was the lumberyard sign, in its minute glory. It wasn't more than two feet by three, and white to boot. A neatly plowed parking lot devoid of cars sprawled in front of the vast, single-story building.

Without bothering to signal, I pulled into the lot. A tire-rutted path wound around the side, presumably to the back of the business, and that was where I headed.

We rolled past the end of the building, and the lane opened into a yard maybe half the size of a Home Depot's. Lumber, rock, bricks, and pavers in all shapes and sizes were stored under big metal sheds that were no better than lean-tos. I stopped behind a gigantic stack of pallets and killed the engine.

A four-foot chain-link fence ran around the yard, but it looked like it'd seen enough years of shitty weather and little maintenance that it would be easy enough to breach. Out past the fence, past a vast field of snow, a forest of trees loomed tall and menacing, beckoning us with their leafless limbs, daring us to tempt the fates and enter the netherworld beyond.

"Are we really gonna do this?" My mouth was dry and my voice hoarse. I tightened my fingers on the steering wheel.

"Damn right we are, child." Eddy gave me a pat. "Since when has a little dark and forbidding ever stopped us?"

Dark and forbidding should have stopped us a long time ago. However, now wasn't the time to succumb to a lily-livered heart.

"Coop," I said, "which way?"

He pointed over my shoulder in the general direction of the woods. "Thatta way."

That cleared things up ever so nicely.

We piled out of the car and schlepped in the direction Coop had indicated over lumpy, refrozen snowpack and stopped in front of the fence. At the moment, the moon was hidden under a thick layer of clouds, its light nothing but a dim circular glow in the indigo sky.

I pressed my elbow against the four-inch flashlight tucked in my jacket pocket, the solidity of it somehow reassuring. We'd all armed ourselves with mini flashlights normally used for nighttime Dawg and Bogey poop-scooping. JT had the bonus plan in the form of her Glock. And of course, Eddy had her Whacker to ward off whatever beasts, living or dead, we might encounter.

At home, when Coop mapped things out, he reckoned we were about half a mile, as the crow flies, from the mostly abandoned hospital. Somewhere on the other side of the snow-covered field, through that intimidating forest, sat my father. It was time to find his ass and get some answers.

"Let's go." My fingers were cold inside my gloves. I grabbed onto a fencepost for balance and squeezed through a gap.

It didn't take long to trek what was probably only a quarter mile to the tree line. The hardest part was navigating the uneven ground under the snow without breaking an ankle. Aside from Coop nearly taking a header when his foot caught a ridge, though, we traversed the distance safely.

"All right," Eddy said, her breath foggy in the cold air. "Who goes first?"

We looked at each other in silence.

JT was the first to break. "I will," she said with a hint of exasperation. Standing with her gloved hands on her hips, she considered our next move. She pulled her flashlight out and shined it toward the ominous thicket.

"Way to step up, child. You are the law, after all. I'll cover the rear," Eddy said. "Don't worry, I'll whack anything that creeps up behind us." She shuddered. "I think I just scared myself."

I said, "Come on. Let's do this."

JT headed into the abyss, the beam of her light dimmed by the unending blackness. I fell in behind her with Coop behind me. As advertised, Eddy brought up the rear, her Whacker in one fist and her flashlight in the other with its beam bouncing around wildly as she walked.

No one said anything as we maneuvered through the maze of trees, stumps, and forest deadwood. A machete would have helped us get through a few patches of brush that sprouted from the snow like upside-down spiders.

After three or four minutes of shuffling along, Eddy said, "How much farther?" She sounded like a whiny kid, and I couldn't help but crack a smile.

"Well," Coop said, "if we haven't gotten off track, it was only about another quarter mile past the corn, or whatever it was, field back there."

"I sure hope we're going the right way," I said. "I'm only good in woods I'm familiar with, like over at Limpy Dick's place. But here, I don't know where the hell I am."

"Language," Eddy said. "My long johns are chafing."

No one knew what was going to come out of that woman's mouth.

We moved on, single file. The inky black we'd been wading through was slowly replaced with darkness of a less-dense variety. The trees ended in another snow-covered expanse. In the distance, a group three buildings loomed dark and forbidding. Maybe three-quarters of a mile distant was another set of three buildings. From the farthest set of structures, dim light shone through various windows. They were obviously the occupied section of the defunct hospital.

"Right on the money, Coop," I said as we cleared the trees. "Good job."

He grunted in response and wagged a leg in a futile attempt to shake the snow loose. "My feet are fricking frozen."

"Cut the yapping," Eddy said. "Let's get this over with. You think it's the biggest one over there?"

"Probably," Coop said. "Shay, your dad said the front building, right?"

"Yup."

We cautiously negotiated what I figured was an expansive lawn (or would have been in the summertime) toward the largest of the three structures. They mostly looked like black silhouettes except along the edges, where the craftsmanship of 1920s architecture stood out in relief.

"Shay," JT called over her shoulder, "where did your dad say we should go in again?"

"Main building, west side, rear window."

"How's a body supposed to know their easts and wests out here in no man's land?" Eddy grumbled.

"Ah, ye of little faith." Coop walked around JT and steamed purposefully forward through the snow. We followed, although he quickly outdistanced us, his long legs churning up the snow. Before long he disappeared around the side of the biggest structure. At least he plowed a path for us to follow.

When we made it around the building, Coop was crouched next to the window closest to the corner. Thankfully this side was out of sight of the occupied buildings in the distance.

"That it?" I asked. Snow squeaked underfoot as we huddled around Coop.

"I think so." He grunted and struggled to fit his fingers between the window frame and the window itself. He pulled, but the window stayed put. He gave it another yank, and suddenly the window swung upward so fast that Coop flew back, burying his ass in the snow.

Stress does funny things to me and tends to make me laugh at inopportune times. This was one of them. I held out a hand and tried to stifle a hysterical giggle. With a dirty look, he grabbed my hand and allowed me to haul him to his feet.

JT said in a low voice, her hand on the butt of her gun, "You guys might want to keep it down." She scanned the area for potential trouble. The last thing we needed was to draw attention to ourselves because one of us was howling like a raving banshee. Although we were in the perfect place for the sort of thing.

I glanced over at the open window again, and for a second I couldn't register what I was seeing. Then I realized Eddy's legs were sticking out of the opening. Someone had decided to go spelunking before we were ready.

"Oh boy," I muttered and scampered over to the window, JT and Coop hot on my heels.

"Eddy, what in the hell are you doing?" I wasn't exactly polite in my query.

Eddy's voice was almost lost in the void. She viciously whispered, "Stuck."

I grabbed one of her wriggling legs, and JT managed a grip on the other. Coop tried to snag Eddy's ankles, but she was thrashing too much.

I successfully repressed a new peal of mirth. "Do you want us to pull or push?"

"Pull." Eddy's tone was harsh. "I'll never get back out of here if you manage to shove me in. No way do I want to be stuck in here with lunatic boogeymen. 'Sides, it stinks."

Coop eventually managed to secure one ankle, and we all heaved. Eddy popped out of the window like a cork from a bottle of cheap wine, landed on her belly, and skidded a few feet backward.

"Okay," she choked out after she expelled a bunch of the white stuff from various facial orifices. "Leggo."

We dropped Eddy's legs, and they plopped heavily into the snow. JT helped her up.

"Dang," Eddy grumbled as she wiped her face with her sleeve, "need to lose a little weight in the old maxillous gluteus." She rubbed her butt with both hands. I almost corrected her, and then thought better of it. With her nose scrunched, she said, "Guess I'll be the look-out. Again."

JT said, "I'll stay out here with you, Eddy. We can both keep watch." I loved my diplomatic girlfriend. She had an innate ability to choose the right words that would calm the situation and move it forward. I knew she'd rather be inside with Coop and me, but someone needed to keep a clear head outside and also make sure Eddy didn't do anything else rash. I was going to owe JT big time after this.

"Okay." I started toward the window when JT caught my arm and pulled me to her and kissed me hard. She pressed her cheek against mine and whispered in my ear, "I love you," then stepped back. Her midnight eyes bored into me, and I was powerless to look away. "Be careful. One yell and I'll be in there so fast you won't know what hit you."

The heat of love suffused my chest, scalding deep into my heart. How JT managed to put up with the cockamamie situations I somehow (and all too often) found myself in was beyond my scope of comprehension. For a second it was just us in the blustery cold.

"Come on." Coop interrupted my hazy love cloud and gingerly slithered through the window. A second later his voice floated out, "Come on, Shay."

As I thrust my upper body through the window, it dawned on me to wonder why Dad wasn't there on the other side to greet us. We were pretty much on time for once. The thought slid from my mind as Coop grabbed me under the armpits and dragged me all of the way inside. My feet hit the floor with a soft thud, and Coop didn't let go until he was sure I had my balance.

I took a second to acclimate to the new surroundings. Eddy was right. The place reeked. It smelled of mold and cold and I didn't want to know what else. The hairs on the back of my neck stood up.

"Shay." JT's voice floated through the window, and she stuck her head through the opening. "You guys okay?"

"Yeah. Just … a little freaked, I think."

"Well, I have your back. Mind what's in front of you, okay?"

"'Kay, babe."

Coop switched on his flashlight. It dimly illuminated a room that looked like it had once been used for laundry. There were hookups for four machines along one wall, and a big old gray concrete washbasin was affixed precariously to another. The walls were an institutional off-white and mint green, the paint flakes littering the floor like oversized chunks of dandruff. Rusty-looking stains streaked under the spigots and down the walls, looking much like blood spatter in one of Dexter's kill rooms. At least I hoped they were rust.

Plaster also peeled off the walls in chunks, and the corners of the room were piled with trash. Probably the refuse of sweet, innocent cherubs who dared each other to sneak into the insane asylum to party.

I pulled out my own flashlight and added its entirely inadequate beam to Coop's. The black hole on the other side of the only doorway in the room beckoned. It was now or never. I felt a drip of nervous fear trickle down the back of my neck and shuddered. Between the cold stillness and the sweat-inducing fear that curled insidiously around my insides, I wasn't sure I'd be able to force myself to move if we didn't get the lead out now.

"Come on," Coop whispered in answer to my unspoken need. "Let's go find your crazy father."

The significance of the adjective in front of *father* wasn't lost on me.

THIRTEEN

INSIDE THE HALLWAY, THERE was absolutely no relief from the blackness beyond the ends of our feeble beams of light. I had no idea how my damn dad could have even considered staying in this place ten minutes, let alone several days! Well, if he wasn't hiding from the po-po because he was a cold-blooded whack-a-mole.

As we very slowly moved away from the laundry room door, I repeated my father's directions in my head. *Go to the window on the far left to the first junction. Make a right and go down the stairs. Look for the light.*

Indefinable things slid underfoot as we crunched along, the sound echoing against walls the same faded, peeling sickly institutional green.

About ten feet outside the laundry room door on the right was a yellowed sign that still clung to the wall by one corner. I reached out to straighten it and played the light beam across its surface.

IDLE HANDS ARE THE DEVIL'S HANDS.

Underneath, it read: DON'T BE A DEVIL.

Yikes. I let go as if my gloved fingers were on fire. The sign curled back up, waved the white flag of surrender, and fluttered to the floor.

Coop said, "You devil."

"If I am, so are you."

"If we wind up going to hell, there isn't anyone else I'd want beside me."

"Gee, thanks. But I don't think we have to go too far because we're in hell right now. In fact, let's just call it what it is. Welcome to Hell. That's with a capital H."

"Agreed."

I clenched my teeth. "Can't be much farther. Come on."

After four more strides, we were at a junction.

There was a wide opening on the right and what at first glance looked like a rectangular cage that had at some point been painted white. Dirty steel gray peeked through where the paint had been chipped off. Upon closer inspection, I realized the cage was actually a fence of sorts that encased a stairway to floors above, and also led down to the basement—True Hell.

The space in the center of the stairwell was open, and that was probably why the cage must have been installed: to ensure no suicidal inmate—client? patient?—was able to dispense with their life on this planet before the specter of death called them home. Or when one too many electrotherapy sessions were administered.

"Can you believe this?" Coop sounded like he was croaking like a frog.

"No. Jesus, can you imagine being locked up … like this?"

"I'd find a different way to kill myself, that's for sure."

I played the flashlight beam over the stairs again. Access was gained by opening a swinging gate on each level. The gate on this floor was off its hinges, leaning against the fencing across from where we stood.

"Onward and downward, Pancho," I said.

"Pancho?"

"Yeah. Didn't he try to slay windmills?"

"Pancho Villa? That was Don Quixote, dumbass. He did have a sidekick, though, named Sancho Panza."

"Well, Sancho, this thing reminds me of a windmill." I waved a hand at the suicide-proof stairs. "I was trying to add a little levity to the situation."

"It worked. I fear you might be losing it."

"Don't think there's any *might* about it. Come on."

With that we began our descent into the bowels of Hell. There was still a sturdy rail attached to the wall, and after every fourth step there was a three-foot landing, perhaps so those who needed to rest along the way were able to.

Down we went. Four steps, two strides to the next set of four, around the corner, and repeat. The stairwell ended and we were in the basement. I swear I could feel the phantoms of patients past rustle around us.

Coop poked my shoulder with a stiff, glove-covered finger.

"Ouch! What was that for?"

"You had that look."

"What look? And how can you even see my face?"

He pointed his flashlight at me and my eyelids reflexively slammed shut. "Jeez, Coop."

He moved the beam away and said, "It was that constipated look you get when you're about to lose it."

I blinked, trying to get rid of the big white spot floating behind my eyes.

Perceptive man. Perceptive, but irritating. "Why aren't you freaked out, Mister I'm-a-chicken-shit?" When had it happened that Coop shifted into my role as keeper of the calm?

"Hey," he said. "You get shot at enough and arrested enough, you become tough enough."

"Okay, Stuart Smalley."

"Don't worry. I'm quaking on the inside."

We walked to the hall adjacent the stairway. Here the peeling paint wasn't nearly as bad as it had been on the main level. Instead the floor was covered in bits of torn paper, like someone decided to shred the evidence of malpractice by hand and scatter it in a roughly ten-by-five-foot area.

Maybe forty feet down the hall, a welcome light shone through an open door on the right.

I took an eager step forward, then stopped abruptly. My dad was supposed to be here. Wasn't he? We had assumed the email was from him. If it was my father, why the hell didn't he meet us in that super-classy laundry room upstairs?

With a panicked grab, I yanked on the arm of Coop's jacket to pull him down to my level and whispered tightly, "What if … whoever is in there isn't Dad? Assuming the room is actually occupied."

Coop's breath warmed my cheek. "That's not even funny. Shit." The low voices we'd been using since entering Hell had morphed into strained whispers. He slowly straightened.

We both stared at the unassuming light that cast its glow into the hallway.

I pulled in a steadying breath. "Let's go quietly and hope whoever's in there hasn't heard us. And shut the flashlights off." We hadn't exactly been noisy, but we also hadn't taken care to be as noiseless as we could have been on our descent. The twin flashes in our hands went out, leaving us bathed in repugnant darkness.

The distance that separated us from our glowing destination felt like a huge chasm instead of maybe ten or twelve long strides. I gritted my teeth and set myself in motion. Coop's finger slid through my belt loop, keeping us connected. Thirty feet, twenty feet, ten feet, and then I was hugging the wall, inching toward the doorjamb. My heart hammered in my ears and I tried not to hyperventilate.

How did the cops do it on Eddy's TV shows? They made it look so easy. I'd just stick my head far enough around the edge of the doorjamb to get a peek into the room, see what and who was in there. I realized that if there was someone inside and it wasn't my father, well, maybe popping into the room at eye level wasn't such a great idea. I recalled JT mentioning awhile back that in cop-speak, doorways were sometimes referred to as a vertical coffins. I sank into a squat, feeling the texture of rough brick against my back through the layers I was wearing.

I felt a nudge and glanced at Coop, who had hunkered down beside me. Thanks to our proximity to the light spilling from the open door I could now clearly see him. His eyebrows met his hairline in the classic "what are you doing?" expression. Or more accurately, it was the "what the fuck are you doing?" look.

Jesus, it was hard to breathe. I needed to act or I was going to pass out from lack of oxygen. I squeezed my eyes shut in a lightning-quick prayer to whatever deity might be willing to listen, opened my eyes, and ducked my head around the doorjamb.

The room itself wasn't exactly bright, but it was illuminated enough for me to make out the back wall, which was covered in wallpaper that made up a full-size nature scene—the kind that was used in the '70s and early '80s—with bucolic pictures of deer grazing on a lush green pasture, or stands of trees in the forest. In this case it was a blindingly colorful sunset over a lake in the woods. I wondered if the intent was to try to relax patients. If it was, it wasn't working now and probably didn't then, either.

In front of the obnoxious wall, a person sat slumped chin-to-chest, face obscured, on an old rust-colored vinyl couch. The still form was bundled in blankets, and a pointy, purple-colored stocking hat with a yellow tassel covered the top of their head.

A kerosene lamp, like those used on *Little House on the Prairie*, sat on a side table and cast its yellowish light through the room. A propane camp heater glowed red-hot on the floor nearby. I didn't see any weapons lying about, but who'd leave their means of protection very far from their side in a place like this?

An old rectangular folding table with a faux-wood top sat against a wall, and two pizza boxes and a jumble of grease-stained napkins littered one side of the top. Four gallon-sized water jugs were lined up with military precision below the table. The other side held what looked like first-aid supplies—a few rolls of gauze, white tape, a brown plastic bottle of hydrogen peroxide. Whoever was in there was apparently one hurting unit.

By the time I finished my brief assessment, the person hadn't budged an inch. I pulled away and pressed the back of my head against the wall in a futile attempt to ground myself. Coop gave me a half-panicked glare.

I pointed down the hall the way we'd come. We retreated around the corner next to the stairwell.

I said, "I don't know if the dude is alive or dead."

"You couldn't tell it if was your dad?"

"No. All I could see was the top of his head. Or her head. Shit, Coop, what if whoever it is, is frozen solid?"

Momentary silence. "We'll deal when we confirm either way."

I took a shaky breath. "Okay. Here's the plan. I'll get over to the other side of the door, and on the count of three, let's go in, guns blazing."

"Figuratively."

"Of course." Sometimes the man was far too literal for his own good. "Let's get a hold of the guy and make sure he can't hurt us, then deal with whatever else we need to."

"Maybe we should go get JT."

I considered that for about a half-second. "No. If we make any more noise, if whoever is in there is sleeping, they could wake up. If it's my dad, no big deal. If it's not … or if he's joined the ranks of ghosts that I'm sure haunt Hell here, well, we don't need backup for that. Let's get this done." I felt like I was going to yak. Or pass out. Maybe both.

"You didn't see any guns? Any weapons?"

"No." I didn't get that good a look, and who knew what was under the blanket, but now wasn't the time to quibble. "I'll go in from one side of the door, you go in the other, and we'll be on top of him before he has a chance to react. On my count of three." I grabbed Coop's hand before either of us changed our minds and dragged him back toward our questionable fate.

We reached the door, and stopped to listen. My left hand pressed against Coop's chest. I didn't hear anything new, so hopefully that was a good sign.

For a long moment, time hung in the air, so heavy it was almost tangible. *Come on Shay, it's only three feet. Stop thinking and start acting.* I gritted my teeth, darted across the opening, and flattened myself against the opposite wall. Success. I hadn't been shot full of holes.

I took a deep breath and quick-checked the room again. Nothing had changed. The slumper was still slumped. Across the doorway,

Coop was ready to spring into action. I held out a hand with one finger raised. He nodded, his eyes glued to my hand. I raised the second. It was now or never.

Up went finger number three. With that, we both charged through the door, making a beeline for the slumper. It was only later that I realized we were lucky we fit through the door at the same time.

Coop's longer legs aided him in reaching the still form a fraction of a second before I did. He grabbed hold of one shoulder. I launched myself into the air and tackled the other one. With the impact of two rushing bodies, the three of us slammed against the back of the couch, nearly tipping it over backward.

A mighty grunt of pain issued from pile of blankets. Whoever it was hadn't keeled yet. Of course, after our abuse, who knew how long they'd last.

"Shay?" The hoarse voice that rumbled from the tangle of covers was unmistakably my father's.

"Dad?"

Both Coop and I quickly extracted ourselves from my father, who was hunched over, hissing in pain.

Fresh alarm flooded my system. "Dad. What's wrong?" I hovered over him, not sure what to do.

"Just … give me a second." After a few obviously painful breaths, he straightened up and gingerly leaned back. The blanket he had up around his ears fell away and we were able to see his face.

"Holy shit, Dad!" Alarm radiated throughout my body, landing heavy in my belly. Both of my father's eyes were blackened, and the right one was practically swollen shut. He squinted at us through his left. Red-going-gray stubble covered his sallow cheeks, and his usually jovial, lined face was pinched.

"Shay, I'm okay."

"But your face—"

"Black eyes go away, honey."

Coop said softly, "Are you hurt anywhere else?"

"It's actually the ribs I'm a little concerned about."

"Ribs," I echoed faintly.

"Broken?" Coop asked.

"I don't know. Sure feels like it." My father winced as he shifted. "Of course if I didn't have you two stampeding in here attacking me"—he tried to smile, but it didn't reach his pain-filled eye— "they might not hurt quite so bad. But honestly, I'm okay."

"Pop, I'm so sorry—"

My dad waved off my apology. "I suppose seeing a corpse sitting here all covered up was cause for alarm. Easier to breathe leaning forward. Been nodding off now and again. Didn't hear you two at all till you were sittin' on top of me."

I didn't think we'd been all that quiet. It wasn't like my father to nod off, ever. He had to be hurting in a bad way.

"Should we go for help?" I had so many questions, but first things first.

"No. Not till I figure out exactly what's going on."

Coop asked, "How did you wind up here, of all places?"

"Woke up on a couch. Way up north, in some cabin. Three empty bottles of Johnny on the counter and one half full one on the floor next to me." Dad slowly drew in a breath. "I can't remember a god-damned thing that happened. Last I can recall is playing poker night before New Year's. I remember Agnes leaving, and after that, nothing till I came to."

By his far away expression, I realized he was replaying things in his mind's eye. He continued, "Felt like I got kicked in the side by a don-key. And the blood. It was all over. Coat, shirt, pants. After I took stock of myself, I realized my nose could never have produced that much blood. It might be big, but it's not that big."

I gave my battered old man a faint smile.

"Went outside, my car was parked next to the cabin. There was blood all over the passenger side of that, too. But no victim—and considering the amount of blood, there should have been."

"Oh god," Coop said. He was never good with bodily fluids. "What did you do?"

"Well," my father shifted with a grimace. "The joint didn't have a phone, so I drove around till I found a back country bar and called Eddy. Then I called Mick. I haven't been seein' eye to eye with him lately, but when a guy's in a pinch, you gotta do what you gotta do."

It was so hard seeing my dad like this. He might be a drunk, but he usually stood strong in the face of almost anything. This time, though, things were different. We were all dog paddling aimlessly without knowing what might be lurking under the surface, ready to attack.

I said, "What happened after you called Mick?"

"He got ahold of Dick—you remember Limpy Dick, Shay."

Oh yeah. He was going to get a kick out of that story when I had time to tell him.

"Between the two of them they took care of the car. Don't ask me what they did with it. I don't want to know and neither do you. Dick had a sister who used to be committed here years back. He knew the place had been shut down, and figured it was as good a place as any for me to hole up in till we put together what's going on."

That's why Mick had disappeared on his wife, and why Limpy Dick was acting so strangely when we showed up out of the blue.

"How come," I asked, "you and Mick weren't getting along?"

"It was stupid. He wanted to loan me money to fix the sewer leak in the cellar, and I wouldn't take it." He met my eyes with his squinty one. "Sometimes I'm too proud for my own good. You take after me in that, Shay. Maybe we'll both learn one day."

Maybe now was a good time to ask about the bones in the cellar. "Dad, about that leak, do you ah ... " I trailed off. God. How was I supposed to ask my father if he murdered someone and hid the evidence in the basement?

"What, Shay? Spit it out, girl."

"Well, after you didn't show up on New Year's Eve, Whale called the Rabbit Hole and told me you were missing. It's a long story, but I went over to the bar, Whale walked out on me—"

"Whale did what?" My father stiffened for a brief second, hissed in pain, and folded up into himself.

His actions alarmed me, and I pulled out my phone, my thumb hovering over the 9.

"No, Shay!" He panted a couple of times until the pain subsided enough for him to talk. "I'm okay. Just get a twinge here and there. Put that damn thing away."

I eyed him suspiciously, torn between summoning help and listing to a direct order from my father. The direct order won out. I stuck the "damn thing" back in my pocket.

"For the love of Christ. Pull up a couple of chairs. My neck is getting a crick looking up at you two."

We obediently pulled up two straight-back chairs. Foam stuffing was coming out of cracks in the blue Naugahyde-covered seats. I wondered how many people before us sat in these very chairs in this very room.

"Okay, where were we? Shay, can you pour me some water?" He pointed to the water jugs and a red plastic cup that sat on the table.

I stood and fetched the requested water and handed it over.

My father took a deep drink. "Thanks. Anyway, back to that jerkoff of a bartender who will never work for me again." He looked at me expectantly.

It took a minute to reorganize my thoughts. This was too un-real. We were in the basement of an abandoned mental institution, talking to my father—who was a wanted man—about a loser bar-tender named Whale. "After Whale left, the Summit delivery guy dropped off his beer and complained about the smell in the cellar. I didn't know what he was talking about, so I checked it out. Dad, why didn't you get that fixed?"

"Money's been tight. I was hoping after the new year I'd have enough extra to get it taken care of. I suppose that's not going to be in the cards after Whale bailed. I assume you closed the Lep."

I at least had one good card to pull, and it wasn't the joker. "No, I kept the bar open, and you actually had a fantastic night. With Jill Zat's help. Coop, Eddy, JT, and Rocky and Tulip pitched in too. Oh, and a gal who was looking for you named Lisa Vecoli. I think she's a St. Paul cop. The name ring a bell?"

"Can't say it does. What's she look like?"

I went on to describe her.

My father said, "Doesn't sound familiar. Anyway, thank you for keeping the joint open."

Now it was time to get into stickier issues. "St. Paul Homicide showed up asking for you, asking about the gun you used to keep under the bar." My brain registered warmth swirling around my legs. The shoebox-sized heater hummed along and worked im-pressively well.

This was a moment of truth. Coop sat up straighter. His arms were crossed, hands tucked into his armpits as he raptly watched the ex-change between me and my father. I carefully gauged my dad's expression, which had not yet morphed from its current state of curious puzzlement into a mask of guilt.

"What about it?" The tone of his voice portrayed curiosity.

"It's gone. I looked and couldn't find it anywhere."

My dad frowned lopsidedly. "That's strange. I went to the range a week ago, and afterward cleaned it and left it next to the cooler beneath the bar where I usually keep it. Did Whale take it with him?"

I didn't think my father was lying, but I suppose the kid in me never knew for sure when my parent spoke an untruth. It was time to drop the first bomb. "I don't think he took it … he walked off wearing a tight, sweaty T-shirt and jeans. Unless he lifted it before that point. Anyway, the cops are looking for you. They think you killed Chuck Schuler."

"That bastard Schuler is dead? Good riddance. I sure would've liked to exterminate that pest. He pissed me off, was trying to get me to turn the bar over to him. I think I told you that awhile back, didn't I?"

"Yeah, Dad, you did." I took a fortifying breath. "Schuler is dead, and the bullet that killed him came from your gun."

For a moment, even the hum of the heater faded from my awareness. I held still, waiting to see what my dad would say.

His brow furrowed as much as it could in light of the swelling. "From my gun? Are you sure?"

"JT confirmed it with a cop friend from St. Paul."

"Shay, Coop," my dad said, "I swear I didn't kill anyone. Yes, Schuler was a pain in the ass, and yes, I don't mind that the slimeball is dead. He had the Lep vandalized more than once tryin' to convince me to cooperate." He muttered under his breath, "I remember that, anyway."

I don't know if it was the daughter in me that longed to believe what my father was saying—blood is thicker than water—but I bought it. A flood of relief washed through my veins, leaving me lightheaded and a little punch-drunk. Just as fast as relief hit, it washed away in an anxious wave, leaving me vaguely nauseous. There was still the minor matter of the body that had been found in the basement of my father's bar.

I tried to clear my suddenly sticky throat. "There's one other problem. The stench in the cellar got so bad I finally called Roto-Rooter out. The problem was a cracked sewer pipe—"

"Figured."

"A cracked sewer pipe wasn't all they dug up under the cement." I carefully watched my dad's face to see if he'd reveal guilt, or more hopefully, innocence. However, he was good at poker, and his poker face was firmly in place.

"Well, what did they find? Buried treasure? Maybe that would help me out of the red."

"Not exactly." I swallowed at the lump that was growing thicker. "They found bones. Human bones and a dress..."

For the second time in as many minutes, silence hovered louder than sound ever could.

"Jesus Christ," my father muttered. His mouth opened and closed a couple of times. "I don't know what to say to that."

Oh god, please don't let him say he did it.

My father's good eye flicked from me to Coop and back again. "Oh no. You can't be serious. You think I offed some woman and buried her in the basement of my bar?" His voice rose in indignation.

I simply shrugged, feeling helpless, way over my head. Maybe there were some things that a kid just didn't need to know about their parents.

"Shay," my dad said, making a concerted effort to remain calm, but a vein in his temple pulsed. He gently reached forward to cup his work-rough palm against my cheek and tilted my head up. "Look at me."

I did.

"I did not bury any bodies in the basement of the Leprechaun or anywhere else. That, I can swear on."

I felt like a puppet that suddenly had its strings cut ... all wobbly and lethargic. "I believe you—"

"Well, well," a voice cut in from behind me. "If it isn't the O' Hanlons and that tall nerdy bastard, all lined up in a nice row."

FOURTEEN

MY FATHER'S HEAD JERKED up. Both Coop and I twisted in our seats toward the speaker and froze. It took a second for me to register the identity of the individual inside the door. He held a humongous handgun that was pointed directly at us.

Without much oomph, Coop said, "Greg? Greg Larson?"

The man in question took a step closer. He was a dozen feet away, too far away to try and charge, but too close for comfort. "Yes. It's little Greg. Remember me, Mr. O'Hanlon?"

"Course I do. Your mug's been plastered all over the city." My father's voice was low, even, and unpanicked. How did he do that?

"So what's with the hardware, Greg?" I asked, trying to keep my pounding heart in my chest.

He waved the cannon. Both Coop and I cringed. "This little thing? I like to call it the Equalizer. It can make the playing field a little more, shall we say, level?" The sneer on his face matched the crazy that now floated behind his striking blue eyes. "You people couldn't leave well enough alone, could you?"

My dad rumbled, "What are you talking about, son?"

"Don't you *son* me, old man. Why can't you follow directions?"

"What directions?" The perplexed tone of my dad's voice echoed my sentiment.

"You were supposed to sell your bar. If you'd sold your bar, none of this would have happened." Spittle flew from Greg's mouth. He stepped closer, within arms reach, and poked me in the forehead with the barrel of his gun. The cold metal seared my skin and I flinched away.

Greg's gaze shifted from me to my father. "You were supposed to freeze to death up there. Your stone cold body would be found with all the evidence the cops would need to convict your corpse of murdering Schuler. All that work … swiping your bar gun, the roofies. Well, they were one thing in this whole mess that worked like clockwork."

I was having problems grasping the finer points, but I was doing well with the big picture: we needed to subdue the lunatic with the great big firearm. Pronto.

Greg's crazed eyes floated back to my face. "And you. You couldn't help but stick your nose where it didn't belong."

"But I—"

Greg shut me up with a backhanded whack across my cheekbone. I momentarily saw stars but clearly heard the bellow of fury from my father. He leaped up and charged Greg. Dad crashed into him as the deafening sound of the gun went off, battering my eardrums in the confines of the concrete room. My father's body bucked in slow motion. Red spray spewed through the blankets covering his back, misting both Coop and me.

"No!" I shouted, trying desperately to shake the cobwebs loose.

"Shay," my father barked, his voice strained, "run!" He tenaciously held on to the shooter. Greg struggled, but Dad locked rock-hard arms locked around the madman.

"Dad! You're—"

"SHAY ELIZABETH O'HANLON! GO!"

I'd never heard my father roar so loudly, and the child in me couldn't help but obey. I grabbed Coop's sleeve. We dodged around the grunt-filled battle between Greg and my father and fled the room like rat-fink cowards.

FIFTEEN

THE SCREAMING IN MY head conflicted with the still silence of the hall. We scrammed down the corridor away from my father's battle for his life.

Get to JT. JT has a gun. She can shoot that little asshole. I repeated that mantra as we hit the stairs in the pitch black and took them two at a time, almost tripping on the longer step in the middle of each flight. Behind me, Coop was running a string of swear words that hadn't stopped since we exited the bloody room.

On the main floor I could actually make out doorways leading into various rooms. Our mad dash ended when we burst into the laundry room, our feet kicking through the chunks of fallen plaster and peeled paint.

"Where—" Coop spun in a circle, looking as hard as I was for our exit window.

I whipped out my flashlight and flicked it on, its beam bouncing off the wall. It caught the edge of an old board, and that board was wedged into the window casing that had been our exit. I tried to yank it out, but my fingers were too cold. The wood was jammed so tightly it didn't budge. Then Coop bumped me out of the way and tried to remove the barrier to our bid for freedom. It was a no-go.

"Shit, Shay," Coop panted, "we need another way out."

The sound of feet echoing as they pounded up the stairs jarred me into action. "Come on," I whispered furiously. "We have to get out of this room." I took off, towing him along behind and we dashed out of the room.

"Where are we going?"

I had no clue. Neither Coop nor I had any idea of the layout of the place other than where we'd already been, so our choices were limited. We were at one end of the building, meaning the hall was pretty much a one-way ride. We were going to have to pass the stairway Crazy Greg was thundering up like a herd of buffalo. I flashed the light in my hand behind us, toward the wall at the end of the hall. There was a narrow doorway just past the entrance to the laundry.

I ran toward the door, praying it wasn't locked. The Irish eyes of some dead ancestor (please not let it be those of my Pop) must have been smiling down at me, because the knob twisted in my hand and the door opened. Coop's coat still clutched in my hand, I darted into the space, which had once been a utility room, if the mummified mop in the corner was any indication, and doused the flashlight. There was no time to close the door before I heard heavy footsteps slowly coming our way.

Coop was pressed tightly against my back and I hugged the doorframe. He whispered in my ear, "Gotta run before he figures out where we went."

He was right. Unless we wanted to be gunned down like the lily-livered gutless wonders we were, we had to keep moving. I tried to slow my ragged breaths. I strained to hear where Greg was going, praying he'd turn into the laundry room. I did a rapid glance around the edge of the door. Greg's dark form was just disappearing into the laundry room entrance.

"Now," I whispered. We both bolted from the closet and raced down the hall.

The hallway was long. The building itself was much larger inside than it appeared from the exterior. Maybe if we could make it to the other end, we'd be able to find another way out. But before we managed to reach the opposite side, an inhuman scream echoed down the corridor. It was followed almost instantaneously by another volley of gunshots and the accompanying zing of bullets hitting walls and ricocheting. We were probably going to get plugged full of lead from a bounce off, if not from a direct shot!

Coop hit the deck and yanked me down beside him. We desperately crab-walked along the litter-filled linoleum, almost scuttling past an open space to the right, but I glanced to the side and realized it was a landing with another set of caged-in stairs. Apparently they'd built a stairwell on each end of the building.

Thank god.

I tugged on Coop's sleeve. He followed my lead, scrambling to the right and onto the landing. This time the swinging gate was still attached. I jerked it open and flicked my flashlight on. I scoured the floor for something to use to jam the gate shut. Coop read my mind and grabbed a thick sliver of wood lying partially beneath the junk on the floor. I realized it was a broken broom handle that could actually make a wicked weapon, but in a flash I could see where Coop was going with it.

"Come out, come out, wherever you are."

What the hell? Greg's singsong lilt sounded like it was still a little ways away. He didn't seem in a hurry to track us down. His pace was casual, almost nonchalant. The sound of his footsteps paused at various intervals. I imagined he was checking each room he passed, just in case. Most likely he figured we were easy pickings, and all he had to do was flush us out to finish us off.

The Protector in me was finally pulling itself together, and the situation started to come into focus so sharply I blinked in reaction. I grabbed the dagger of wood from Coop's hands and shoved him in front of me to the gate. We both grabbed it, and it swung open so easily we nearly lost our balance. Coop pulled me through the opening and the gate slammed shut. The sound of metal clashing against metal vibrated my brain.

I desperately lined up the two circular loops and crammed the pointy end of the broom handle through it. Coop added his weight, and we both backed off. I gave the wood a good pull, and it didn't budge.

"I hear youuuu," Greg sang. It sounded like he was almost on top of us.

We didn't stick around. Instead we hit the stairway, leaping to the longer landing in the middle of each flight, down and around until we were back in the basement. Coop flicked his flashlight on. There was another gate, meaning this stairwell led down another story past the basement. It was either play ring around the insane asylum or go for uncharted territory.

"Down!" I frantically whispered to Coop. We dashed forward and the beam from Coop's light bounced off a lock that secured the gate shut. There was no time to try to pick the fucker, even if we had the capability. Maybe that was something I should take up in my spare time—if I lived to have any spare time after this.

The good news was the gate was only chest high. I took a flying leap, swung my leg, shimmied over the top, and dropped to the opposite side. Coop was after me in a flash, landing lightly on his feet, knees bent to absorb the impact.

As soon as he regained his balance, we were pounding down the steps into the unknown. My light bounced around as I pumped my arms, reflecting at crazy angles off the walls. Thankfully the steps were clear of debris, and we made it to the next level without incident. We had maybe a fifteen-second lead on Greg, assuming he scaled the gate as easily we had. I took a moment to shine the light down one end of the corridor. It ended in a whitewashed wall. I whipped around and pointed the beam the opposite direction. The walls were pristine compared to the neglected and crumbling structure above.

"What is this?" I asked.

"I don't know, but come on." He pulled out his flashlight and added the beam to mine. Here the surface under our feet was curiously clear of trash and collapsed drywall.

A rattling bang and colorful cursing propelled us into flight. Maybe Greg hurt himself as he tried to scale the gate. One could hope.

Our footsteps pounded along the narrow passageway, which felt like a tunnel. After about fifty feet we hit a T in the road, and we skidded to a stop.

"Which way?" I asked.

Coop's flashlight caught a list of locations painted in black script. The top read INFIRMARY, with an arrow pointing to the right. Below it read CABIN 3, with another arrow to the right. LABORATORY arrowed to the left, and the last location on the list read BOILER ROOM 4 to the left. Going left was definitely much less appealing than going to the right.

Coop whispered, "I like the sound of the infirmary."

Greg's voice echoed weirdly as he singsonged, "Where are you, you two shitheads?" It was hard to tell how close he was.

"To the right it is," I agreed, and that's the direction in which we flat out ran. I didn't dare douse my light, because the tunnel curved this way and that before it momentarily straightened out again.

The pounding echo of our footsteps left little doubt that Greg would figure out which direction we'd taken. Sure enough, we came around a sharp corner into another straightaway, and I could hear his shoes slap against the pavement. At least he'd stopped singing to us.

Ahead, a tunnel branched off to our left, and the sign painted on the wall read LIZARDSPIT INFIRMARY, 200 FEET. I didn't have time to wonder what in the freaking world Lizardspit was, and I didn't much care. We hit the spurs and dodged down it. After about a hundred feet, we curved sharply and hit another straightway. Broken glass crunched beneath our feet. The volume of garbage increased as we closed in on the end of the tunnel. Musty mattresses leaned against the walls. Metal bedpans, kidney-shaped tin barf buckets, tubing, and other pharmaceutical castoffs were on the floor. Metal headboards and footboards from mid-century hospital beds were propped against a set of striped mattresses. We carefully but rapidly picked our way through the medical minefield to the gate that stood between us and a stairway to freedom. This time the gate wasn't chest high. It rose to the ceiling of the tunnel. We weren't going to be climbing that behemoth. A length of chain was wound around the door and the frame.

Greg's voice echoed ever closer. "Yoo hoo, my foolish friends!"

"Shit," Coop hissed and pointed his flashlight at the gate. I followed the beam. It illuminated a fist-sized, silver padlock that would probably take a couple of sticks of dynamite to blast open.

I yanked on the lock. It was as sturdy as it had been the day it was attached.

"Holy fuck, Shay, what are we gonna do now?" The desperation in Coop's voice made it crack.

I glanced at my best friend. His eyes were wide, almost wild with panic. For a moment, despair and terror nearly immobilized me. We were going to die in the bowels of an insane asylum. My father got shot for me, and I was going to let him down.

No, goddamn it. No. I was not going to disappoint him, make his sacrifice worthless. Newfound determination stiffened my back. I muttered, "Grab something hard and hold your ground." Adrenaline surged so fast it made me lightheaded. The familiar red haze of fury flared, narrowing my vision, focusing my attention. I welcomed it.

Greg would pay, even if it was the last thing I did. And that was a very real possibility.

I bent and scooped up the closest thing to a weapon I could find. It was one of those ancient metal bedpans, and it hefted nicely in my hand.

Coop rummaged around the floor and pulled up an old metal cane with a hook on the end. "Ready."

Creepy silence rang in my ears for a few tense seconds. I realized Greg had stopped his sing-song chanting. I suddenly heard his footsteps—slow and hesitant—crunching ever closer through the slew of waste. I figured he had to be close to the last bend in the tunnel.

I whispered, "Let's do a blacked-out Broadway Broadside when he gets close enough."

A Broadway Broadside was a not-so-clean move we'd come up with when we played broomball, in order to keep someone away from the ball at faceoff. Occasionally it came in handy to rush some irritating opposing player, nail them at chest level between linked arms, and lay them flat out. Of course, the refs didn't appreciate that, and we often wound up sidelined for two minutes for obstruction or roughing, but it was usually worth the penalty.

Without any referees in this deadly game, the threat of penalties flew out the basement window. We had absolutely nothing left to lose.

Coop held his flashlight up, his other arm toward me. I dropped mine and gripped the bedpan tighter. I wrapped my other arm around his, locking us together at the elbow and said, "Go on my mark—when it sounds like he's within striking range." How we were going to judge that was beyond me, but the plan was better than nothing. With a dual nod, we doused our flashlights at the same time.

Suffocating blackness settled in and Greg's footsteps stopped abruptly. There was no telltale glow from his direction. Either the shit didn't have a flashlight of his own, or he was playing our game.

No matter.

For the first time since this nightmare started, I didn't feel fear. I had no second thoughts. It was time to kick some madman ass and get my father help.

Welcome to the last stand at the Lizardspit Infirmary corral.

I breathed slowly through my nose and tried not to hyperventilate. "Greg, let's talk about this."

Glass crunched as he took another step. "Yes, Shay, let's talk."

Good. As long as he spoke, we could get a rough idea of where he was. The downside was that he could get a lock on our general whereabouts too.

Since our chances of making it out of here in one piece pretty well sucked, I figured we at least deserved the full story. "How did this all start?" I tugged on Coop's arm and pulled him a step to the right. Might as well make the target hard to hit.

Instead of being shot dead, glass crunched again, closer but still not quite close enough. Greg said conversationally, "You're going to die. Oh, those high school memories."

"High school?" I repeated. The man was truly off his rocker. He was a long way from high school. I pushed against Coop and we both leaned his way.

Two more footsteps echoed through the tunnel. He was probably fifteen or twenty feet away now. Still not close enough to run him over before he realized what we were doing. "Damn right. Sweet sixteen."

I had no idea where he was going with this. What I'd give for a pair of night vision goggles about now. "High school or college?" I asked.

"Sophie Brady."

Sophie Brady. The name did ring a bell.

"The Sophie Brady rumor. In high school," Coop murmured. "Seniors scared the freshmen, told 'em if they weren't careful they'd disappear just like she did. Remember?" He dragged me down into a crouch.

Greg let out a sound that was a cross between a laugh and grunt.

It was coming back to me. I remembered underground whispers surrounding a student named Sophie Brady. She was our school's urban legend. There was always debate as to whether or not she actually existed or if the older kids had created a convoluted ghost story to scare the underclassmen. It seemed like it ramped up right around Halloween—stupid teens trying to out-scare each other. I always figured that if she were indeed real, she'd run away or dropped out years before I showed up on the scene.

Who knows, maybe she got herself knocked up and moved somewhere no one knew her.

Greg took another step forward. He was almost within striking range.

Coop's elbow tightened on mine and I squeezed his in response.

"Oh, yes," Greg said, doing that weird singsong chant again. "She ran away, yes she did. But I found her."

One more step, two at the most, and we'd have a slim chance to mow down Crazy Boy if he didn't start firing his hand cannon first. *Come on, man... come just a little farther.*

Hoping to draw him closer, I said, "Where did you find her?"

"I saved her." Greg's tone shifted. He sounded almost dreamy, like he'd mentally checked out of this terrifying tunnel and into his memories. "I found her and I saved her."

He took another step. The sound of his foot impacting something was muffled by his pained yelp. "Dangerous down here," he said after a second's silence. "If you aren't careful, you could get yourself killed. Your father wasn't careful enough, Shay."

Bastard! I hissed in a breath and Coop's grip tightened on me. I opened my mouth, but before I could retort, Greg mumbled, "Sophie wasn't careful either. She got herself killed."

"How'd she get herself killed, Greg?" Coop's voice was gentle, coaxing. He was always better in finesse-necessary situations than I was. I was more like a wrecking ball.

"I found her. With those drug-dealing dirtballs. I took her. I saved her."

From the sound of Greg's voice, he was finally close enough. From the sudden tension of Coop's arm against mine, I knew he realized it too.

"I loved her. It wasn't my fault I loved her to death."

What the hell? Did Greg just confess to murder? Maybe Sophie Brady wasn't fictional after all.

"I loved her, but she wouldn't stop screaming." Greg's cultured voice became ragged. I imagined his eyes spinning around their sockets in a demonic frenzy. "I tried so hard to shut her up. Then she stopped fighting me. Oh, it was good. So good."

We needed to take him down before he decided to pull the trigger, but his fractured tale was morbidly mesmerizing. I couldn't help myself. "What was good?"

Greg ignored my question. "If your worthless, drunken, idiot father would have sold the bar, none of this would be happening." With no warning, Greg went from lost in the past to high-pitched, present-moment fury. "Schuler was supposed to fix the problem! But your dad woke up before he froze to death. And you. Couldn't keep your nose out of it, you dyke bitch. We had it all set up and you ruined everything!"

"GO!" I shouted. Coop and I surged blindly forward. We had one chance. I prayed our aim was more accurate than Greg's might be.

A brilliant flash lit the tunnel for the briefest instant, followed immediately by a thunderous explosion that battered my eardrums. I couldn't tell if either Coop or I was hit. With the adrenaline spike, I probably wouldn't notice anything unless the shot took me out then and there.

By some miracle our raised elbows slammed smack dab into human flesh. The impact was so hard I thought the arm I'd entwined with Coop's was going to pop right out of its socket. The bedpan in my free hand went flying.

For a moment, Greg was motionless, hung up between us. He gurgled as he tried to breathe. We'd nailed the weasel right in the larynx.

Coop and I unlinked our arms. Greg dropped to the ground. I went with him, groping blindly for his gun hand. Through the violent ringing in my ears, I heard a familiar voice shout, "Police! Don't move!"

Thirty seconds later, after speed-cuffing Greg and securing his gun, JT had her arms wrapped around me so tight I could hardly breathe. Her entire body was quaking. She whispered fiercely in my ear, "You are going to be the death of me. Jesus Christ."

Coop, his voice snarky and shaky at the same time, said, "Shay kind of has that effect on people." He stood off to one side, hanging onto a disheveled Greg Larson. I wondered what potential constituents would think seeing Greg half-crazed and handcuffed.

"Sorry, babe," I said. "It's not like I mean for these things to happen. How the hell did you find us?"

"Long story," JT mumbled into my neck.

Eddy was a human light post, with a flashlight in each hand and another in her armpit. She said, "Let's skedaddle. That father of yours is an ornery old cuss. Told us to find you two and Trigger-Finger over there. Lisa's with Pete now, doing some fancy first-aid stuff. She called the police and an ambulance while your white knight and I did our thing."

"Lisa? Lisa's here?" That little weasel! I pulled back away from JT in alarm.

"Come on." JT grabbed Greg by the scruff. "We can explain and walk."

On the return trip, Eddy and JT gave us the down and dirty of what had transpired since Coop and I descended into Hell.

Greg must have tagged along when we drove up to Princeton. He'd somehow managed to get the drop on Eddy and JT. The bastard cracked JT over the head with something, knocked her senseless. After JT hit the snow, Eddy went after Greg with her Whacker, but he slammed her up against the wall. Once Greg crawled into building, he jammed a chunk of wood in the window frame to block it.

After that, he most likely followed the sound of our voices, and the rest was history.

I led the charge into the room where we'd left my father and skidded to a halt. My dad was seated on the couch, hunched over, his bruised face ashen. Lisa kneeled next to him, pressing something against his back.

My father looked up, relief cascading over his strained features. "Shay," he wheezed. "You okay?"

I nodded. My throat constricted painfully. I'd never seen him like this.

"What ... " wheeze, "about the ... " wheeze, "vegetable muncher?"

Coop stepped up beside me. "I'm fine, Mr. O."

JT dragged Greg around us and shoved him into a chair so hard he almost flipped over backward. "Please move, and make my day," she told him and then glanced at my dad. "You'll be happy to know your assailant is in custody."

Greg glared at my father. "Too bad. My aim was a little off."

"You asshole." My composure crumbled. I belted him square in the kisser. God that felt good, even if my knuckles smarted like hell.

"What the thuck!" Greg tried to lob a loogie at me. Blood and saliva dripped off his chin. "Polith brutality!"

JT said, "She's not a cop."

Lisa looked like a skittish raccoon in the headlights. "Help's on the way, should be here any second. Shay, can you hold this against your dad's back if I go let the police in?"

"Yeah, sure." I hustled to my father's side.

Lisa showed me where she was putting pressure on my father's wound. He grunted softly as my hand replaced hers, and I nearly passed out at the amount of red that had soaked into the bunched cloth.

Eddy went with Lisa in search of the front door. I wondered how they were going to open it. If they couldn't, the cops would be able to.

Greg sat slumped, scowling blankly. Blood continued to dribble from his lip. I wondered if he was having a mental break. Well, more of a break than he'd already had.

Every second that went by felt like an hour. In reality, less than ten minutes later we were outside Hell, surrounded by a sea of various emergency vehicles flashing red, white, and blue lights.

After the Princeton cops were briefed on what had gone down, Greg had been stuffed into the back of a squad.

An ambulance crew stabilized my dad and whisked him to the Cambridge Medical Center, a hospital about twenty miles away. One of the medics patiently explained to me that if Cambridge couldn't handle the gunshot wound, he'd be transferred to Hennepin County Medical Center in Minneapolis.

I briefly gave my version of events to a pimply faced Princeton police officer, and then sat on a gurney next to JT in an ambulance in front of the Asylum of Horror.

A paramedic busied himself checking out a good-sized gash on the back of my woman's head while she tried to justify to another cop standing outside the rear doors why we broke into abandoned state property in the first place.

JT gave a condensed recitation of what brought us up here. The cop jotted occasional notes, pausing now and again for clarification.

"Tell me again what happened outside the window," the man asked, his pen poised above the paper.

JT said, "Eddy and I were waiting outside the window when *wham*! The lights pretty much went—ow!" she yelped, wincing as prodding fingers continued their examination.

The paramedic doing the poking said, "You should probably come in and get this checked out. I don't think it needs stitches, but it's a mess."

"No, I'll be fine. Just patch me up. I'll have Shay bring me in if I need to." JT listened about as well as I did to medical advice.

The medic dabbed at the wound with a piece of gauze. "All you cops types are alike." He leveled a pointed look at me. "Watch her for changes in alertness, confusion, a headache worse than the one she's got now. Confusion." The hint of a grin softened his otherwise stern countenance. "Oh, did I say that?" He shifted his eyes back to JT's scalp. "Seriously, any vomiting, seizures … unlikely, but you never know."

I gave my own pointed look at JT, who rolled her eyes at me. "I'll drag her in kicking and screaming if need be."

The cop cleared his throat none too quietly, and JT resumed her recitation. "Anyway, between Lisa Vecoli shaking the snot out of me and Eddy trying to turn me into a snowman, I came around pretty fast." She nodded at Lisa, who was milling with Coop and Eddy a few steps from the ambulance.

"You two," the cop called to Lisa and Eddy, "can you please come over here?"

Coop remained where he was, happy, I was sure, to have some distance between himself and the po-po.

Eddy and Lisa shuffled toward the bumper of the ambulance. It took a few minutes for both of them to run down their vitals and contact information.

I waited for Lisa to identify herself as a St. Paul police officer, but she didn't. Now would be the perfect time to bring up the fact I knew she was a lying sack of horse hockey. I said, "Lisa, don't you think you should tell him your little secret?"

Lisa frowned. "What secret?"

"Come on," I said. "You don't need to hide it any more. You might as well come out and say it."

"Say what? I came out in high school." She did a great job of looking perplexed.

The cop stared at Lisa. "I don't give a crock about anyone's sexual orientation. Just tell me what happened."

Before I could needle her any further, Lisa said, "Earlier today I was about to swing by the Rabbit Hole—the café Shay owns—to find out if Shay's dad had come back. I've been trying to give him something my mother wanted him to have. Anyway, I saw that her car was parked close to the front door of the Rabbit Hole. She, or whoever was driving, pulled out as I pulled into a space on the other side of the street. A huge, gray, four-door Chevy truck two spots behind her came out almost at the same time. It nearly sideswiped a bus. For a second I thought it was a coincidence until the truck swerved into the opposite lane of traffic to pass the bus and three other cars before cutting back in behind Shay." Lisa shrugged. "I guess I'm suspicious by nature. So I flipped a U turn and followed them both. I never expected to wind up here."

If you ask me, that didn't sound exactly suspicious. What did make sense was that the little liar had been watching us herself, and the fact that she lucked out and someone was indeed tailing me gave her a great excuse now.

Lisa said, "I tracked Greg—at a distance—through the field and into the woods, where I lost sight of him. Luckily there were plenty of tracks in the snow.

"I found Eddy trying to revive JT. Between the two of us we got her back on her feet. Then we kicked out the plank blocking the window. Eddy refused to be left behind, so we helped her inside and she came with."

I wondered how many bruises Eddy was going to have after that.

JT said, "We didn't know what we were going to find once we got in, but we followed the same path you did, Shay. We found your dad, got him up on the couch. Lisa called for backup and an ambulance, and your dad ordered Eddy and me to find the two of you." She glanced at the cop, who had his head down and was writing furiously on a palm-sized notepad.

"And," Eddy said, "all we had to do was listen to Greg sing his way through the corridors. The Pied Piper of the Princeton Mental Institution led us right to them." She paused. "Ah, you might not want to include that in your notes."

"Got you covered," the cop said without looking up. "Go on."

JT said, "We stopped, listened to Greg ramble about a gal named Sophie Brady until we heard Coop and Shay trounce him and a gunshot. Then I moved in and threw the cuffs on."

A grudging part of me was thankful Lisa came along when she had to help JT and Eddy. Even if she was still staunchly playing the, "I simply want to find Pete to carry out my mother's last wishes" gambit.

After what Greg had said down in the bowels of Hell, Lisa'd be hard pressed to continue to question my father's participation in Schuler's demise. I wondered if the body in the cellar of the Leprechaun could be Sophie Brady. That concept gave me a kind of potential, bittersweet relief. Regardless, there were still so many unanswered questions. The one thing I felt I could rest easy about was that my father had no hand in creating any corpses.

SIXTEEN

Two days later, I sat perched on the edge of my dad's hospital bed, and Coop was parked in one of those vinyl recliners that looked comfortable until you actually used it.

My dad had certainly been through a few rough days. He wound up with bruised ribs, a broken nose, and a bullet that passed through his lower right side, missing the most vital of organs. The doc said he didn't need his appendix anyway, and after two hours of surgery to repair the damage, we were told he should be almost as good as new once he healed.

The cops had been in three times to question my father since I'd come up at nine that morning. It was closing in on two thirty, and I wondered how many more visits from law enforcement he was going to get before this neverending Thursday would be done. My dad had firmly denied knowledge of either Chuck Schuler's demise or how Jane Doe wound up beneath the cement in his basement.

The police were checking into my dad's story, looking into who owned the cabin my dad "claimed" (their quotes, not mine) he had found himself in, and trying to nail down a timeline of what exactly had transpired since last Friday night. The good news was that there was physical evidence that my dad had been beaten. The bad news was that my father's memory of the time between the poker game Friday night and waking up bruised and battered Monday was still nonexistent.

Not a lot of information had come from any of the cops regarding Greg Larson's status except that he was being held while the investigation continued. I was dying to know—and that was certainly a bad choice of words—if Greg really had something to do with Jane Doe. Was the body in the Leprechaun Sophie Brady?

The door creaked open, and a hand holding a brightly colored bouquet of flowers in a glass vase preceded JT into the room. She'd made a run down to Pam's Pawhouse, retrieved Bogey and Dawg, and dropped both of them off at the Rabbit Hole before driving back up to Cambridge. At this point most of our vacation time was pretty well shot, and we'd be going home tonight instead of heading to Duluth after all. Sooner or later we'd find another chance to get away.

"Hey guys," JT said and set the vase on the windowsill. "Though these might cheer you up, Pete."

Coop gave her a thumbs up. "Nice."

She came over to stand next to me and assessed my father. "You're looking a little more lively. How you feeling?"

"Hard to feel too bad with the stuff they're pumping into me." My dad motioned at the IV stand and the various tubes that carried various drugs into his arm. "Thanks for the pick-me-up."

JT leaned her hip against my thigh. "No problem. Any more visitors?"

"Nope," I said. "Not yet anyway. Did you see Eddy at the Hole?"

A conspiratorial grin brightened JT's features. "I did. She rode here with me and will be up in a couple of minutes."

I knew that look, and whatever Eddy was cooking up was going to be interesting.

Coop asked JT, "You get in hot water for what happened?"

"No. I had some explaining to do, but as long as I keep cooperating with the investigation, I should be okay. Busting into a locked, abandoned building with the intent to save a life was a worthy reason for breaking the law."

The door opened again, this time admitting Eddy, whose smooth brown face was split by one of the largest I've-done-it-this-time smiles I'd seen from her in a long time. In her hands she clutched a weirdly shaped object beneath a hand towel.

"What've you got under there, Eddy?" my father asked cautiously.

"You'll have to take the towel off and see." With barely restrained glee, she plunked the thing down with a metallic thump on the hospital tray table that hovered over my dad's lap.

Gingerly he reached a hand out and took hold of the edge of the towel. "It's not going to blow up or smoke or do anything like that, is it?"

"No, it's not going to bite. Go ahead."

With a flick of his wrist, the towel went flying. Underneath was an old, metallic-silver bedpan, like the one I'd grabbed from the tunnel floor in the Lizardspit section of Hell. The bowl was filled with chocolate Tootsie Roll midgees.

My dad said, "Where did you get that shit pot? You clean it before you put that crap in there? And yes, I know what a pun is, and yes, I meant to say it."

Eddy's dark eyes sparkled. "I swiped it after we took down that rascal in the crazy house. Figured it would be a souvenir."

"That's some souvenir." JT reached over and grabbed a handful of Tootsie Rolls. "You did wash it out, right?

"What do you take me for?" Eddy said. "Of course. I disinfected it and ran it through the dishwasher at the Hole."

I wasn't sure if I was okay with that or not. But in the end, the poop-catcher was clean, so what the hell. I grabbed a few midgees too.

Coop's face was a mask of horror. "That's disgusting on so many levels. The fact that you're eating nothing but a bunch of chemicals is bad enough, but eating them out of a bed pan?"

I unwrapped a roll and stuck it in my mouth, chewed for a while, and swallowed. "Tastes okay to me."

Coop tossed the magazine he'd been reading at me. With a delighted howl, I fired off the Tootsie Rolls that were in my hand, catching him center mass.

"Oh, you're in trouble now." Coop snagged the Kleenex box from the side table by the bed and flung it Frisbee-style at my head. The door swung open just as I ducked. The box narrowly missed the door-jamb, and bounced off the shoulder of a man dressed neatly in a suit and tie.

My laughter choked in my throat when I realized the victim of the flyaway box of tissues was Roy Larson, Greg's dad.

"That's some welcome." The surprised look on his face smoothly morphed into concern. Roy stepped into the room and the door swung shut behind him. "Pete. I wanted to stop by and see how you're doing."

Coop said somberly, "Sorry about the Kleenex attack."

"Hey. If you can't have a good time in a hospital . . ." Roy trailed off with a shrug and refocused on my dad. "Really, Pete, how are you?"

"Doc says I'll mend." I could tell from my dad's tentative tone he was wondering how to handle Roy.

What was appropriate to say to the father of a probable murderer?

"Oh. Good. That's good. Wanted to stop by, apologize. For my son. He's been under stress. A lot of stress. Lately."

Like *stress* was a reason to shoot my father?

My dad waved off the words. "Politics are a dirty business. Pressure. Strain. Not a good combination."

"No, it's not," Roy agreed. "There's a lot of dirty business. Too much dirty business." His shoulders drooped, and it was like he deflated, folded into himself. "Dirty, dirty business."

I glanced at JT, and she was watching Roy with a look of concern. She said, "You okay, Mr. Larson?"

Roy's gaze slid off my dad and his eyes landed somewhere between the mattress and the floor. "Oh, yes. I'm fine. Just fine. Couldn't be finer. No."

Eddy cocked her head as she studied Roy. "You having a stroke or something?"

"No, ma'am. Not yet, anyway." Roy pushed his hands into his pants pockets.

"Roy," my dad said, "I told you, it's okay. I'm okay."

"Okay," Roy said, his voice sounding weak. "Not okay. It's not okay." Suddenly his head snapped back up. "It's not at all okay, Pete."

"I know it's got to be hard to deal with—with your son in the clink, and ... " My father trailed off, leaving the obvious unspoken.

"It's not okay, Pete." Roy was stuck on repeat. Maybe he *was* having a stroke. I glanced around the bed for the nurse call button.

Roy's face flushed a deep maroon. His ears turned red and his neck became suffused with blood. He muttered, "Nothing is ever going to be okay again. If nothing is going to be okay for me, it's not going to be okay for you either."

"What—" my dad said, but Roy cut him off.

"No, nothing will be okay."

Roy pivoted to face me. In one motion, he pulled his hand out of his pocket and raised it to chest level. My chest level. It took me a second to realize there was something in his hand. And it was pointed at me.

That something was a black, palm-sized handgun.

My arms flew up. "Wait a minute," I said. "Just wait a second."

"Roy," my father barked. "What in the sam hell are you doing?"

JT stiffened, eased away from me.

"You took my son away from me, Pete. So I'm going to take away something you care about."

Roy's gun hand was remarkably steady. "You," he said to me, "over there, by your father."

I didn't argue. I shifted to stand next to the head of the bed.

"You two." Roy looked at Coop and Eddy. "Over there." He motioned with his gunless hand at the space next to the window. "You too, police girl."

Eddy and Coop shuffled over to the window. JT slowly backed up, her hands at shoulder level. "Take it easy, Roy."

Roy glared at JT. "You know I'm the king of kitty litter, right?"

JT frowned, but she nodded with gusto. "I sure do." I could imagine her saying that whatever the madman wants, the madman gets. Maybe psychotic breaks run in the family.

Roy said, "Do you think I wanted to be the king of kitty litter?"

JT said, "I don't think I can answer that."

"No!" The volume of Roy's voice caused a group jerk reaction. "I was supposed to be governor! But that didn't work out so well, did it?" He didn't wait for an answer. "No it didn't. Everything fell apart when Greg…"

"When Greg what?" I asked, keeping my hands by my ears.

"Boys will be boys, you know. Things get a little carried away. Happens all the time." This was turning into a like son, like father fiasco.

I finally saw that the remote with the nurse call button had slid down between the side rails.

Suddenly Roy growled, "You look at me, Shay."

I snapped my head up and met his eyes. They were eerily similar to his son's in a loony bin sort of way.

He said, "You have no idea what it's like to have to protect your offspring. The lengths you'll go, even if it means sacrificing everything. Everything you've worked your entire life for."

Roy shifted to better see my father and me. The hand holding the gun was now trembling. A lot.

"If only," Roy's tone was wistful, "if only Greg hadn't started seeing that girl, none of this would ever have happened. I wouldn't have had to take care of her. I wouldn't have had to jackhammer concrete in the middle of the night and hope no one noticed. I wouldn't have had to lay new cement. We would've been home free. And we were, until the goddamn sewer line broke."

Oh my god.

Roy's voice hardened. He glared at my father. "If only you'd sold the Leprechaun when Schuler came knocking, we wouldn't be here."

Out of the corner of my eye, I saw Eddy reach toward the bedpan and then jerk her hand back. How could she be hungry at a time like this?

"When you refused to sell, Pete, I had to take matters into my own hands. Again. I had to make this pesky little problem go away. Again."

The Protector starting revving up and my core vibrated.

Hoarsely my father parroted, "Pesky little problem?"

"It was the perfect setup, you know. Your gun was so easy to take. And that damn Hanssen. He actually came though. Found someone to dispatch Schuler. Do you know how to freeze a body in a block of ice? A chest freezer works amazingly well. We even remembered to drop your gun in there with him. Oh yes." He laughed harshly. "Do you have any idea how heavy a block of ice that size is? We actually had to cut the freezer away from it in pieces! Took Greg and I forever. After that it was easy. Pushed that monstrosity right out of the back end of Greg's truck and dumped it next to the other ice blocks in Rice Park. It was rather artistic, if I do say so myself."

The man was certifiable. Shouldn't the nurse be coming in any time? I couldn't remember how long it had been since she was in last.

"We smeared his blood all over you. Your clothes. Inside your car. Even had someone mess you up. All the proof was there."

Roy took two quick steps forward and pressed the barrel of the gun against my dad's head. "You're stubborn, Pete. Too stubborn for your own good. You were supposed to die. Everyone knows you're a drunk. On the wagon, off the wagon, no one would have questioned anything. No heat, the cold. You were catatonic when we left. You were supposed to be unconscious long enough that you'd die of hypothermia. That's what the man said. The stuff was strong, he said. A couple drops would take care of it. If only I'd put a few more into your scotch, Pete. It wouldn't have hurt. Freezing to death." His eyes were wide now, the whites showing. "Why won't that bitch fucking leave me alone?" Spittle flew from his mouth and his lips trembled.

Talk about a cluster of a confession. Holy shit on a shingle. If we lived through this, my dad was home free.

My father said, "You've had my back all these years, Roy. We were there for each other. How could you do this?"

"You betrayed me. You were supposed to die. Greg was so close! So close to my dream. I did everything I could to make his career happen. I made his mistakes disappear. Do you know how much that's cost me? Do you? And now it's all washed down the goddamn sewer."

It felt like the hot end of the betrayal poker had been shoved down my own throat. Everything I had understood about Roy's role in my past was being reframed. Right here, right now. And I didn't like it one bit.

While Roy's attention was on my father and me, JT had slowly shifted, trying to ease around the end of the bed. I glanced furtively, trying to gauge her progress without being obvious. Her face was weirdly scrunched up, and her chest jerked once and then again.

Oh shit. She was trying not to sneeze. I held my breath. *Come on babe, hold it back.*

She explosively lost the battle.

Roy whipped around, his gun stopping directly in front of JT's drippy nose. "Don't even think about it, lady cop. You move again and I'll do it. I'll shoot her." He jerked his head at me.

"Easy," JT said. "I'm not moving, see?" She held her arms up higher. For a second I was afraid her jacket would ride up enough to expose the gun in the holster at her side. If Roy saw that, all bets would be off.

Thankfully Roy turned his attention and his weapon back to my dad and me. "You two are nothing but a huge pain in my butt. It's time to get rid of that pain."

The door opened. Roy spun around as Lisa Vecoli stepped in. The smile on her lips rapidly faded as she saw what was pointed at her.

With Roy distracted, Eddy scrambled on top of the bed with surprising agility and grabbed the bedpan. Tootsie Rolls flew as she hefted it over her head and leaped off the bed, aiming for Roy. The pan nailed him square in the back. Eddy's momentum knocked him off balance and they both landed in a heap at Lisa's feet.

JT and I pounced on Roy like hungry cheetahs after a dry spell. I held him down and JT slammed cuffs on his wrists.

Coop pulled Eddy to her feet and she looked derisively down her nose at Roy. "Teach you to mess with my family."

Astonishment and confusion battled for dominance on Lisa's face. She said, "Sorry to crash your S&M party."

———

Visit number four from the cops included a drop-in by St. Paul's Sergeant DeSilvero, who was almost apologetic. He informed us that he'd keep us abreast of the progress on the case, and he actually told my father he wished him a speedy recovery. DeSilvero might have been an asshole on the outside, but I suspected inside might be another story entirely.

This time one uniform was left behind, standing guard outside my dad's door, just in case. It was too little too late by then, but I suppose they felt they needed to cover their butts. It had taken almost two hours to get everyone's statements after Roy was led away mumbling about Tootsie Rolls and broken dreams.

It was sad.

We reconvened in my dad's room, excited chatter flowing freely. I hopped back onto the foot of my dad's bed, and JT leaned against the window ledge, looking exhausted. Coop had given up the recliner for Eddy. He sat on a padded folding chair, elbows on his knees and head in his hands. Lisa propped herself up against the wall next to the door, mostly being quiet, taking in what was being said.

I hoped after all this she'd come clean. In fact, maybe it was time to force the issue. "So, Lisa," I said, and she glanced my way. "Which department do you work for?"

The blank look on her face didn't fade.

I said, "You have to know by now my dad didn't have anything to do with Schuler."

Now she frowned. "Of course I know that."

"So cough it up. You're with St. Paul, right?"

"St. Paul? Shay, what are you talking about?"

"Come on." I laughed incredulously. "I was onto you by Monday. I know you were hoping to find my father by getting close to me. You're smooth. I'll give you that."

"What? No. I was trying to help." Now Lisa was starting to get agitated. Her eyes flashed and the muscles in her jaw clenched.

My father, Coop, JT, and Eddy warily watched our exchange.

"You're a cop Lisa, just fess up."

"I am not a cop. Where on earth did you get that idea?"

"You can't believe I'd fall for a stupid story like your mom died and left you instructions to find my dad and give him a stupid coin. What do you take me for?"

Now Lisa was really getting revved up. She stepped close, leaned into my face. *Bring it on, baby.* Maybe it was time to duke it out. My fists were itching to do some damage to something.

"I do a good deed and this is the thanks I get?"

"If you weren't a liar," I shot back and poked her in shoulder.

She poked me right back, raised her voice. "I'm not a liar and you're nuts."

Steam started pouring from my ears. I slid off the bed to my feet and gave her a shove.

She gave me a withering glare and shoved back.

I grabbed her leather jacket in one hand and cocked my other arm back, about to pop her when my dad bellowed, "Girls! Knock it off. Now!"

After a few long seconds I let go of her jacket.

Emotion flickered across Lisa's face, the anger melting away, replaced with an almost perplexed expression. "I'm sorry," she murmured, her wide eyes locked on mine. "I don't know what came over me."

I held my hands out, palms up, and took a step back. "I'm sorry too." And I was. I felt like I'd been taken over by an alien.

"Lisa," my dad said, "what's this about a coin?"

She said, "It's an old nickel." Lisa broke our gaze and rummaged around her pants pocket. She handed the item in question over to my dad.

He flipped it over in his palm and stared at it for a few long heartbeats. "Where...where did you get this?" He wrapped his fingers slowly around the nickel.

Lisa took a shuddery breath. "It was my mom's. She recently passed away. She told me to find Pete O'Hanlon—you, maybe—and give it to him. I don't even know if you're the right person."

JT, Coop, Eddy, and I silently watched the interchange.

My dad asked softly, "What was your mom's name?"

"Connie Vecoli."

"She have a maiden name?"

"Yeah. Rockwell."

"When did she get married?"

"When did she—" Lisa shook her head. "I don't know. My dad bailed when I was little. She never talked much about it. I don't remember a whole lot about him. I kind of got the feeling they hooked up because he got her pregnant."

276

My dad stared at Lisa for a long moment. "How old are you?"

"Twenty-five."

"I think," my dad said, his face more serious than I'd ever seen it, "we might have a situation."

All of us stared at him, waiting for the punch line.

"Lisa," he said in a gentle tone, the same tone he used when he needed to tell me something I didn't want to hear. "I think... I think you might be my daughter."

It felt like all the air was sucked out of the room in one whoosh.

I stared at Lisa with my mouth hanging open, my eyebrows buried in my hairline. I surveyed her face, her eyes.

She had blond hair, I had black.

She was taller than I was, but just as angular.

She had a temper. A serious temper.

A temper much like mine?

Holy crap on a cracker. I had a sister.

The End

Photo © April McGuire

ABOUT THE AUTHOR

Jessie Chandler is a board member-at-large of the Midwest chapter of Mystery Writers of America and a member of Sisters in Crime. In her spare time, Chandler sells unique, artsy T-shirts and other assorted trinkets to unsuspecting conference and festival goers. She is a former police officer and resides in Minneapolis. Visit her online at JessieChandler.com.